THE GLA

The Glass House

Sophie Cooke

arrow books

Published by Arrow in 2005

1 3 5 7 9 10 8 6 4 2

Copyright © Sophie Cooke 2004

Sophie Cooke has asserted her right under the Copyright,
Designs and Patents Act, 1988 to be identified as the
author of this work

First published in the United Kingdom by
Hutchinson in 2004

Arrow Books
The Random House Group Limited
20 Vauxhall Bridge Road, London SW1V 2SA

Random House Australia (Pty) Limited
20 Alfred Street, Milsons Point, Sydney
New South Wales 2061, Australia

Random House New Zealand Limited
18 Poland Road, Glenfield
Auckland 10, New Zealand

Random House (Pty) Limited
Endulini, 5a Jubilee Road, Parktown 2193, South Africa

The Random House Group Limited Reg. No. 954009

www.randomhouse.co.uk

A CIP catalogue record for this book
is available from the British Library

Papers used by Random House are natural, recyclable products
made from wood grown in sustainable forests. The manufacturing
processes conform to the environmental regulations
of the country of origin

Printed and bound in Great Britain by
Cox & Wyman Ltd, Reading, Berkshire

ISBN 0 09 946553 1

In memory of my uncle
Charlie Shiffner

Acknowledgements

Huge thanks are due to my family and friends for their encouragement and support, the Scottish Arts Council for affording me a space in which to write, my agent Clare Alexander for her expert advice, and to Clare Smith and Tiffany Stansfield at Hutchinson for turning a manuscript into a book. Most of all, thanks to Norman for keeping me sane.

Chapter One

HER VOICE IS going like a kettle, faster and faster, higher and higher, a squawking song. I do not like her face when she does this. She is waving a spoon, bits of boiling-hot soup are spattering off it as she screams.

Lucy yells back at her. She always does. 'Shut up!' Mum slaps her face with the back of the spoon. Bryony is crying with her eyes closed. Her face is slimy and sad. She always cries. Mum is busy shouting in Lucy's face. I slide backwards to the wall with gentle movements. Invisibly I slip from the room, I am a clever little crab, though turning the door handle seemed to take an age.

I can hear them howling from the other side of the door. I pick up my anorak from off the floor and creep out of the back door.

The sun is shining. I pass through the gap in the mossy dyke at the back of the garden and take the path up the hill. It is quite steep, which is good because you don't have to walk far to feel like you've come a long way. The house is quickly far below you – just a little roof in a little garden, grass and mum's flowers.

She only grows them to dry them. She hangs them upside down and then when she's taken all the juice out of them she arranges them in wreaths and stuff and sells them at the craft fairs to her friends. 'Oh Mary you're so clever' they say, and look at me and Lucy and Bryony like we're lucky, arranged beside her.

I turn round and carry on up the path. There are sheep droppings and big stones in it, and short grass either side. I walk hard, getting hot inside my jacket and my head so I stop again. I take off my anorak and tie it round my waist. The glen is goldish green in the late sunshine, the trees down by the river look happy. That's where I used to go, I used to curl up between their roots and feel kind of safe. Now I am fourteen and I'm a good walker so I come up the hills instead. It makes you feel like a bird just flying away.

Up and up I go, over the heathery top. Now I can see the lochan the other side; the wind is roughening up the surface and reeds are lilting at its edges. I smile. It's not far. I wade down through the heather rustling its bells at my passing.

The near edge of the lochan comes into view again from behind a great hump in the hill, and there's someone there. It is a boy wearing a camouflage jacket and standing with a fishing rod, it is Alan. Standing on a rock, he hasn't seen me yet. I stand still for a while, watching his back. He stands very still, like a tree. Then there is his arc of movement and the swish of the line slicing through the air as he casts, and then he is still again. I like Alan.

I want him to see me so I walk right on, into the side of his field of vision. He looks round. I stand still. We both just stand here, looking across at each other. My arms are down by my sides, my yellow hair is blowing across my face, I wish I didn't have my anorak tied round my waist. Do I look good? He does.

His face is round beneath crumpled reddish-brown hair, his camouflage jacket and his jeans are beautiful upon him. His Def Leppard T-shirt is flapping gently against his body as if it wants to stroke him. He is looking at me and his eyes are like they always are, like he's not a person but an old tree or a big rock and doesn't mind me being there at all.

After a while he grins at me. It is the greatest smile you ever saw. It is like the feeling of the sun on your eyes, nuzzling at your eyelashes, before you fully wake up, before it remembers who you are and you remember too. His smile is like that, something perfect. I turn my head and try to smile back and start walking on and away.

I wonder if he is looking at me as I tramp round the edge of the water. I sit down on a rocky bit. I tug a piece of heather out of the ground and pluck it.

Up here, you wouldn't know there was anywhere else. It is a secret cradle in the sky with just the lochan and its peaty bog, lush with pink and green mosses like cake rot. The wind blows and a buzzard flies. Rocks and water and sky.

Up here, I can feel the numbness. Why don't you cry, says mum. Because I can't. Not that I say that, I just say nothing.

I glance through my hair and he is still there. A small figure fishing. I look back.

I like the water. One day I will go to the sea and climb in a boat and just sail away. Wide waves and no land in sight, just wind and gulls and jellyfish bobbing by. I'd come ashore and people wouldn't know me and they'd wonder who was I.

Sometimes mum wonders if I'm her daughter. I've got no feelings, and those horrid little eyes. 'Stop looking at me like that!' she says. Other times, though, she knows exactly who I am. I am her clever little Nesspot and she loves me and I am so pretty. So, it's not all bad. I had better go home. My bum's going numb anyway.

I stand and look over at the fisherboy again. He's still there. I skirt quite widely around him and back up to the brow of the hill. I can feel him watching me for part of the way but I don't look round.

There it is again, the glen, laid out below me. I start down the path. Everything is beautiful and I feel sick. Closer and closer comes the house, lower and lower come I. And I am at the bottom again, with the hills struck up around me in a song that can sometimes go on too long. I like the hills but only because they end the glen if you climb over them. They hold you in and they let you out. If the world was flat you could always see out but would always look back.

I'm at the dyke, past it and crossing the garden, I stop and stand still by the corner of the house.

I can't hear anything from inside so I open the back door and climb the stairs. Lucy opens her bedroom door and comes to stand in the passage, facing me on my ascent. 'You always run away,' she says. She turns round and goes back into her room.

I go to the bathroom, pull down my jeans and sit on the loo. Mummy comes in. She has changed into a clean short-sleeved white shirt. She asks me very gently where I have been and I say 'up the hill'. She looks at me like I am a puppy caught with a sock in its mouth. Seeing as I dislike being with everyone else in the house so much, I needn't sleep in it tonight. Firmly but kindly done. She kisses my head and then she goes out and leaves the bathroom door open behind her.

I finish off and go downstairs. She is waiting. I go outside and she is right behind me all the way, overtaking in time to open the door of the stone shed for me. 'No supper,' she says and kisses me again. 'Sleep tight.' She closes the door and puts the bolt through. It is only six o'clock.

The sun is still streaming in through the window which faces out over the dyke. I sit down in the square of light with my back against the wall, head turned upwards to the warmth, back of my head resting on the sill of the window facing into the garden. I close my eyes.

There is a tapping at the sunny window-pane. I open my eyes and squint at the person, it is Alan again. I am pleased to see him. I sit still, looking at him until he taps again and then I stand up and climb on to the sunny wooden workbench. Kneeling on it, I push open the tiny top part of the window. It only opens a few inches. I peer down at him through the gap.

He is standing in the field on the other side of the dyke and he gazes up at me without saying anything. The pause lengthens into a dare and so eventually I say 'Hi.'

He grins right away. 'Hi Vanessa,' he says. 'Are you all right?'
'Yes.'

He nods for some time. 'Why are you in the shed?' I shrug.
There's a pause. Then Alan says, 'I heard you got expelled from
your boarding school.'

'Yes.' I look over his shoulder and then back at him. 'I'm a
vandal.'

He smiles.

'I defaced the pavilion.'

'What did you write?'

'Just pictures.'

We both look sideways. Then I say, 'They'd given me
warnings and stuff.'

Alan nods and looks up at my face again. 'Is that why you're
in the shed?'

I shake my head and don't say anything. I just watch the way
his hair blazes in the evening sun, strands of it burning bright
like metal wire in the bunsen flame. I seem to watch it for a long
time but maybe it is just a few seconds.

'It's not padlocked. I could let you out.'

'No,' I say. 'No, I'm fine.'

He looks away.

I don't want him to go. 'I drew a whale.'

He looks back at me.

'It had eaten loads of people. They were all climbing out
through its skin and being sick on it.' It was a stupid thing to
draw.

Alan laughs. 'You didn't paint it on the dinner hall.'

'They call it the refectory there.'

'Do they?'

I nod.

'Your sisters are still there?'

I nod. 'Back to the perfectory in September.'

He grins.

Then he stops smiling. He looks as if he wants to say something, you can see the words making it halfway up his throat and tumbling back. 'I hope you don't miss them,' is what he says.

He was avoiding my eyes but now he looks right at me. I don't react.

There is another small silence.

'I've got a fish for you.' He holds up a trout. Light from the sky collects on its scales and runs off them. 'Hold your hand out,' he says.

I think about it.

I draw back from the window and awkwardly angle my elbow through the gap so that my forearm is dangling out over the dyke. We look funny, my arm and the fish, hanging in the air, both out of place. Alan passes the fish into my hand and waits till I have closed my fingers before letting go. Slowly I reel my arm back in through the window and I look at the handsome trout for a second before laying it on the workbench beside me. I felt his hand touching mine. I look through the window and see him looking at me. Through the dirty glass, it seems that I am under a calm water looking up at him on the other side. He is looking a wee bit worried.

I straighten up so that my face is at the gap once more and he grins. Everything is all right. We are back in the same world.

'It's a nice fish,' I say.

'Thanks,' says Alan. 'Please can I let you out.'

'No.'

'Then can I come in?'

I shake my head. He just can't come in here, not really. He would drown in here.

His eyes are moving over my face. He raises his hand very slowly and I stay dead still as if there is a wasp on my nose. But he isn't going for my face at all. He lays his palm under a thick ribbon of my hair that has tumbled out the window. I look at it

6

as he draws his fingers through it. I expect he can feel it in his hands but I cannot feel him at all. My dead hair in his live fingers. Only when he reaches a tangle is there a quick jerk of feeling in my scalp.

'Ow.'

'Sorry.'

He is carefully teasing out the knot. He stops before he is finished, though, stops with his suntanned fingers still embroiled in me and looks straight ahead without moving. He is looking into the murky glass and then he looks up at me. At the inches of my face. He looks me in the eyes and he says, 'I really like you Vanessa.'

I don't know what to do. I can't move and I can't speak, so I don't. I just stay very still and keep breathing. He is looking at me and I don't know how to answer. I don't know anything. I look down at his shoulder. His hand is still in my hair. The cloth of his jacket moves as he pulls his arm away and my hair flaps free again.

I look back at his face. We both stay very still: Alan standing in the field on the other side of the grey stones, me kneeling on the bench in the shed, my hand splayed against the wall and my feet over the edge behind me, hanging in the damp air. The sun and the sky are behind him and he stands in the whole thing quite surely. He is like a boy, but me, I am not like a girl.

'I'm sorry you can't come in,' I say.

His gold-green eyes spark up and he looks at me gladly although he is not smiling. 'It's okay,' he says, shaking his head.

He stretches out his hand and presses the pad of his forefinger against the glass, watching it with a look of concentration as he runs it down the pane. He looks up again and smiles. I like it when he smiles. I try to smile back.

Anyway, I draw my face back from the window gap and he watches me lurking there and I look sideways and he departs. He walks like a boy, a graceful lurch, with his fishing rod over his shoulder. I watch him go, a camouflage jacket and a rusty halo.

I turn round to face my shed. It is a little chilly so I pull out the tarpaulin and wrap myself in it like a sausage roll. It feels cold but it will warm up. I stand in it, looking out of the window. Alan is on his way down the road now.

I turn and look out of the other window, into the garden where mum is stooping in a far-off flower bed. She has a head-scarf to keep her glossy dark hair off her face. She is very pretty, my mother. I love her. I watch her for ages, tending to her plants. Mary Mary quite contrary, how does your garden grow?

Lucy and Bryony move past the kitchen window. Mum goes inside, the sky darkens. I lie down on the workbench, all wrapped up but still a little shivery and glad I have got my anorak. I lie on the bench because the concrete floor is colder and not as good.

I have got the trout beside me, it is quite smelly but I like it. It is watching me. I smile. I look out of the window at the stars. The dirty glass is like a skin of ice now, the water has frozen over and me and the fish are under it looking up at the sky. There is a hole in the ice where Alan ran his warm finger through it, a little line where the sky is blacker and the stars are brighter. Stars.

Sun comes nuzzling at my eyelashes, kiss kiss kiss you're lovely. I wake up. I sit up. My neck aches. I look away from the sun and out across the field where it was burning in the evening.

A leg under a blanket. Something close catches my eye, just below me, on the other side. Over the dyke, a human bundle has appeared like a mushroom in the night. Dark reddish-brown hair and closed eyelids, lips parted, breathing sleep. Cardboard under him and a blanket over the top, pulled up to his chin. How can you be there? Beautiful boy. I like looking at

8

him. Did he watch me sleeping under the ice when he came in the night? Did he see me through the hole his hand had made? Waiting beside me on the earth. I watch him as the shadow of my shed slowly shortens. It is rolling back towards me and soon the sun will be falling on his face.

The bolt clanks open and mum is standing in the door in a blue cotton dress. She smiles. I sit still. 'I don't know why you insist on wrapping yourself in that filthy shroud,' she says, striding towards me and kissing me and taking the tarpaulin off my shoulders. 'Come inside and have a bath before breakfast.' She is close to me and smelling of green shampoo. She turns her back and moves towards the door.

I look again at the boy lying in the field and then I follow her.

I lie on my tummy in the big white bath, racing witches. It is a race between the droplets of water sliding down the enamel. I call them witches because of the way they change shape. They start off plump and clear, and then they streak away into dark fishes.

'I need the bathroom!'

I slip down towards the plughole, my head going under. Escaping bubbles of oxygen tickle around my scalp, fizzing out along my seaweed hair and up through the bathwater. In this tank there are loud clankings, echoing in my eardrums. The air in my cheeks runs out and I lift my head out of the water.

'Fucking hell.'

I am still for a second. I don't understand why Lucy hasn't come in. I get out of the bath, squeezing my hair out first, careful not to drip too much on the floor. In a small towel I open the door.

'What were you doing in there?'

'Nothing.'

'Do you mind leaving, or do you want to watch me change my tampon?'

*

I go to my room. It looks like a nice day again. I pull on a pair of red cycling shorts and a white T-shirt. I sit on my bed and comb my hair, thinking about Alan's fingers. I wonder if he is still in the field? I expect not. I wonder why he came? I turn on the hairdryer, hot and loud. It burns my scalp. We don't have to get our hair completely dry, just dry enough not to drip. I hang the towel on the peg on the back of my door and I bounce downstairs.

'Hello, darling,' says mum.

'Hi,' I reply with a small grin. I sit down at the table, next to Bryony. On the kitchen clock, the time is two minutes to nine. Out of the window lupins are swaying while Bryony chatters away. I'm hungry. At thirty seconds to nine Lucy saunters through the door and drops into her chair. She always cuts it fine. Mum says, 'Pass the milk, darling.' We can start now.

'Vanessa,' she says and I look up. 'Are you looking forward to starting at your new school?'

I shrug. 'Yes,' I say.

She expels a clod of air through her nose while cracking a closed-lip smile. Her gaze becomes fixated on the salt. Then she looks up at me fondly and says, 'Try not to get expelled.'

'Yes,' I say. I stick my knife in the jar and start spreading stiff honey on my cold toast.

Lucy says, 'You have to inject heroin in the corridor to get expelled from there.'

'Don't be silly, Lucy,' answers mum. But she's not really paying attention. She's staring out the window at the lupins, her eyes strung through their petals and into herself. We don't say anything else.

There is a bench in front of the house where mum often sits with a book. She goes there after breakfast is done, with a big hardback book about the gardens of Gertrude Jekyll. You can

10

see the top of her head through the kitchen window. Wisps of her dark-brown hair are ruffling in the breeze. So I go out the back door and turn left. I cross the back garden and come to the dyke running up the side, and I get a foothold and lean right over it. There is no sign of Alan. I lean further out and bend double, dipping my head right down, just in case he has burrowed into the very stone. I gaze the length of the dyke, the grass inverted into the roof of my vision. Sky falls away below me. Breakfast rises in my throat. I straighten up. He's not there. I glance around the valley bottom and go back into the house.

The telephone rings. I hate telephone calls. I sneak away from it, into the sitting room, and wait for Bryony to answer it. 'Dad!' she squeals. Damn. I wish I'd picked it up. She is telling him about her new trainers (except she calls them 'sneakers' because she thinks it sounds cool); and now she is telling him about me getting expelled: 'Dad, it was so embarrassing!' Even though he already knows about it. I roll up the hem of my T-shirt. Now Bryony is telling dad about the wildcat that was found dead on the road, and how nobody could understand what it was doing so far from its natural habitat. I come out of the sitting room and stand nearby, leaning against the wall. After she's babbled on for another minute and told him everything of interest, she passes me the phone and skips off into the garden.

'Hi, dad.'

'How's my girl?'

'Okay.'

'What are we going to do with you?'

I think he knows exactly what will have been done with me.

'I don't know.'

'So. What's your news?'

I can see him on the other end of the line, big, broad and fair, planted in the desert. I always imagine him in a telephone box on a flat expanse of empty sand, although he tells me

Saudia Arabia isn't really like that. He says it's very modern. He went there after he got made redundant from his job in Edinburgh, went to work on the oil engineering since that is his field. He wasn't too upset about leaving Scotland. I get the impression he likes living in the Middle East. He gave me a book called *Welcome to Saudi Arabia* and the cities were shown in glossy photographs on its pages. Cities in Saudi Arabia are very clean, with tall shining buildings made of black glass, and black cars, with dark glass, all of it the colour of oil. It is very sleek and fine. There are no camels in the cities any more. They would make too much mess and besides, nobody needs them.

'Nothing of note,' I say.

Dad laughs.

'When are you coming home?' I ask casually.

'I don't know,' comes his breezy reply across two thousand miles. 'I love you,' he says. He waves it at me like a big feathery pampas grass from a departing aeroplane.

'I know.'

Mum comes in and I pass her the phone.

My bedroom is hot. I fling the window wide open. My book is lying ready for me: *Force 10 from Navarone*. I grab it, curl up on my bed and open it at the place marked with a postcard. In two pages I am gone.

'Vanessa!' shouts Lucy from the bottom of the stairs. I wish I wasn't here. She calls again. I post the card in my new place and I go. As soon as she sees me in the stairwell she disappears into the kitchen. I follow her. I am cutting tomatoes and cucumber, washing lettuce as she talks. 'I can't believe you've been inside all morning, Vanessa, stuck in your room, Jesus, I've been sunbathing, look, I've got a tan line already.' She pulls her watch strap to one side, showing off its white imprint on her pale brown arm.

'Very nice,' I say.

'You've just got no idea.' But she looks happy, dancing round the table with vinaigrette and a basket of bread. There's a beautiful butterfly printed on her T-shirt. Its wings stretch right over her bosom, and light comes through the loose cloth under her arms and between her legs, every time she moves. You can see the dark shape of her swimsuit underneath.

'What sort of butterfly is that?'

Her face flicks towards me. She examines me for a second. Then she peers down at her T-shirt, pulling the hem out and away from her body. 'I don't know,' she says. But she is pleased that I asked.

'It looks like a swallowtail.'

'No. I think it's just a made-up one.'

'Is it new?'

'Yep.' She walks round the table, laying down knives.

'Where did you get it?'

'On the school trip to the butterfly farm.'

'Didn't they tell you? If it was a swallowtail?'

'No.' She goes out the door. I can see her through the open window, standing on the front terrace next to the top of mum's head. I sit down at the table.

Mum comes in first, taking off her sunglasses. My sisters are with her. We are eating, and then mum says, 'That was nice, speaking to dad, wasn't it.'

'Yes!' says Bryony eagerly.

'Funny, isn't it. He buggers off and leaves us and – oh! – we all just love it when he calls.' The strands of hair around her face are shaking. We eat very slowly now, so as to be quiet. She's staring out the window again, and then she says, 'Someone left their bath water in.' I can't swallow. 'Who was it?' asks mum, in an interested voice, as if she were asking Who was that man who explored Antarctica? Just remind me.

'Me.'

The bit of cucumber between my molars is becoming unbearable.

'Well.'

I'm staring at the block of cheddar between us, glorious orange, please don't fade.

'Never mind,' she says. We all sit very still. Then she says, 'I'm going into Perth this afternoon.' Everything is all right. Lucy pours a loud glass of water.

I watch the Range Rover skate into the distance, sticking like magic to the tarmac road. The hot noise fades, rears up with the gear changes and fades again. It sounds like mum is making the noise and not the car. I run my fingertips over the rough stone of the terrace where I sit. The glen sifts slowly round me as I watch her disappear. I breathe out and squint into the blue sky.

'You'll get wrinkles,' says Lucy without looking at me. She is lying on her back, on a towel, in swimsuit and sunglasses. Her arms are by her sides. Bryony is lying next to her, doing the same.

'You'll get bored,' I say. Bryony giggles. I smile.

I can see Alan's house from here, the white bungalow far down to the right. I wish he was standing outside.

'Vanessa,' says Lucy. 'Don't you think – are you listening? – don't you think mum's out of order, having a go at dad like that?'

I tilt my head and follow the skyline. Then I follow a trail of scree down to the tree line. From here you can take any line you like around the geometric contours of the conifer plot, and then follow the track down to the road, and the road out to the silhouette of the hill. It all joins up.

'The only reason he went to Saudi was to keep earning money for us. Poor guy.'

'I think he likes it.'

'Necessity is the mother of invention.' Lucy is always coming out with the wrong proverb. She sighs.

I felt Alan's hand touching mine. I follow the swallow that dips overhead. He ran his fingers through my hair and he said: I really like you, Vanessa. The swallow flies right into the sun. I can't go with it any more because the glare is too strong for my eyes. I look away through orange rings into the green of the low grazing by the river. Fish! I had forgotten. He gave me a trout. How did I forget? He gave me a fish, to swim through the night with me. How strangely awful to forget. Shit and shame for leaving it behind. I stare angrily at the shed where it lies. I must rescue that fish. Only, there's no way I can get to it without my sisters seeing. I drum my fingertips on the stone. Such a handsome trout. I exhale loudly and close my eyes. My skin melts away in the sunshine. I open my eyes. Lucy and Bryony stubbornly remain, unmelted.

'I'm going for a walk,' I say.

'Right,' says Lucy.

'Okay,' echoes Bryony. I can see her cheeks trying to hold in another giggle. She's a funny child, always laughing or crying. Worse than usual since Janet left. She was always Janet's favourite, got the biggest flapjacks and smiles.

'See you,' I call, stepping across the garden. I head down the track towards the gateposts. I swing my arms hard, trying to shake the tightness like water drops from my fingertips. On the road, the hot hardness of the tarmac presses through the soles of my trainers. I kick one foot up behind me and now I am running, very fast, down the road, towards the sun. I swing my fists up to my chin and shoot them out behind me as I go. Fresh air pours into the sweating back of my neck, old hair slapping around it. My mouth opens and my eyes half close. A red car comes roaring up behind me and I breathe harder as it hoots. The roar disintegrates into the distance ahead, chasing the exhaust. There is pain in the muscle below my ribcage and in hoops round my back. I slow down, jogging now, stopping when I reach the lay-by. I stand with my hands on my hips and grab short breaths.

I'm really hot now. I'm going to go and lie in the river. So I look both ways and cross the road. I get a foothold in the fence and a hand upon the post and I feel the barbed wire wobble under the sole of my trainer as I hover here, half-sprung, catching my balance on top of the world.

I jump. I glance at the white bungalow nearby. There's nobody there.

I blow my hair out of my face and watch the clumps of grass coming towards my feet. I don't look up again until I'm under the tree. Its leaves are making sense against the sky. Jeez, I'm hot. I jump and land on the shingle. The water sounds so good. I step out on the stones, getting my trainers damp. And then I stick my leg right in it and the cold water rushes into the sweaty towelling around my swollen foot. Oh man. And the other leg. I stand, with the river flowing round my calves, quite happy with me being part of it, as if I were a pair of fence posts. It feels so good.

I sit down and cool my crotch. The water makes sucking noises in my clothes. I kind of laugh, and lie down backwards, settling carefully among the rocks. Water flows all around me, streaming through my clothes and out my fingertips spread wide like webbed feet. Ah, it soothes the sore skin on my back.

The sky is so deep overhead. It's hard to imagine the blueness ending in atmosphere and space. It doesn't seem to have a back to it. But I suppose it does. I close my eyes. I am an aquatic plant. I make food from sunlight. I smile. My tendrils are delicious.

After a bit my skin gets cold and soggy. My palms pucker and my bottom goes like metal jelly. I stand, and stagger under the weight of my waterlogged clothes. My trainers stumble in the stones. I lurch forward. My arms fly wide. I grab my balance and straighten up. I look quickly around. It's all right, he isn't here, he didn't see. I clamber on to the bank and lay myself down to dry. I am breathing too fast.

I pick at the grass growing next to me but it is not all that entertaining and I am getting bored of lying here. I sit up and look at the white bungalow. There is no car outside and no sign of Alan.

I cross the river and walk up the field the other side. Three sheep start trotting, swerving nervously in circles. Stupid animals. I cut up to the corner of Alan's back garden. There is nobody there. I stand by the fence for a while. I don't know what to do. I squat down and listen. There is nothing, nothing but the small wind blowing and the faint hum of his washing machine. I slide sideways between the wires of the fence. His garden isn't barbed.

It isn't much like a garden at all. The grass hasn't been mown for a while and grows in tussocks with daisies and dock leaves in. I stand on it. I move across it and stop behind the rosebush that grows like a lone cowboy in the middle of the lawn. The flowers have enormous bright pink petals and open themselves wide around rings of yellow pollen. I glance down at the faint outline of what was once a flower bed, circling the rose bush on the ground. Like an ancient settlement, it tells secrets beneath my aerial photographing eyes. It is grassed over. I am in Alan's garden. I look up.

Alan's face is at the window. He is sitting silhouetted, busy doing something. I look around me, but no one else is here. I'm the only one.

He raises his head. Wind ruffles the pink petals at my waist. I stay behind them. I am being very still, but not as still as him because the wind has got into my damp hair tails. Half of what I see in the window is me in the garden reflected back at myself, but I can see enough of Alan's face behind it to know that now he is looking at me. He has seen me. I want to fly away. Or stay, and just be part of the garden. A bird table, perhaps. He goes away, to get a sandwich or watch TV.

I thank God, in spite of the flapping little disappointment. I walk fast towards the track that leads away from the front of the house. I get to the white corner. It is encrusted with little bits of broken shell. I look over my shoulder. I see Alan, standing in the garden. He is just wearing a pair of shorts made of jeans cut off at the knee. I can see his nipples.

'Hi there,' I say.

'What are you doing?' he asks.

I wonder where they got all these shells from. It looks very prickly. Not the sort of wall you would like to be thrown against. 'Going for a walk,' I say.

'In my garden.'

I lean with my hand against the wall. The pain is kind of reassuring. 'Yeah.'

'Do you want to come inside?'

I press my hand harder. 'Is your mum and dad home?'

'No.'

'Yeah.' I walk towards him, brave like a paratrooper, and follow him to the back door.

It is dark inside and it smells of modern things. It smells of thick carpets and air fresheners. I remember it.

'Take your shoes off,' says Alan. 'Do you want some squash?'

I shake my head, although I am thirsty.

He moves from one foot to the other, slowly. 'Do you want to see my room?'

'Okay.'

His brown back glides ahead like a beautiful flatfish.

There is a light in his bedroom, on a bent stalk angled over a desk by the window.

'What are these?' I ask, picking up one of the figurines from off the desk.

'Warhammer,' says Alan. 'Do you know it?'

'No.' I wish I did.

I feel funny, being in Alan's room again and not being a child any more. 'I like your room,' I say. 'The way you've got it.'

'Do you?' He looks surprised.

I nod.

I am desperate to say something. I'm not sure what it is or how to say it. I glance around his walls. Time swells up in my head, squeezing out my brain. All I can think is a big noisy silence. I turn my back on the room and stare straight ahead at the map of Scotland on the wall above the desk. Dumfries! Dumfries! It won't go away.

'Thank you,' I rudely say. 'You know, for before. Thanks.' I sneak a glance over my shoulder. He is standing looking embarrassed. Thank God it's done. Oh look, there's Loch Leven.

'We've been doing Mary Queen of Scots at school,' I say.

'You'll probably be ahead,' mumbles Alan.

'I don't think so.' The pause is awkward. 'Have you done her?' I wish I could think of something cool to talk about instead of school work.

'No.' He sits down on the bed and shuffles backwards so that he is leaning against the wall with his bare knees bent up in front of him. 'We did Early Peoples of Scotland, but. And King Canute and Eisenhower.'

'I don't know Eisenhower.'

'He's an American president.' He is going a bit red, embarrassed about knowing. But he ploughs ahead. 'I like the Early Peoples,' he says. 'You know, the brochs and crannogs and stuff.'

'Yeah! It's ace.'

His face brightens. 'You've done it too?'

'Yes,' I say, although really I read it in books from the library. I love the pictures in them, the aerial photographs of Iron Age hill forts and neolithic tombs mumbling a lumpy old truth out of the land. I love the drawings of hairy families from six thousand years ago, sitting grinding in the grass. People lived here and they were just like you and now they are dead but it's okay. It all fits.

'There's a Pictish stone up at Dunfallandy,' says Alan.

'Really?'

'Aye, it's totally cool. All carved and stuff.'

I nod. 'Cool.'

'Maybe you'll be in my class,' says Alan. My heart starts beating fast. I shrug and look at the map. I put my finger on the place where we are, up from Perth and then west, and I stand there. I hope he's not looking at me.

'Have you been to Inverness?' I ask.

'Aye.'

Why did I ask him that?

'Vanessa,' he says, 'why are you wet?'

I take my finger off the map and turn round. 'I was in the river.'

'What, you fell in?' He is looking at me, amazed.

'No. Just lay down. I was hot.' I don't mind him laughing. I like it. I smile. 'What, don't you get hot?' I say.

'Aye,' says Alan, 'I go in the river when I'm hot. It's just that I take my clothes off first.'

I stare at him.

He looks offended. 'Uch, I keep my pants on, Vanessa. I'm not a tink.'

'I didn't—'

'Doesn't matter.' He is still smiling, that perfect smile. 'Do you want a biscuit?'

'Yeah,' I say, although I'm not hungry. I smile back.

We sit on the back doorstep with the biscuit tin between us. I unwrap a Wagon Wheel and Alan says, 'Were you cold last night?' I shake my head. He looks at his feet and then he carries on. 'Is everything okay at home?' he asks.

'Yup.' I say it like a suitcase lock snapping in and hope he gets the message. Don't ask me anything else please. For revenge, I say, 'Is everything okay with you?' Ha ha.

But he cocks his head thoughtfully and slowly says, 'I suppose so. My folks are fighting a bit.' I look down at my cheery red biscuit wrapper in embarrassment. 'They shout and stuff, but I don't think they're going to divorce. I think they love each other.' He just sits there, eyeing the hillside.

Suddenly I am angry. 'Why are you telling me?' I turn to him with tight shoulders.

He stares. 'You asked me!'

'Well, I didn't mean it.' I stand up, wishing my cycling shorts had pockets, somewhere to put my hands. They are feeling shy. The biscuit wrapper flutters around my purple trainer. I glance down at Alan and see that he is looking sideways, away from me. The look in his eyes is strange. My skin is cold. But now I've stood up, I can't sit down again. I can't stay standing here, either. I look like an idiot. I am going to have to leave. I push my foot off the doorstep and walk across the grass. Please shout after me. Please say something. But he doesn't. I'm nearly at the fence, and still no words. I go as slow as I can. I put it off, but eventually I am standing at the wire, looking out at the field of sheep. I turn round. 'Do you want to come for a walk?' I say.

He looks at me. 'Where are you going?'

'Don't know.'

He doesn't move.

'Up to the wood.'

He is not looking friendly but he says, 'Okay.' He gets his trainers and he comes.

The trees grow very close, farmed in furrows. We have to duck down and squeeze between. It is dark and green, with a floor of rocks and orange needles. We are building a bivouac, so we don't say much. We just crawl on our knees and pass each other branches.

When it is done, we sit in it. I see the red scratches that the prickly sitka has scraped on Alan's ribcage. He is scattered with criss-crossing lines. 'You're scratched,' I say.

'Not as badly as you,' he answers.

He is wrong, because I am mostly protected by the cloth of my T-shirt. I check my forearms, but the marks there are only white ones – light, surface scratches. 'I'm not,' I say.

'On your back,' says Alan, looking at me soft. 'I saw the marks on your back.' He looks down at the ground.

'How did you?'

'When you were leaning forward. Your T-shirt went up. I was behind you.' His face is flushing under the tan. 'I wasn't perving or anything. I just saw.'

'So?'

'It looked sore.'

'It's not. It only hurt at the time.' I should probably not have got expelled. But I did, and it is better to get punished like that and have it over with. After she's done, you know you're going to be all right. It's the end. She slaps it shut. Sometimes she cries. I shrug. 'I shouldn't have got expelled,' I tell him.

Alan just looks at me.

'Don't tell anyone,' I say. 'It's the only time, you know. My mum is really cool.' I crawl out of the bivouac. 'Are you staying here?'

He nods.

'I'm going home,' I say.

'Hey,' says Alan. 'Do you want to come round tomorrow?'

I don't know if I will be able to. I smile at his serious face. 'Maybe.'

*

As I come down the hill I can see my sisters still laid out in front of our house on the other side of the glen. Mum's car is not back yet. I hop across the rocks in the river.

'Hi, dead bodies,' I say, stepping over Lucy and Bryony. They have been rolled on to their fronts. Lucy has got a Walkman on her head.

Bryony is reading a book about cheerleaders. She beams. 'Hi, Vanessa.'

I smile and say, 'Spanner,' as I walk into the house. Maybe I'll see Alan tomorrow. I like being with him. I take three apples out the bowl and I juggle. I like juggling. The less you think about it, the better you get.

At last, Lucy comes inside. Bryony is following her. I sneak out of the back door and hurry round to the front of the house. And very slowly raise my head so that I can peer into the kitchen window. They aren't there. They must have gone upstairs. I run across the garden to the shed. The bolt is well-oiled. I burst inside, into the familiar damp coolness. I don't want to be in here long. I want to get out. I grab the fish from off the bench. My body slackens the second I get outside again. I slide the bolt back through and my fingers bounce away from it as if it is burning hot, but it is not. I walk back, with the trout concealed behind the side of my leg.

Little fish, little fish. I lay it on a plate and I put it in the fridge. I stroke its sticky scales and then I shut the fridge door and wash my hands.

Mum's car bumps up the track. She goes straight to the garden and sits on her bench. I don't know what she is doing. She hasn't got her book. Oh well. I take out a pad of paper and sit drawing at the kitchen table. I draw a city filled with trees and wild plants. There is a big cathedral with foxgloves growing from its windows, and all the houses have blue speedwell and clumps of ferns sprouting between their bricks. Ivy and dog roses grow over some of the roads, turning them into green tunnels. There is grass instead of tarmac, and the houses are tall and graceful.

Next time I look out the window mum has got her secateurs out. She is bending over by a flower bed. 'Hello, darling,' she says, walking off the terrace and into the kitchen in her glamorous shades. She is holding three white lilies.

'Hi,' I say, following her with my eyes as she props them in a vase. She keeps rearranging them, although there are only three. She seems a million miles away. I go back to my picture.

'Oh!'

I look up. Mum is standing at the open fridge, looking like an alien. I concentrate very hard and very obviously on my drawing. 'Vanessa,' she says.

'Mmm?' I look up, clearly torn away from my work.

'Do you know why there's a trout in the fridge?' It is a genuine question.

'No.' I carry on drawing.

'It wasn't there at lunchtime.' She shrugs and pulls out the bottle of Coke. She wanders back to the vase and stands there sipping her drink, made with a little splash of vodka.

'Maybe it's a miracle,' I say.

I surround the Senate with cow parsley.

'Yes,' says mum vaguely. She swallows her drink and makes another. 'We'll have it for supper.'

I nip my tongue between my teeth and smile at my pencil.

'Let's see your drawing!' says Bryony.

'It's not finished.'

'Come on, darling.' Mum is walking over to me. I take my hands off it. She lowers her sunglasses a little, peering over the top and scanning my page. 'Bit lopsided, isn't it. Why's it full of weeds?' She wanders off, saying, 'I'd stick to the sums if I were you, darling.'

Lucy glances down. 'Ha ha!' She starts laughing. 'Interesting,' she says, as I cover it with my hands. 'I take it you haven't come to grips with perspective yet.' As if I care.

Bryony is looking at me. She wants to be nice but she wants to agree with the others. She fidgets awkwardly. 'It hasn't got any people in,' she gabbles, and scurries to the window.

I just stare at her. That child is weird. She is standing with her back to me as I pick up my pad and leave the room. When I close my bedroom door, I hear her feet running up the stairs and down the passage to Lucy's room. I take my drawing out of the pad and tack it on the wall.

At supper, I smile over my tender trout mouthful. I eat the rest of my plate first – pea and mushroom rice – so it is saved till last. So its taste sits smoking in my mouth for ages afterwards. I enjoy watching the others eat it. I know something good, as Bryony cries as usual about having to eat slimy mushrooms. It is strange how mum doesn't hold her mouth open and force them down. She is just sitting there, still wearing her sunglasses. I can't see her eyes but I think she is staring at the wall. I shift in my chair. Bryony stops crying and looks at mum. You can see her wondering if maybe she can get away with leaving the mushrooms on her plate. But she doesn't dare and so she sits there forcing them down all by herself, crying again. Lucy starts staring at the wall as well, but she stares hard, as if she hates us all. I don't care. I've eaten a secret fish.

Sun wakes me. I'm a sleeping warrior with long strong hair. Like scissors, my eyelashes cut into the day. I roll around yawning and wanting something. I lie on my back and hang upside down over the side of the bed. The courage of last night is gone, but that looks better. Blood thrashes around in my temples.

Breakfast in my belly and still I don't feel right. I stand on the terrace bouncing a ball. The morning air is still cold. Mum is in the kitchen, washing up. It is ever since yesterday morning that she has been going round with that funny look on her face. She looks the way people look on buses and trains and in doctors' waiting rooms. I wish she would go back to normal. Anyway. The ball sucks into my hand. Slaps the ground. It comes back again, and again, flying between my hand and the stone. I fall into its even beat.

Mum glides past me, slow with her new inertia. I can hear her secateurs clip-clip-clipping, dragged out like the tune in a wound-down Walkman. Cliiip. Space. Cliiip. Space. Bang, bang, bang, I bounce the ball faster. The clipping stops and she glides slowly back past me. She is going to the kitchen with a basket of flowers to hang from the rack above the range. 'Hi darling,' she says to me as she disappears through the door.

'Hi,' I say to the empty space. I keep bouncing the ball. I can hear morning kids' TV squawking out the sitting-room window. I chuck my ball high up in the air and turn my back. I walk away and hear it landing behind me. The bouncing dribbles away.

He said to come round. I stand at the bottom of his track looking at his house. It squats, and the sun climbs higher behind it. It's going to be another hot day. I start walking towards it.

The bell rings behind the front door. I hear him coming.

'Vanessa,' he says when he opens the door.

'You said to come round.'

'Come in.' He holds the door open and we both stand in the hall.

I fix my eyes on his black T-shirt. Laughter bursts from a nearby room. My eyes shoot up to his face. 'Who's that?' I whisper.

'Who is it, Alan?' calls a voice. It sounds like his mother. I look at Alan very hard, mainly because I don't know what else to do.

He looks unsure. 'It's Vanessa,' he calls back, slowly, as if to make it better.

'Gordon,' I hear her say to herself, speaking my surname as if it is some kind of radioactive element. Alan hears it too and his eyes seem very careful. His mother comes into the hall. Lilian McAlpine is much plainer than my mother and also she is quite small. Still, I am scared of her. I don't know anyone else like her; she is completely different from all the other adults who are my mother's friends or my friends' mothers. I am sure that she hates me and thinks I'm posh. She certainly doesn't like my family.

'Hello Vanessa,' she says.

'Hello,' I say, glancing at her and staring at the wallpaper. Nobody says anything. My face starts going red.

'Well,' says Mrs McAlpine, 'why don't you come into the lounge.' Oh no. Please can I go home. But I follow her and Alan follows behind me.

His older sister Morna is sitting on the sofa. This is getting awful. 'Hi Vanessa,' she says.

'Hi,' I say, looking at the patch of brown velour sofa above her shoulder.

'Have a seat,' says Mrs McAlpine. There is nowhere except the sofa. I slide on to its far end and clasp my hands. Alan squats down on the footstool. Mrs McAlpine leans over the glass coffee table. 'Do you drink tea these days, Vanessa?'

'Er, no.'

'Have a biscuit.' They have got some on a plate. I take one. It makes crumbs down my T-shirt. I glance over at Alan. He is looking at the carpet.

'Does your mother know you're here?' asks Mrs McAlpine.

'No.'

That makes her smile.

'I hear you're coming to the High,' says Morna from the other end of the sofa.

'Aye,' I answer, trying to sound more like them. Alan stares at me. I can feel the redness flooding back.

'Well, it's a good school.' Mrs McAlpine sips her tea. The brass carriage clock ticks away on the mantelpiece.

'I've not seen Lucy for a while,' says Morna with a snag in her voice.

I want to say It's not my fault.

'Is she home?'

I nod. She laughs. She is laughing at Lucy for thinking she wasn't good enough. They used to be friends. We were all friends. It went a bit wrong, though. One day when we were all five of us watching telly in the sitting room in my house, and Morna asked Lucy when she was having her birthday party, and Lucy rolled on to her back and lay there on the carpet with her hair fanned out around her head. She was gazing at the ceiling and she said, 'Morna, I don't think you should come.'

'Why?' asked Morna.

And Lucy just said, 'You're common. You wouldn't fit in.' And then she sighed dramatically. Me and Alan looked at each other and Morna stormed home. Mr McAlpine came round and spoke to my mother. It started off very polite and ended in a shouting match in the kitchen.

'Well, Alan,' says Morna, 'I hope you feel honoured.'

'Vanessa's been here before,' says Alan.

'Not within living memory.'

'She came here yesterday.'

'And so how's your dad, Vanessa?' says Mrs McAlpine.

'Fine thanks.'

'Well, that's good. Where is he again?'

'Saudi Arabia.'

'I bet you get some good postcards, do you?'

I nod. 'Quite sandy.' Nobody says anything for a few seconds after and I wish I had said something more sensible. But what could be more sensible than sand? All the little shells that sheltered the soft creatures, finally ground down into something to make glass and sandcastles from.

'He's an engineer, isn't he?' I actually look Mrs McAlpine in the eye when she says that, because I am so grateful.

'Yes,' I say. I'm feeling brave now. I'm going to be sociable. 'You work in the, um, Job Centre, don't you?' I ask. I am glad I remembered that. Morna makes a funny noise and gets up and walks out of the room.

'Yes,' says Mrs McAlpine. This clock is very loud. 'I expect you'll be wanting to get outside. Alan, don't forget you're helping your dad with the car this afternoon. Come back for five, will you.'

'Aye,' drawls Alan, getting to his feet. I stand up, and a few biscuit crumbs float down through the air. I examine the carpet and shuffle out the door, following Alan. Mrs McAlpine is still sitting in the armchair, looking out the window with a funny smile.

'Why isn't your mum at work?' I say as soon as we get outside.

'It's Saturday.'

'Oh.' In the holidays, the days of the week run together like mud. 'Hey Alan,' I say, as we slide through the fence. Or rather, I slide through it and Alan climbs over the top. He looks at me. 'We had your fish for supper last night.' I open my mouth and smile at him, showing my teeth and everything.

He stands in the field grinning back at me. 'Good,' he says, turning his back and walking on. Jeez, I love his walk. I want to wrap myself around his leg. I don't know why. He turns and finds me staring at him. 'What are you doing?' he says.

'Admiring your lovely legs.'

'Ach, fuck off.'

I run to catch up.

Chapter Two

My uniform sits folded on the chair beside my bed. I come in
clean from the shower and pull on my pants and vest. Mum has
washed and ironed them for me and they smell of warmth. My
heart swells up like a loving bullfrog. I pull on my navy-blue
opaque tights. They hide the marks on my legs.

'Very smart,' says mum, and I believe her, when I walk into
the kitchen. She stoops and kisses my cheek. 'Breakfast!' she
says. It's like a party, with just the two of us. We have eggs and
toast, and mum makes me laugh with my mouth full. I pull my
hair into a ponytail and pick up my bag. Mum bought me a new
one, and I have a selection of brand-new writing tools inside it.
Anyway, I put on my anorak, sling the bag over my shoulder
and kiss her goodbye.

'I love you, darling,' says mum.

'I love you too.'

I walk down the track and wait at the gate for the bus to
come. I turn round a couple of times and Mum is always at the
window, looking out and smiling at me. She waves. Beautiful
face at the window, you can look so different. But it's okay, I
know the real one.

The minibus pulls up. It is white, and people's heads are in
the windows. I pull in my stomach, getting ready. Duck my
head and climb through the sliding door. All the heads look at
me. Ten faces. I try to smile but my mouth feels tight. I take the
single seat by the window and hold my bag on my lap. I glance
at the others. They are all looking at me. An older girl at the
back is whispering into a pale boy's ear. I face out of the window
as the bus pulls away.

'Hey!' says one of the boys. 'You're that new girl.'

'So?' I have lit little fires in my eyes to scare away wolves from my cave. Stone Age girls weren't stupid.

'Are you Vanessa Gordon?' He has short black hair and a skinny face. His eyes wrinkle up when he speaks.

'Yes.'

'Ma mum was talkin about you. You went tae a private school.'

'So?'

He looks at me and grimaces.

I look back.

He turns round to someone sitting behind him. 'Did ye see the Rangers game?'

Alan comes sliding towards me on the verge. The minibus pulls to a halt at his track. The door shudders and slides sideways. His reddish-brown hair is in the bus and then his face. He grins at me. Oh thank you. Morna climbs in after him. Oh no. She gives me a dead look and brushes past to a seat at the back. 'Hi Robbie,' says Alan, sliding on to the seat at the front. Him and the boy Robbie start talking about rock bands. Interrupting himself, Alan turns round to me and says, over the top of the seat, 'Hi Vanessa.' He smiles at me again and goes back to his conversation. Morna and the older girl at the back of the bus are watching. Me, I watch the fields go by. A girl shouts 'posh girl' from a few rows behind but nobody takes her up on it. I hear her whispering to the friend sitting next to her. The friend mutters 'posh girl' half-heartedly. I smile out the window.

'Hey Alan,' shouts the louder girl, 'who's your girrilfriend?' She giggles.

'Fuck off, Aileen,' says Alan, considerately, like he's telling her she should be getting more rest. Morna says nothing.

It looks a lot uglier than my old school, all dirty concrete and tarmac instead of butter-painted stone and lawns. The bus drops us off in the big tarmac rectangle in front of the building. It is very colourful because everyone is wearing different coloured jackets, walking across the tarmac, flitting between concrete pillars, sitting on benches, red, blue, black and orange. At St Peter's, everyone was a matching shade of aubergine.

I must report to the office. I am to go in the main doors and turn left. I look up. Sun bounces off the rows of windows. Red paint peels off their frames. I look straight ahead. There is the main door, under a concrete overhang to protect you from rain or bird shit.

'Vanessa,' says Alan at my side.

'Hi there.'

'How're you doing? Don't mind Aileen. She's a silly bisom.'

'I'm fine.' I hoik up the bag strap on my shoulder. 'I've got to go to the office.'

He stands around.

'See you later,' I say, heading off across the tarmac.

'Aye,' says Alan.

The woman at the office says yes, I am in 2B. She goes out the door into the entrance hall. I can see her standing with her hands on her hips, scanning the people going past. 'Siobhan!' she yells.

A girl stops and turns her head. 'Mrs Mackie.'

The woman jerks her head and Siobhan rolls her eyeballs and comes walking towards the office. I pick up my bag and stand in the doorway.

'This is Vanessa,' says the woman. 'She's joining 2B.'

'Hiya,' says Siobhan, looking at me like I'm a jar in a sweet shop. Wondering whether to buy me. Trying to see what I've got inside. Chewing her gum.

'Hi,' I say.

'Take her down to registration,' says the woman.

We walk down red linoleum corridors. Siobhan's hair is

cherry coloured and shiny with spray. It moves in a solid mass. 'You're new?' she says.

'Yeah.' I don't know why she asks me.

'Ha ha.'

She pushes through a swing door. We're outside again. There is a warren of concrete paths among prefabs and our classroom is inside one of these.

Twenty faces in the classroom turn and look. They murmur and then the noise grows back to where it was, shouting and jabbering about holidays and new clothes. Hi, hi, hi.

'Ah!' says the voice of the man at the big desk. He has the look of a clever fool about him. 'Vanessa Gordon, I presume.'

'Yeah.'

'I've heard all about you!' I smile politely at the bald head. 'Quiet, everyone!' shouts the man. 'Everyone, this is Vanessa Gordon. She is new.' I would have thought that was obvious.

'Hi,' I murmur, but they are all talking again.

'We are honoured to have her with us,' he says. Jesus.

'Gordon,' shouts Siobhan. 'You're over here.'

I squeeze between backs of chairs and fronts of desks. A boy is getting out of a chair next to her. Everyone is shuffling around and changing places.

'What's going on?' shouts the man.

'G comes between F and H,' says Siobhan.

He doesn't reply, just looks down at some reading.

The girl's name is Siobhan Hare, the teacher calls it out on the registration list.

'Mr Horace is a total arse,' explains the girl sitting just behind me, when the list is done and the noise is back. I turn round in my chair. Siobhan breaks in, 'Aye, he's a fuckin eejit. This is Ruth.'

'Hi,' I say. Ruth has a seriously ugly mouth but it doesn't seem to bother her. It is better when she's talking. When she's resting, her lips fold inwards and completely disappear into a spooky crack across her face.

'You jist moved here?' asks Siobhan.

'No.'

'Eh, she talks very nicely!' Siobhan turns round to other people. 'See the way she says 'no'! Say no again.'

'No,' I say, meaning that I won't.

Siobhan crows. I am not sure I like her. 'Gnoh,' she mimics. 'Ah, you're deid posh.'

I shrug.

She looks at me. 'Eh,' she says. 'Only jokin, eh.'

'I don't mind,' I say. I turn round and say to Ruth, 'Where do you live?' It's a crap question but it will do. Siobhan sits sulking against the wall. No one's going to get me.

I look around and take them all in. A girl on the other side of the room stares back at me. She is sitting in the centre of a trio, flanked by a dark girl and a good-looking boy. She sticks her tongue out at me. The girl and boy turn to see me and they all start laughing. I look at my desk. I catch her wrinkling her nose at me later on.

'Hey, Vanessa!' calls the girl, as we leave the maths room. I wait for her. She doesn't bother rushing, just ambles gently towards me. Her permed brown hair sways either side of her pretty green-eyed face. 'Walk with us to french,' she says.

'All right.'

'I'm Angie. Angie Cameron.' She sounds very proud of it. 'You're friends with Alan, aren't you.'

'Kind of. Yes.'

'Alan's lovely, isn't he.'

I shrug.

She continues. 'Me and Debbie are really good friends with him.'

I say nothing.

'God, you're not very talkative, are ye?'

We turn a corner.

'No.'

She starts laughing. Then she stops.

She makes me sit next to her in french. French is a piece of piss. I've been learning it since I was seven, and here we are back buying a handbag with Marie-Claire. I pretend I can't do it, because I'm not stupid.

The bell rings. 'Come with me,' says Angie Cameron. I follow her outside and the dark girl is walking behind us. 'This is Laura,' says Angie, introducing her friend.

'Hiya,' says Laura, collapsing on to an outdoor bench. 'I'm supposed to sit next to you in Reggie but I can't be arsed.' She drops a mint into her mouth. 'Giuliani, Gordon, Hare, ken. Siobhan is such a pain, though. I can't stand that side of the room. So I defecated to the other side. I told Mr Horace that my name was actually spelt with a C. I told him that an Italian C is pronounced J.' She examines her shiny purple fingernails, very cool. 'He's a total moron, you can get away with anything.'

'You mean defected,' I say, without thinking.

'What?'

'Doesn't matter.'

'Then why did you say it?'

'Defecating means shitting.'

Angie cracks up. The laughter just tears right out of her. She peeks around to soak up all the people who have turned to look at her. She giggles for a bit and then stops.

'Hi,' says a tall girl with blonde hair, an undernourished Viking princess.

'Debbie,' says Angie, 'this is the new girl, Vanessa.'

Debbie examines me very thoroughly. Her eyes are rimmed with black to match the scrap of black lycra loitering under her baggy jumper and above her DM boots. The others wear the same, but with dark-grey or purple jumpers instead of black. They all wear the same skirts, that scoop their bottoms and stop just under. Debbie has her straight blonde hair pulled up into a high ponytail like mine, with waxed ends and fringe. I see her take in my hair colour with displeasure. Her pale-blue eyes look a wee bit scared. In the same way that dogs look scared of postmen, before they bite. What are you doing on my patch, foreign intruder in your shiny red van?

'Nice skirt,' she says very sweetly. Mine is a short navy kilt made of wool. Me and mum chose it together.

'Thanks,' I say.

Debbie raises an eyebrow and laughs. She stretches a hand down to Laura, who is sitting on the bench enjoying this.

'I was joking,' says Debbie. She walks off, linking arms with her two friends. Oh well. I sit down on the bench and lean back with my eyes closed, waiting for the bell.

Mum wants to know if I have had a nice day. I say yes, it was fine, and pour a glass of milk.

'Have you made friends with any of them?' Have you made contact with Mars?

'Yeah.'

'Well, tell me then.' She is intent and nervous.

'I sat with this girl Siobhan in the canteen for lunch.'

'And she's all right, is she?'

'Kind of. She teased me a bit, but she's okay.'

Mum throws her arms in the air. I follow them, but her hands have not fallen off. She is so strong, you sometimes expect her to accidentally break herself. 'Heh!' says mum. 'She teased you?' Her voice starts rising. 'And you're going to be friends with her? For God's sake Vanessa, don't be such a doormat! For crying out loud!' She grabs my shoulders and starts shaking me. The milk in the glass I am holding sloshes from side to side. 'You've got to be harder!' shouts mum. Her face is very close to mine and her eyes are wide open, demanding me. I see her mouth going open and closed, enormous and full of breath. I am trying not to spill my milk. 'Harder!' she repeats. She lets me go. I put my glass down on the shelf.

'But not with me, Vanessa.' Her voice has changed to soft and gentle. She steps towards me and wraps her arms around me. Something in my chest falls down. 'You don't ever have to be hard with me.' She strokes my hair. 'Now, what shall we have for tea?' Malt loaf, mum, let's have malt loaf and butter. I love your soft jumper against my cheek. She pushes me away and fills the kettle.

I change out of my uniform, peeling my tights down very slowly. The cuts are not too bad. It wasn't mum's fault, I was just running away from her and I fell. She had caught me reading a novel with lots of sex in, *Blue Diamonds* by Giselle Harris. I got it in a bag of books from the PTA jumble sale in the village, you get ten for 50p. I don't know what happens at the end of the story because mum caught me reading it and started screaming. Dirt, filth, you little idiot, do you think this is going to teach you anything? You don't have a clue about sex and if you think reading drivel like this is going to help you understand then you're sorely mistaken. She started reading off the back cover in an acid voice: ' "Rich, spoilt Cecily De Vere seems to have everything . . . except satisfaction. Ha! She embarks on an erotic journey of sexual discovery bla fuckity bla searching for love" – Love! Golly gosh! Well that will make it all turn out fine. And in the meantime, sex is just something you can muck about with, isn't it. Isn't it, Vanessa! Won't hurt anyone! Bullshit! It's a load of utter bullshit.' Crap. Rubbish. You. Pervert. Idiot.

She told me to wait while she went downstairs but I wasn't going to do that. I ran outside and into the garden. She saw me and came chasing after, screaming at me to get back in the house. She chased me round and round the flower beds till the grass beneath my feet was a speeding green blur. I looked over my shoulder as I ran. My foot hooked into the ground and tripped. I flew very slowly, and, when I landed, wire frames for the flowers came out to meet me. The sharp metal ends ripped my skin. I lay in the ruined plants with my eyes wide open as mum caught up with me.

'Are you all right?' she enquired, looming over me.

I nodded.

'Then get out of my plants!'

I staggered out and she saw the gashes on my legs.

'Bloody oaf,' said mum. 'Get inside.'

I hovered there behind her, thinking that maybe I could do something to make it better. She knelt, trying to heal the damage I had done to her flowers. They were totally mangled. I looked at all the broken stems and squashed leaves and then I felt sick.

'Get inside,' said mum again, and this time I went. I went inside and kicked the book round my room. Anyway, that's how I cut my legs.

I am putting on a pair of leggings and the jumper with the big sheep on the front. I lie on my bedroom floor, flat on my tummy, and stretch my arm out under my bed. My arm swipes around like a windscreen wiper until I find it.

I get a blue biro and sit down with *Blue Diamonds*. I give the lady on the front cover lots of snot droplets around her nose, and a pair of horns. Then I black out some of her teeth and give her spots. I write 'Debbie' next to her and start laughing.

It wasn't even a very good book. I prefer the ones about war and spies.

I look at the picture again and suddenly I think *No*. I score out Debbie's name and throw the book back under my bed. I could read the ending, if I wanted to. But I can't be bothered, and I stand in the middle of my room.

Siobhan wants to be my best friend now. 'Dinna mind Angie

and Laura,' she says. 'They awny hate you cos you're beautiful.' Then she laughs sarcastically.

'And you only hate them because they're popular.' I laugh sarcastically back.

She shuts up. 'I don't hate them,' she says, toying with a chip. She is telling the truth. 'Comin for a dander?' she says, rocking back on the canteen chair.

'Okay.'

'Hey,' says Siobhan, as we walk down the corridor. 'What did the number zero say to the number eight?'

'I don't know.'

'Nice belt.'

I start coughing. 'That's crap,' I say. I start laughing.

Alan is approaching. He is parallel. He halts, and I'm still giggling. 'Hi, Vanessa,' he says.

'Hi,' I say, wavering. This is not how it was meant to be. I've been wanting to speak to him ever since Monday. 'Sorry,' I say.

'What for?'

'I don't know.'

He is looking at me very closely, and his eyes seem to be thinking I've been avoiding him. He isn't sure and he just says 'Right,' and looks at his shoes. Then he says, very casual: 'Do you want to come down the street with me for lunch tomorrow?'

'Okay.' I hope I sound cool.

'Good,' says Alan.

'Okay,' I say again and start walking on down the corridor.

Siobhan is chattering. 'You jammy wee bint, Alan jist asked you out.'

My head is light like my skull is filled with sherbet. I shrug and say: 'Yeah.'

There is a cluster of other second years at the end of the corridor. Two pairs of legs are swinging from bums perched on the window ledge. Angie and Debbie, sitting with Laura on the ground beside them. Debbie's boyfriend Pete is there too, sitting further back on the window shelf with his legs wrapped round Debbie's slender body from behind. Now and again he pulls her hair. She doesn't seem to mind the opportunity to squeal. Every time he does it the audience laughs. There are about five of them standing by.

Debbie looks up as we approach. 'Hi, Siobhan!' she calls cheerily. Everyone turns round and Siobhan looks surprised.

'Hiya,' she says in response.

'I love your necklace,' says Debbie. 'It's gorgeous!' It is a silver CND logo on a leather thong. Siobhan stops and Debbie motions her to come closer. Siobhan hesitates for a second and then she steps forward.

'Wicked,' says Debbie, raising the necklace a few centimetres in her fingers. 'Where did you get it?'

Siobhan is glowing. 'Bits'n'Pieces.'

'It's cool,' says a satellite called Sarah Black. One of Debbie's henchladies.

'Yeah,' echo the others.

Even Pete says, 'Cool, Siobhan,' and smiles at her over Debbie's shoulder.

I start walking on alone towards the swing doors. Debbie calls after me, 'Oh, hi Vanessa.' I chew my lip. She is transparent. I hit the doors gladly, a cowboy swinging through the saloon with pistols loaded beneath my coat. The doors burst open behind me a few seconds later and footsteps come thudding quickly until they catch me up.

'Hiya,' says Siobhan, out of breath. She looks embarrassed.

'Hi there,' I say. I look at her again and a small balloon of sympathy bursts inside me. She looks like a hunger striker who has just gorged herself on chocolate cake. Man, it was delicious, but oh – so undignified. She smiles weakly at me.

'Did you hear about the man who drowned in muesli?' I say.

'Nuh,' she says, perking up, laughing before I have even given the punchline.

'He was pulled down by a strong currant.'

She finds it hysterical. I lean against the wall and look up at the grey sky. I don't care about them, but she does. Poor girl. Ah well, I am going down the street with Alan tomorrow.

I am too scared to look at him on the bus home. I feel him watching me from time to time. I dig my eyes deeper into the passing streets, the brown fields, the road shrinking narrower into the hills. When he gets off the bus, I watch his back. It is funny seeing him in his school jumper when I have seen his naked chest and the knobbles of his spine.

I am thinking about his back as I sit in English, chewing my biro and staring at the redundant inkwell in my desk. Miss Roker asks me what I think about Juliet Capulet and my head snaps back. 'I think she was a little hasty,' I say. Laura sniggers.

'Yes,' says Miss Roker, 'good. Juliet is a very impetuous character, but she is also very fearful, with a slightly unattractive streak of nit-picking practicality. Swear not by the moon.'

'Bloody fuckin moon,' says Dave.

Worst of both worlds, I think, chewing my pen again. Between safety and magnificence there must be an awful lot of soggy crap. You have to plump for one or the other, or you just end up with the shite in the middle. And then, I wonder if Alan's back is still brown under his shirt?

The bell rings and we clatter out into the corridor. I am thinking pleasant thoughts as I wander, and Siobhan is chatting at my side. Debbie has joined our crowd from the classroom next door; she is walking with Angie. I catch them both smiling at me. Angie's foot springs out and trips my ankle. I stumble forward and hit the floor sprawling. It bangs my hands. Some people snigger, but mostly they just keep walking and talking. I smell the floor. I see their legs. Siobhan is looking uncertain, and then she walks away as well. She goes very slowly and keeps looking over her shoulder.

'Siobhan!' It is Angie calling, and Siobhan turns round. 'Why are you friends wi her?' asks Angie.

'She's all right,' says Siobhan, but she keeps walking away. I watch her, and then I just get up and start walking away as well.

Debbie and Angie are laughing their heads off, going, 'Ooo, ooo, Vanessa Gordon-Bleu,' in posh voices.

My bag has slid a long way along the red floor. I keep my eyes on it as I walk, getting closer. I am nearly there when Pete appears and snatches it away. He holds it high above my head. I jump. Only once, and then I shrug and I say: 'Fine, have it,' and I walk away. My face is burning. I breathe deeply, instructing the flush to leave me.

'Come an get it!' calls Pete. 'Ya English coward!'

I raise two fingers over my shoulder and keep going. I don't know why they all call me English. I haven't got a drop of English blood in all my body. Something hard blows into my ankles, fast and heavy. I lurch forward, but I don't begin to fall. I'm steady now. When I turn round I see that it's my bag. My ankles throb. 'Thank you,' I call to Pete, picking up the strap.

'Tharnk yoo!' he mocks behind me.

'What's going on?' Morna is here in her prefect's blazer, with Katie Macaloney by her side. Katie is Debbie's older sister and she is also Morna McAlpine's buddy. They sneer down their noses at me like I'm a foreign body on a microscope slide.

'Nothing.'

I go down the stairs and I hear the whole lot of them laughing behind me. Sour-bellied shit-brains.

Alan is standing at the gate waiting for me. He scuffs his trainers on the ground and looks at the clouds. I stand still, watching him. A raindrop lands on my cheek. Maybe I'll go back. But I don't, I walk forward, and he sees me. 'I thought you weren't coming,' he says.

'I'm late.' I'm not saying sorry. I look at him like it's his fault and we start walking, drifting down the pavement.

'Is something wrong, Vanessa?'

I laugh. I am feeling cynical today. Then I shut up. We walk along in silence, and then Alan says, 'I haven't spoken to you for ages.' He doesn't speak to me for a little bit longer. 'Pete and Debbie and that lot.' I look at him but he doesn't go on.

I tug a sycamore leaf off a passing branch. 'They all think I'm English.'

'It's the way you talk. You don't sound Scottish.'

'So? I'm as Scottish as they are. It's got nothing to do with being Scottish — Hari's Indian, Laura's frigging Italian, and nobody minds that. It's a load of shite.' I am angry with him. 'My dad's from here, my mum's from Helensburgh, and I was born in Perth.' I am carefully shredding the leaf.

'Nuh.' He glances at the leaf in my hands and looks at me sideways. 'It's not where you're from. It's the way you talk.'

'What's wrong with the way I talk?'

'Nothin. It sounds really nice. It's just that it's the way posh people speak. You know.'

'Oh yeah. And posh people can't be Scottish.'

Alan grins at me. 'You are quite posh, Vanessa.' He says it like a compliment and I start to smile at his shining face, just when I didn't expect to. This boy. I want to climb all over him and go to sleep in his armpit with a fistful of reddish-brown hair. He smiles and speaks to me in that way and everything breathes out.

We get chips and cans of Irn Bru from the Wallace Fry, and we find a wall to sit on.

Alan is tapping the side of his can in a rapid drum. 'Has anyone asked you out?' he says.

'No.'

The tapping slows down. 'Good.' I look at him and find him eyeing me with a slow spark. The metal tap runs even as he puts his hand over mine and leaves it there. He is looking at my ear. He looks as scared as I am. I don't know how we are going to eat the rest of our chips like this. An engine roars in the car park behind us. Wheels crunch over the gritty tarmac, and Alan's hand is resting on mine. It presses and holds me. A woman in a black mac walks past us, carrying Co-Op bags. My heart thuds. I look at the pigeons mucking around on the roof opposite, and I see the heat and weight of his hand. Please don't take it away, please don't take it away from me. Something like need spurts through me. Like I need to urinate or eat. It's strange, and makes me look at him. We're a pair of skeletons now, and we smile.

Wind chills my legs and blows a crisp packet under my shoes. His pale lips move. 'Will you come to see me?'

'Yeah.'

We sit on the wall for a minute or two, just sitting in the middle of the world. Then we get back to eating our chips and swigging from the cans. A pocket of uncomfortable gas rides down my throat and sits in my belly like a bullet. I glance up at Alan. He's got a lick of brown sauce at the side of his mouth. I smile. He looks at me as his tongue flicks out to clean it. I am unsure of a lot. I stop smiling and look away.

Mum is absent from herself when I come home. In fact, she looks startled to see me. She strains an enormous smile, runs her hand through her beautiful hair and buries her face in a big book. I take advantage, changing quickly out of my uniform and into a pair of jeans and a black long-sleeved T-shirt. I think Alan likes black. I want to cry. I tug the velcro strap on my purple trainers and I listen. She coughs in the kitchen. She has the radio on.

I tiptoe down to the telephone. I find the directory and look him up. McAlpine, and his father's name is Frank. McAlpine F. I find it: 241 982. The line rings.

'Two four one nine eight two, hello?' It is his mum.

'Hi,' I say, quietly. 'Is Alan in?'

'Who's calling?'

'Vanessa Gordon.'

It goes quiet, and then I hear Alan: 'Hi there. How are you doing.'

'Okay.'

'Are you comin round?' Not with Morna there, and your mum and dad who make me feel like a clumsy alien.

I stroke the phone book. 'Maybe we could just meet in the lay-by.'

'Why are you whispering?'

'I'm not.' I am.

'Why do you want to meet in the lay-by?'

'I just do.'

'Okay.'

'When?'

'Um. Five minutes?'

'Okay. Bye.'

'See you, Vanessa.'

I put the phone down. I poke my head round the kitchen door. 'Mum,' I say, and she looks up from somewhere else. She is a bit flushed, glowing above the red jersey dress she is wearing today. I tilt my head. 'Mum,' I say again, 'is it okay if I go out for a bit?'

'Yes!' She looks relieved. 'Yes, of course it is.'

I keep looking at her as I retreat and shut the door between us.

I hug my anorak round me as I walk down the road. Maybe he won't come. I try to walk more slowly, so that I won't be standing there on my own.

The road flattens sideways into the lay-by. It is empty of Alan. There is just the white concrete litter bin. I knew it. I knew he wouldn't come. But I thought he might. Maybe he will. Well, I'm not waiting around. I shift from foot to foot in the chilly wind. I push up my elasticated anorak cuff and check the watch dad gave me for my birthday. It is six minutes since the phone call.

Nice watch, though. It has got a moon and stars on it, and it cost one hundred and fifty pounds. You can get imitation ones for twenty. Dad couldn't make it home, but he sent me this and a card in which he wrote that fifteen was a lucky number. I don't know if that's true. Probably not.

Alan is not coming. Anyway, that's easier. I hit the litter bin hard with a swipe of my hand. It hurts. I start walking away. I walk away even slower than I came.

'Hoi! Vanessa!'

He's here, and now I pretend I haven't heard him. It's too embarrassing. I was here waiting for him, and he didn't come.

'Vanessa!' He starts running and now he is right behind me.

I turn round. 'Oh, hi.' I smile.

He is looking at me like I've just stuck my finger in his eye. 'Where are you going?'

'Nowhere.'

'Aye you are. You were going away home.'

Please don't look at me like that. Anyway, you were the one who didn't turn up on time. 'No I wasn't.'

He sighs sharply. 'Whatever.' He stands planted in the middle of the road. 'Well, you can go home if you've changed your mind.' He is staring at me.

'I haven't changed my mind,' I say casually. I walk back up the road towards him. When I reach him, I look into his eyes and see that the goldness has gone, leaving green stones. 'What shall we do?' I say.

He shrugs. 'I don't know, Vanessa.'

He goes over to the litter bin and rests on its edge. I go and sit beside him. Geese fly overhead. I reach my hand out and I put it on his. He doesn't move, just loosens. He is looking at the geese as if he may pardon them. He sighs and looks down at my hand. I watch him as he lifts it and holds my fingers up in front of his face. He clasps my hand very tight between his two palms and he stares at the three. 'I don't understand you.' He looks up at me and I look back. I think: you don't need to. I put my other hand on his neck and stroke him.

It looks like we're doing a funny kind of waltz, sitting here on the edge of the bin. He is so close to me. I feel the softness of his skin.

Alan pulls my hand in close between us and brings it up to his jaw. I hold his head between my hands. He slides his arms upwards, pushing his fingers between the roots of my hair, cradling the back of my skull. His face is very near, and his eyes are very curious. What do you want to know? I lean forward and rest my mouth on his. I feel his hands stiffen in my hair as I kiss him. It is very slow, the breaking of our tongues into each other's mouths. They steal around like loving burglars, our tongues, poking at teeth. They push against each other in a house made by our open lips. They push and tussle and they set off tripwires inside me. It is like they are fighting, faster and faster. Alan is grabbing at my hair, pulling me even closer. It is him, I try to tell myself. It is his tongue inside me, it is his mouth that I have broken into. I kiss harder still. I want him to press a stone against my groin. Blood and nerves are running loose. I push my body against him. He throws a hand out to steady us. We kiss more slowly now, licking and gently sucking on each other's tongues. Now he will understand. I do. I understand everything now. Everything in the world makes sense. Happiness pulses through me. I tell him it with my silent tongue.

I pull away at last and wipe my mouth with the sleeve of my anorak.

Alan grins at me. 'That was all right,' he says.

'Yeah,' I answer, smiling at him.

'Where did you learn to kiss like that?'

'In my dreams.' You are the first boy I've kissed, isn't it obvious, sitting there laughing next to me with dark clouds scooting over your head. He reaches out a finger and lays it on my lips. Gently, he pokes it inside, feeling my front teeth with his fingertip. It makes me feel uncomfortable. I shake my head and his finger falls away.

'How many people have you kissed?' asks Alan.

I shrug. 'Five, or something,' I lie.

'Oh.' He looks at the ground. Oh. I reach out and touch his knee. He looks up at me and smiles. Then he frowns. He says, 'You're beautiful.'

'No I'm not.'

'You are.' He leans forward and kisses me again. 'I love kissing you,' he says.

I smile, and it's as if all the sun and the rain is inside me. 'Yeah,' I say, 'it's all right.' I want to stay with him.

We go walking up the hill. There is a sheltered spot near the top where we stop and sit down. The glen seems harassed, down below, windy and pierced with our houses. We are above it, out of the wind. We huddle into each other. 'I really like you,' I say.

Alan stares at me. 'Do you?'

I would have thought it was quite clear. 'Yes,' I say, running my hand over the starved anaemic grass. I am not looking at him. His arms come round me, young branches purring around my body. I tilt my head into his neck so that he can't see my face and I kiss him there. I smell his skin. It smells of washing powder and rain and I breathe it in. He is so warm. We press into each other, pushing hardness against hardness, I feel it through soft layers of clothes. Alan runs his hand over the front of my anorak, over my chest. Maybe he knows I am afraid, or maybe he is afraid himself, because he takes his hand away even though I want it to stay. He strokes my hair. And then he wraps his arms around me so tight, like steel hoops, squeezing me so close to him that I nearly stop breathing. He says, 'I'm never going to let you go.'

My eyes are wide open. I don't know what to say, so I say: 'Okay.' He relaxes his grip on me but he is still holding me, and we lie there until Alan asks me for the time. I say six o'clock and he says shit, he has to go home for his tea. We run down the hillside.

I know it is easy to fall. In fact, it is harder to come down than it is to go up. You can stumble very easily. I find that it is better if you skip when you are on a steep downhill slope. For some reason dancing is safer than walking. So I dance down the hill, but Alan runs. He grabs my hand and pulls me with him. I scream at him to let me go. I am laughing but I am terrified. I can't control my feet any more, they are just jolting after him. I have lost my dance steps. The ground rushes beneath us like we're a pair of hawks, not a boy and a girl. It is a mess of grass and rocks half blinded by waves of my yellow hair. Alan's camouflage jacket slices in front of me like a kite, with a wicked set of limbs and a hand pulling me onwards. I'm going to fall. I know I'm going to fall. Please let go. Don't let go. I will fall, either way. The slope flattens out. Our thundering stride slows. The land rocks up through my calves. We come to a stop, and we haven't fallen over. We are lucky. My knees are trembling. We climb the fence by the lay-by and we stand close to each other.

I smile at Alan. 'Well, fuck off home then.' I am breathless.

'Cheers,' he says. He kisses me again. I grab the sleeve of his jacket tight in my fingers. I kiss him hard. 'I'll see you,' he says.

I nod. 'You will.'

He grins at me and stands there for a second while the grin slides smoothly off his face. His eyes are serious now. 'Aye,' he says, looking down the road. 'Let's go.'

So we set off simultaneously in opposite directions. I turn

round when I have gone a little distance and I see his figure moving up the track to his house. I turn back to the road and carry on.

'Hi!' I call, opening the door. There is no answer. Oh well. I think I'll watch some telly.

The sofa cushions in the sitting room are low and battered. They look like mum's been trampolining on them. I smile at the thought as I pick up the cushions and shake them. Mum jumping up and down in the red dress, her brown knees zigzagging in the air and her dark hair tumbling up to the ceiling as she falls. But she isn't laughing. Her face is looking worried, wondering: What am I doing here? Why am I trampolining on the sofa?

I pick up the remote control. I would like to go trampolining with Alan. We would jump up and down and just kill ourselves laughing. I smile. He said I was beautiful. I wonder if I am.

Something bright catches my eye. The light is shining on a piece of bright metal. I pick it up off the carpet. It is a gold ring. I think it is mum's wedding ring. I try it on but it is enormous.

'Mum!' I say, entering the kitchen. She is sitting at the table with a newspaper. She looks like a rather lovely tulip, red and black. Her left hand is holding the edge of the page nearest to me. A gold band twinkles round its middle finger. I don't understand. I put the ring down on the table very quickly. Her face tightens.

'Is this yours?' I ask casually.

'Yes,' says mum. Her ringed finger slips behind the newspaper and out stretches her bare right hand to pick it up. 'Thank you, darling. I thought I'd lost it.' She smiles at me. She looks back at her newspaper and pretends to be reading it.

I quickly slide away, but I haven't closed the door properly. I stand in the dark hall, peering through the crack. Mum glances right at me but she doesn't see me. She puts down the newspaper. The new ring glints in the palm of her hand. She tugs off her own gold ring and sits there sliding the two rings together from hand to hand, pouring them between her palms. The metals chime against each other. It is a high, tinny sound. She is staring out the window again like she was in June. The rings drop on to the table. Mum leans back in her chair. Her face falls apart into a grimace, her mouth turned into a shivering rectangle. Her eyes are closed and she is making choking sounds. I slip away.

She knows that I know. I see her checking in my eyes and finding. 'You're a clever little thing, aren't you?' says mum. She is looking at me like I'm a lizard about to dart away. I wish I could. Dart away. She knows.

I wonder who he is. Or she, perhaps my mother is having it off with a thick-fingered lesbian. Who does the ring fit, I wonder? Some adulterous Cinderella with a wedding band for a slipper. Are they better than dad? I kick my head into the wall. Dad, you should be at home.

And Alan comes to meet me in private places, my one true love. We go to the bothy over the hill. I tell mum I'm away to stay with Siobhan and Alan tells his mum something different and we go there. It is very cold. When you take your shirt off, the cold swirls over your body like a milky film. We bring condoms and cheese rolls. Alan lays out his sleeping bag and we get inside it and cuddle each other closely.

We converse on many topics. Alan tells me about how he is going to leave Scotland and work abroad. He says that I will come with him and we'll have children in a house in a hot country. There will be a veranda and lots of palm trees, red flowers and a black car and a big piano. I think he put the piano part in for me. I think it sounds nice. I don't say anything, though, I just listen. If you ask him why he wants to leave

Scotland, he says, 'Ach, it's too cold. And nobody ever dis anything.' I quite like Scotland, myself. Maybe being shut out by your own country isn't so bad. You get to live it through the eyes of a tourist.

I once said to Alan, 'I am part of the lost tribe, you know. We're not allowed to be Scottish because we're rich and happy. I mean, you have to be poor and oppressed to get membership, don't you.'

Alan just said, 'Are you happy?' – as if I might be wrong.

And I said, 'Yes.' He looked at me, inquisitively. I don't like it when he does that. I kissed him to stop his eyes.

We make love quite often. I was glad there was no blood the first time. Alan wasn't. He looked at me strangely, as if he thought I had secretly been doing it with someone else. He didn't say anything. Nor did I.

I am first into the morning. I wake up on his chest, the safe pillow of his breathing, and hear the low beloved beat thud beneath my cheek. I open my eyes very slowly. Sleepy muck clogs my eyelashes. The pale half-light is gathering. I like watching him as it comes slipping through the small and dusty window, etching his face in milk out of the shadows. His brow is drawn down into a frown, puzzled at his own dreamings. His lips are parted, interrupted. Dear sound. Two curves whose quirky beauty could never be formed in marble. I know his face by heart. It is all so close to me. I drop my mouth on to his skin. I whisper to him, kissing him as I talk. 'Darling Alan,' I say, and I am not even embarrassed. 'I love you so much, I love you so much. I'm yours. Always.' I like him best when he's asleep, because then I can tell him everything.

When he wakes, I pull up and away from him. He tries to lean after me and kiss me. But once I've started I have to finish. I can't turn back. So I keep moving away from him. He ducks crossly after me and fastens his mouth round the tip of my breast. He is holding my nipple too hard in his teeth. It hurts me. It makes my eyes wet in a flash. I grab his head and force him off me.

'Why did you do that!' He looks at me, stubbornly. Then he sees my eyes. 'Oh, I'm sorry, oh Vanessa, I didn't mean to hurt you!' But I am clambering right out of the sleeping bag. My foot catches him across the chest. I hope I haven't kicked him hard. Sorry, Alan, I'm sorry. I stand with my back to him, freezing cold all over, pulling on my vest bra and my shirt.

'Vanessa! I'm really sorry. Honest I didn't mean to hurt you. Please!'

I don't turn round. I pull on my jeans. My legs are shaking. Button, zip, socks, hop. I hear him scrambling out of the sleeping bag behind me.

'Vanessa!' There is something in his voice like a breaking dog. I turn round. He is standing naked in front of me. His arms are by his sides, his chest bare and hairless, his cock half-hard in the mat of hair between his thighs. And his familiar face is part of it all, looking at me so honestly it hurts to see. Behind my breastbone, something blows. I start crying. My neck shakes under it as the tears bolt from my face, eager to leave me.

He steps towards me. He pulls on a jumper over his shivering body and he puts his arms around me. 'What's the matter? What's wrong?'

I can't stop crying. 'I don't know,' I say, and it's the truth. The tears keep coming, streams of them, mingling with mucus from my nose.

'Vanessa, Vanessa,' says Alan, very gentle, burying my head in his jumper. The wool is prickly on my hot-skinned face. I am so unhappy, and I don't know why. He strokes my hair as I cry.

We sit outside, leaning against the wall of the bothy and leaning into each other. I let him shelter me, for a while.

'I don't understand you,' says Alan.

I wish he would stop saying that. I look out across the high land and it is empty. It swells and dips in folds of rock and scrubby grass. Wind blows clean across it. Sheep graze, battered and daubed with farmer's paint, blue or red markings on their knotted woollen flanks. They'll be going down soon. But me and Alan are going to be coming here right through the winter. It's the only place. The wind blows right into my soul, and calms it. There is nothing here. Nothing, I realise. This is an empty place. A kind of gratitude flows over my tear-wrecked innards.

I turn to Alan and I say: 'It's all right.' I smile, and he reads it in my eyes. His own eyes sparkle and his smile fans out like wings. He kisses my face all over. Playful lover. I start laughing underneath it.

We sit together until we get too cold. We talk about politics. Alan says he is a socialist. I am an environmentalist, when he makes me think about it. Alan tells me about seeing Alice Cooper in concert. I say I've never heard of her and Alan bursts out laughing. His laugh always sounds so unexpected and large. I love it. It makes me start laughing too, even as I am asking: 'What? What's so funny?'

'Alice Cooper is a man.'

'Funny name for a guy. Is it one of those ones that's an anagram of something else?'

'Like what?' he says, laughing again.

'I don't know.' I stare at the clean wide sky, thinking. 'Crool ice pea.'

'Aye, Vanessa. Great rock name.'

'Terror of the deep-freeze.'

We both start laughing.

We seem to laugh a lot. We laugh at the whole wide world, because it doesn't understand.

Alan and I belong together. We fit together like buckets and spades, spooning life into each other and tipping it out in brand-new shapes. Everything is made new. I would like to tell him, but maybe he can read my mind. I would like to tell him, but maybe it will all be washed away. The thing with words is that they take so long to say. What if I start to speak and halfway through, something changes? He could turn cold and leave my words spoken and hanging in the air, set going and crawling on towards him. I would have to watch them land and cringe as they flopped, stupid-looking things. Alan says he loves me. Is it safe? You never can tell. I just laugh with him and hope that we stay together always. The wind blows nakedly on our soft faces.

Alan and I go inside the bothy and touch each other. We are all wrapped up and burrow our fingers through the layers of clothing. It looks like something from another world, his penis, fit for the strange purple creature between my own legs. Our genitals are so sexual and so unbeautiful, and I like that because it makes them more secret. They sneak smooth in the pulled-aside folds of wool and buttons and denim.

My green checked shirt falls down, covering my breast again. His hand is pulled away from me, hovering in the air around me, its fingers all pointing towards me, gently. As if a piece of music has just finished. He is looking at me directly. He is looking very serious. There is something almost hollow in the widening pupils of his eyes. Something very terrible and fragile. I look back at him and I wonder what he sees in my own eyes. Nothing, I hope. I squeeze his penis and stroke it faster.

Alan's lovely hand is tugging at my jeans zip. I breathe in, trying to make it easier for him. He gets it at last, combing into the metallic pubic hair on me. We slide around each other and I stretch my vocal cords, closing my eyes. Please do it, Alan. Please succeed in being inside me. I want you to be. You're so good and beautiful. But it's all so far away.

Still, there is the moment where I almost come, and it all becomes blisteringly crystal perfect, somewhere up ahead. Two seconds that make me want to howl at the sight of it. Come back.

I feel sad afterwards. Alan is lying heavily on my chest, still breathing hard. I lay one arm around him, one hand splayed across his back. My other hand is circling in the dust upon the floor. I close my eyes to stop them leaking.

Alan is suggesting that we go for a walk. He is packing up our bags and putting them in the corner while I stand against the wall, watching him. I watch him slipping the knotted condom into one of the compartments in his small rucksack. I wonder if it was designed for that, by some bearded man at a drawing board in Oslo. Side pocket with spunk-proof lining. Take your litter home. Alan's litter, not mine.

'What?' I ask him.

'Let's go along the hill a bit. See if we can find any wolves.'

'There aren't any wolves.'

'I know.' He is standing with his hands on his hips, looking at me.

I look back. 'Okay,' I say. We close the door behind us.

We have not gone very far when a man comes into view. I am surprised. It is the first time I have seen another person up here. The man is wearing a green cagoule, with the hood drawn up over his head although it is not raining yet. He is walking towards us. I try to steer Alan in another direction, away from the stranger. I don't want to be meeting any new people. But Alan just smiles at me and says, 'It's Gavin.' I don't want to meet Gavin. I'm not in the mood. And why is it that nobody is a stranger to Alan?

Gavin is upon us now. I stare at the way he has tied the drawstring of his hood tight under his chin, so that his face is framed by a puckering oval of green synthetic fibres. Gavin must be in his fifties. It is an old face, hacked and battered by the wind. His nose and cheeks are pinky brown and his eyes are brown as well. They are very warm.

'Alan,' says Gavin, by way of a greeting.

'Hi, how y'doin,' answers Alan, like a man.

'No too bad, no too bad.' The man looks at us both. He looks especially at me, checking out my face. 'The wee Gordon lass, isn't it?'

I nod. I want him to go away. He is annoying me. But he just keeps standing there, and Alan isn't moving on either.

'Aye,' says Gavin, looking at us in that very close way. 'I've seen the two of you up here.' He pulls a small piece of silver paper from his green pocket. He removes a ball of chewing gum from his mouth and wraps it up slowly, nodding while he does it. 'Often,' he says, depositing the silver ball back into the pocket. He is looking at Alan now, not me. I don't know what his eyes are saying. It is all in code. It looks like something important, but I cannot read these men. Alan stands tense and still, looking back at Gavin stubbornly.

Gavin moves. He turns towards me and stretches out his hand. He is wearing orange gloves. 'Gavin McCann,' he says, as I shake his hand. He smiles at me very brightly and it's awfully fake but I appreciate it.

'Pleased to meet you,' I say. My hand falls down again, resting by my side. No one speaks for a second or two.

'This is Vanessa,' says Alan. Gavin nods, not looking at either of us, and then he walks past us.

'That was a bit weird,' I say, as we carry on towards the ridge. Alan says, 'How do you mean?' and I don't answer.

'I can't see any wolves,' I say.

Alan's face swivels towards me, grinning. It takes up the sky. His eyes bedazzle and he says, 'I can.' He is pointing at the sheep below us. I know what he means and I smile. I smile because I think that we are different. The sheep are very small, after all, and far, far below us. We are walking on the ridge now, on the crust of rock that juts like blood through the high, cold air. I don't care about Gavin McCann, or anyone else.

We sit on the rock at the highest point, leaning our backs against the cairn. It shelters us a little from the wind. I tell Alan about the wildcat. I tell him how I found it down on the road to Crieff. He doesn't ask me what I was doing there. I tell him how I found it lumpy and mangled by the side of the road. I saw its eyes and they were wet. I touched its fur. I squatted down and stroked it for ages, still warm. It was really beautiful, I tell him. Some other people came along in a car after I had gone, and they found it properly.

'I didny ken there were wildcats this far south any more,' says Alan.

'Me neither,' I say. Nobody knows what it was doing down here, especially in July, which was when it happened. I found it the day after I'd come home from being expelled. Everyone else knew about it the following day, after the proper people had found it. But I found it first, and I squatted there with my stinging back and thought maybe it had come south to find me. I was glad it was dead. I sat and spoke to it for a while, and it lay and let me stroke it. Its face was broad and beautiful with proud tiger stripes. It reminded me a little bit of mum, except of course it was covered in fur. The fatal wound was in its flank, a bloody mess. The strong body lay still, except for the long whiskers above its white dagger teeth, bared stupidly at the car which had gone past ages ago.

It is funny, now I come to think about it. I found the wildcat that day, and then the next day Alan gave me that trout. Two dead animals in a row were both my friends.

Alan says that when he dies he wants people to eat him. Just like a trout, I think. It makes me laugh. I say: 'Yeah, but the problem is, how do you know who's going to eat you? You wouldn't have any control over it. You might end up being a corpuscle in a psycho.'

'I wouldn't mind.'

'Yeah you would.'

'I wouldn't. Anyway, you could decide, before you died, which people were going to eat you. If you minded. You could leave it in a will.'

'I bet it's illegal.'

'So?'

I shrug. 'I'm going to be buried. But not in a graveyard. I'm going to be buried on top of a hill, miles away from everyone else.' Stalks will hide me.

'That's sociable.'

'Oh right, and cannibalism isn't remotely antisocial.'

'Cannibalism is extremely sociable,' says Alan. 'You carry on, inside all these other people who are still alive. Better than mouldering away underground all on your own. I reckon it's quite a nice idea.'

'Yeah. Lovely.' Sometimes I think Alan is a bit unhealthy. I never met anyone who was quite so into the idea of other people. It wouldn't be possible for him to be anything other than a human being.

'It means you don't really die,' explains Alan.

'What's so bad about dying?' I say.

'I don't know.' He frowns. Alan is funny about things like that. He's quite soft, in a way. I lean over and kiss him.

Mum watches me very closely these days. She is waiting for me to say something. What does she think I am going to say? Nothing. I just watch her stirring pots guiltily. I have a secret of my own.

And then it is not a secret. Mum says, 'I know what you've been doing.' She is standing in my bedroom door while I do my homework at my desk. My pencil is still on the page of sums. Quadratic equations. You multiply two lots of brackets together and a minus times a minus becomes a positive.

I don't answer. I look at the wooden door frame adjacent to her head.

'I know what you've been doing with Alan McAlpine,' says mum. My head starts heating up. My brain is glowing orange. I can't move my lips, so I don't bother trying to answer. I just blink.

'And you know what I've been doing,' says mum. My gaze sloshes on to her face. She is looking very steady and cool. Like a lovely salamander. She says it all, as if it were nothing. I am in awe of her as she stands there, announcing, 'Obviously I am having an affair. I am having an affair with John Crawford.' It is funny the way that mum's skin almost shines. Like a stone under water. 'Your father doesn't know about it,' says mum, 'And nor does Diane Crawford, nor the Crawford boys. I would like to keep it that way. '

I nod. 'Good girl,' says mum. And then she laughs. 'Ha! Well. You're as good a girl as I am.' Her expression evens itself out. 'So, darling. I won't stop you from your sordid little antics if you won't tell your father about mine. Do we have a deal?'

I still can't move my lips. I am just staring at her face. I nod, but I feel sick. Mum nods back at me, just the once, briskly, and she disappears back along the passage. I sit very still. I am still holding my pencil on the page of my jotter. It hasn't moved. I stare at the quadratic equations and I try to make them come right, but I don't move the pencil. There isn't any point in doing them on paper. It's the equations in your head that matter.

I lie on my bed and look at my photos of dad. Dad and mum, dad and me, dad and my sisters, dad and grandpa. Everyone says that I have my mother's face and my father's colouring. Mum drew the picture of me and dad just shaded it in. Dad, why did you go? The arguments weren't that bad. He should be here. Dad doesn't belong in the desert, you only have to take one look at him. Big and pale-skinned, freckled and fair-haired. Now mum is sleeping with Mr Crawford. Why is she doing it? I wish dad would come home and put a stop to it. If I told him what was going on, he would come home right away. Maybe he would be here by Tuesday. And then that would be the end of the deal. Who do you love, Vanessa? Who do you need? This horrid sick feeling is not a reason for breaking the deal. Though it feels like it is eating me from the inside out, a dirtiness creeping up and out through my skin, and I wrap my arms tight around my tummy to try and contain the dirt inside me as I lie on my back on my duvet. I close my eyes and I begin to breathe. I breathe very slowly and deeply. In and out. This is how mammals stay alive.

Mum comes into my bedroom again. I open my eyes and they swivel sideways to see her while my head stays perfectly still. She is holding a paper bag.

'You should be using something,' says mum.

She puts the package down on my desk beside the maths. 'Some condoms,' she explains. 'For Christ's sake, don't get pregnant.'

I lie motionless. She is looking at the photographs.

'You shouldn't feel sorry for your father,' says mum. 'He's been screwing around for years.' She turns lightly and patters down the stairs.

All the careful breathing swells up inside me. I am out the bedroom door and down the stairs behind her, in a moment. The banister flies under my hand. The back of her head is right close in front of me. I have got her. But I stop. I don't do it. I just stand there, watching her recede ahead of me. She turns round as she opens the kitchen door. I am perched ridiculously on the stairs, fists clenched, like a too-scared cliff diver. And then I scream: 'I hate you!' I scream so loud, the stairwell sounds like cardboard. I don't take my eyes off her.

Her glowing tiger face is turned keenly on me. The face twitches a little as she says, 'Don't be silly, darling.' She disappears into the kitchen. I want to strangle her and make her a beautiful grave. I storm into the kitchen after her. She looks at me, raising a warning eyebrow as I stand here hunched and breathing hard. 'Stop following me around,' says mum. 'I'm going to start getting angry soon.'

My jaw tightens.

'Vanessa, go to your room. Stop looking at me like that! Go to your room!'

I'm not budging.

She is coming towards me and she has whipped a wooden spoon from out the jar by the range. I am very aware of the spoon as she advances. 'I'm sorry!' I scream. But it is too late now. My body stretches up to the ceiling, pulled up by the roots of my hair. We are going to the laundry room. My feet scuffle clumsily. She pushes the choke chain over my head. The handle of the leash is looped round a coat peg. The dull flagstone floor swoops through my eyesight. Her hands push me over the tumble-dryer. The chain tightens round my neck as she jerks my body upwards with the motion of raising my jumper. The spoon starts. And then on my bum. Slap slap bang. It doesn't really hurt, but I bite my lips. I can taste the blood in them. Bang. It's the words that go with it that scare me. I bite harder.

She isn't hitting me very hard at all. She just uses the beat of the spoon to give her words rhythm, and the choke chain is just to make sure that I stay and listen. It's the words that she knows she can get me with. Nasty girl. Snotty-nosed little madam. Vile. You don't deserve. Hated most of all my children. You the worst. Bad. Awful. Wish you'd never been born. Who do you think. Horrid child. Pain in the arse. Insolent. Stupid. Bleeding idiot. You make me. Little worm. Not my daughter. I wish. Cold little bitch.

I lurch forward on the end of the chain. It tightens. Air can't pass. Just lightness and no world. Ha ha ha. I push away harder. Ha ha. It all goes swirling into the colour of oil. The oil is curling into flowers. Here I go. Her voice falls up the cliff.

*

My eyelids flicker.

Mum is on an old cine-camera through the shutters. Her hands are at my throat, digging the chain out of my skin. Her fingers scrabble and tug. She is saying words loudly. She is saying my name. She is slapping my cheeks and screaming. 'You did that on purpose!' she screams. 'You could have died!' Tears are stripping down her cheeks. She is holding my chin and raising it gently. She examines my neck. 'Oh God,' she says. She looks at my face. My face is blank. I know it is. I know, because my mind is blank. I just look back at her. 'Jesus Christ,' says mum. She is looking in my eyes. 'What on earth are you?' She says it softly. Then she holds my head against her chest. But I'm not here. Not really. I am just observing. I observe the navy-blue of her jumper and the feel of the lambswool. I observe her shaking as she holds me. I wonder why she is shaking. She is holding me very tight.

I walk to see Alan on Monday afternoon. I haven't been to school. I have spent all day at home with mum. She has been bringing me jigsaw puzzles of German fairy tale castles and scuba divers. We have had a fun day together. We had lunch on the sofa, watching telly. Mum kept rumpling my hair and kissing me. She tells me that she loves me very often. I am wearing a polo-neck to hide the big ring round my neck.

I watch the school minibus go past my window and I lie on my bed reading for a while. It is late when I start off and go walking down the road towards the bungalow. It is getting dark and there is a bit of rain falling.

'Hi,' says Morna, answering the door. She smirks at my polo-neck. 'Alan been giving you lovebites? Nnh.'

'Hi Vanessa,' says Alan. He looks kind of relieved to see me.

'Hi,' I say.

'Do you want to come in?'

What the hell. I shrug and step across the doormat.

'Hi there!' says Mrs McAlpine, cheerily. She is leaning her head round the sitting-room door.

'Hi.' I look at my trainers.

Alan says: 'Hey, I got that guitar. D'you want to see it?'

I smile broadly. I feel it stretching out across my face. 'Yeah.' I know he has been wanting a guitar for ages.

Morna snorts. 'Guitar ma arse,' she says, staccato and under her breath. She goes into the sitting room. Alan's chin tilts up after her. He looks at me to see what I think, but I don't think anything.

We go into his bedroom and he shows me the guitar. 'It was thirty pounds,' he says. 'Second-hand, but it's a good one. Well, all right for learning.' He plays some chords. 'I'm going to write a song about you,' he says.

'Don't be daft.'

He smiles and plays some more chords. They don't sound very musical. 'Were you sick?' says Alan.

'When?'

'Today.'

'Oh. Yeah.'

He laughs. 'Right. Skiving.'

'Yeah.' I smile and laugh.

I lean against him and he lays down his guitar. His arms come up around me. I close my eyes. Please can we sleep. Please can we just sit like this for ever. I feel safe in the crooked cove of his arm. I clasp my arms around his waist and hold on. Hold me well, Alan. Don't let me go. My lips fall apart as I drift away.

He dances through all the people, holding me. He has me steady in his arms as we move through the coloured disco lights. Warm orange flashes on our cool skin.

There is a swimming pool in the disco. We run along the diving board and we jump right in. The lights fall away into a garden around us, full of flowers as we hit the water. Clear splashes in my eyes. Perfectly clear. Everything seems closer for a moment. In slow motion I try to reach the sky with my arms as I go down. I can see everything so clearly. The world is full and lucid. And then the world is silent and blue. Alan is down here somewhere. Where is he? Ah, here is his hand, reaching out towards me. I take it. Bubbles are pouring upwards from his mouth as he smiles. We move towards each other through the water. He kisses me. We kiss for a long time, melding arms and legs around it. His face is still smiling, and his hair waves vertically up from his head. But now he is drifting after it, moving upwards to the glimmering light above us. He wants me to go with him. Our fingers stroke each other as we separate out into two. I see his face, looking worried as he moves on upwards and away from me. It makes me laugh. I open my mouth, laughing. Water rushes into my throat. It is water that I am breathing, but I can't stop laughing. I glimpse the white sole of his worried foot and water fills my lungs.

It chokes at me and I jolt awake.

'Hey,' says Alan, stroking my hair. 'Sleepyhead.'

I sit up. I laugh. Then I am quiet, resting my head against him once more. I put my hand up to my neck. It is all right. The polo-neck is still concealing the marks round my throat. I leave my hand there to be sure it doesn't slip.

Chapter Three

She tries not to make a lot of noise. I hear her cry, though, even through her stifling pillow, as I open my book.

Mr Crawford arrived at five thirty p.m. He comes here once or twice a week. I go to my room when I see his car and I stay there until it is gone. Sometimes they call me down to have supper with them, but usually I am allowed to take a snack through to the telly, which is a privilege. When I see him, I say: 'Hi, Mr Crawford.' And he always says, 'Hello there, Vanessa,' in a voice which exaggerates my childish status. I never look at him.

I read a lot of books when he is here. I put a tape in my cassette player and the music makes the books into films.

Sometimes my films get interrupted by their sounds. Mr Crawford must be very good in bed. But not better than dad. If dad was here, she would never have looked twice at him.

Mr Crawford cries out in ecstasy. I nudge up the sliding volume control on my cassette player. Lou Reed growls louder, singing, *Satellite of Love*. It annoys me. I pull it out the machine and stuff in a different one.

> *There's a good tradition of love and hate, stand by the fireside.*
> *The rain may fall, your father's ignoring you, you still feel safe inside.*

The song is big and mellow like a dark wooden bowl. I like Tanita Tikaram. I also like my dad. I am glad he is coming home tomorrow. He is coming back for Christmas. My sisters will be back on the same day. So this is mum and Mr Crawford's last fling of 1993. Now they will have to wait until January 1994. I smile and pay attention to my book.

Mum drives away to fetch my sisters from St Peter's. I telephone Alan once she has gone. 'Hi,' I say. 'Do you want to come round? My mum's away.'

'What. Oh. Do you want me to come?'

Fine, Alan. Fine. 'Only if you want to.'

There is no answer. The silence pierces my ears.

'Well. It wasn't important. I was just a bit bored, but there's loads of things I can do.' My stomach is churning. He doesn't want me any more. I knew it. I knew this would happen. I slam the receiver back down on the telephone and kick the skirting board. There is a tearful growl rising in my throat. It is trying to push its way out through the whole of my face.

I run upstairs and rip my pictures off the walls. I tear them up and it makes me feel much worse. It feels good. The imaginary places in the pictures fall in tatters to the floor. I kick my bed. I pick up the scraps of paper and crumple them into little balls. I try to throw them at the wall but they just flop and fall through the air once they have gone a few centimetres. I pick them up and throw them harder. It still doesn't work. The growl starts escaping from my mouth.

Fine. There are loads of things I can do. I look around me and run out of my house.

It is cold outside. December rain is not falling but jumping from the sky. It is leaping into the sodden grass. I run as fast as I can, aiming towards the gap in the dyke at the back of the garden. By the time I stop, I am halfway up the hill. I keep walking, shaking my arms as I go. I am cold and soaked through. Good. I keep going further and further.

I reach the top of the hill and look down towards the lochan. It is stormy grey today, not summer blue. I start walking towards it. There is no boy. There is no boy standing on the rock. The emptiness of the landscape is wrong. It is too obvious. There is a space where he should fit, and I should fit beside him.

In summer we came here together. He stood fishing and I lay down beside him. When he caught a fish, he was almost as glad as me. Sometimes I went wandering off to inspect the bog, but I always came back. We lay back on the heather and looked up at the sky without speaking, except for Alan sometimes saying, 'This is nice.' I lost my virginity there three months ago, under the deep blue sky and his suntanned, straining face.

I don't know why virginity is something you lose. I always thought that sex would be something you won. But maybe this way round is right after all. Something is losing itself through my fingers. It is tugging at my insides as it goes.

A gurgling noise comes up my throat. I jump around the edge of the water from stone to stone. The stones are slippery in the rain. The rain batters the lochan in loud lines and I wonder why I don't fall into the rapping bed of nails. I get to the end of the stones and jump onwards. I take a long leap through the air and when I land the earth opens up beneath me. Did I know it was here? My friend the peat bog. It sucks around my legs and I feel them sinking quickly deeper as they pedal. The world is liquid under the pink and green mosses. It is thickly soft and endlessly deep. I just keep going down. I reach out a hand. It clasps the edge of a rock. I swing my other hand round, too. I am holding the cold rock with both my hands. My body is under the ground, but I can breathe for as long as I want to hold on. And now I am calm. Rain dashes my hands but I just leave them there. I am hanging in the ground. It is peculiar and quite nice. I have no desire to try and pull myself out. I think I will just stay here for a while. I move my body closer to the rock so that I can rest my cheek against it. I am happy. The peaty water between my clothes and skin turns warm with the slow heat from my heart. Rain cleans my head.

There is something godly in it. A sense of peace washes over me.

A dog barks. For a second I think it is Cloudy, our old dog, and then I remember that he died ages ago. We only kept his leash. The dog is coming nearer. I try to hide behind the rock. My hands feel big and overly visible.

I see a man and I shut my eyes. The dog has got its nose all over me. Bugger off, both of you. Get away from my home. And the man's hands come down on the rock, as he squats forward on it, levering himself towards me.

Fuck. It's Mr McAlpine. I quickly close my eyes again. I can hear his hard breathing.

'Jist haud tight, Vanessa.'

'I'm fine. Please, I'm fine.' My voice is rising, like hers does.

'Ye dinna look that fine to me.'

'I am.'

He sighs. He thinks I'm stupid.

'Yer five feet doon in a bog. It's pishin wi rain an you're wearin a T-shirt.' That's why he came, he tells me. Cause Lilian saw me while she was doing the dishes and reckoned I should not be belting up the hill in a T-shirt in this weather.

Mr McAlpine has got me under the armpits and he is pulling me out of the bog. It slurps kisses round my feet. It doesn't want me to go. Why couldn't he just leave me here? Or preferably not have found me in the first place. My legs are warm and sleepy as they clatter up on to the rock, dragged horizontal behind me. Mr McAlpine is taking off his jacket. He must be hot from the trouble.

I'm sorry, I'm sorry for the trouble. But you really didn't have to.

'Here,' says Mr McAlpine, holding out his jacket. 'Git this on ye.'

'Oh no, I'm fine.' I smile to prove it. 'I think I'll just go home.'

'Too right. Wi a coat on. Ah'm no havin ye dyin o hypothermia.'

'Really. I'm fine.'

'Put the coat on.'

Mr McAlpine is bigger than me. And I think he does actually want me to take his coat. So I put it on, and it feels surprisingly good. 'Thanks.'

'Right.' He doesn't smile. He isn't much like Alan.

We walk down the hillside and he says, 'Where's yer mither?'

'She's out.'

'You'll have to come back wi me, then.'

We go the rest of the way in silence, down to the car by the road. I am pleased at how the rain makes a bit of noise to fill our squelching footsteps.

Alan is in his bedroom when we enter their house. He doesn't come out until his mother makes him. He clearly doesn't want to see me. He can't think of anything to say. He just stands there.

'You're wet.'

'Yeah.'

'Get her some clothes, Alan.'

We all sit in the McAlpines' sitting room. They call it their lounge. I like the sound of that. Somewhere for lounging in. Or a departure lounge, somewhere to fly from. An arrivals lounge, somewhere to come back to. And then lounge in, some more. A place where you rest between voyages. Lounge, lounge.

I am happy wearing Alan's clothes. I feel very close to him, even though he is sitting as far away from me as possible, a quiet moon in the chair while I sit hot by the electric fire with pretend coals glowing. I am wearing his Def Leppard T-shirt and his black jumper, and I am wearing his jeans, baggy on me. His socks are warm. I wriggle my toes inside them. I am so happy. I love being in his clothes. They sit all around me and when I move they move with me. It is magic. Even if Alan doesn't want me here. Sometimes he glances at my face and I can see out of the corner of my eye that he looks cross. Behind him, the glen in the big window matches in its bored coldness.

Alan's mum is talking lots. I must be excited about seeing my dad, that'll be nice having all the family home, what am I doing at Hogmanay, I'm welcome to celebrate it with them. I don't know what she wants me to say. I say: 'Oh, right,' and look at my feet. Mrs McAlpine is looking at me funny. She starts talking about her work in Perth Job Centre, but she is still talking to me. Her voice comes out in long thin ovals. It is very restful to listen to her. The ovals link together, one word starting before another one has finished, like running water. They could go on and on for ever, except after a while she says she is going into the kitchen to get the dinner on. She gives Alan a look and the words are stopped as she rises from the sofa and leaves us alone in the room.

Neither of us speaks. We sit in the lounge as if we were just waiting for our planes. It is very warm and I can hear the rain outside. The carriage clock on the mantelpiece is going tick-tock. Tick-tock. I pinch my toes between my fingers to give myself something to do. To distract myself from my silent lover in the chair. Tick-tock.

Twenty minutes of life pass by. The longer it goes, the less we can speak. Now we cannot move, either. It is like when you think there is someone in your room at night and you can not move to switch on the light that would tell you there was nobody there. We sit rigid. His mother calls him. When he gets up to go to her, the movement is like a tidal wave of relief.

He is gone. I jump up from the floor and walk over to the window. It takes up almost the whole of one wall, looking west up the glen to where the sun sets. There is no sunshine today. Just the clouds and the cold fat river, spreading up over its edges. The sheep on the hills must be pretty miserable, but they just carry on eating their grass.

Alan, Alan, why has it all gone wrong? I won't leave you.

Mum will be back in an hour or two. She might go mental if I'm not at home. On the other hand, she might not mind at all.

We sit and eat lunch in the McAlpines' dining room. It is small and dark. Mr McAlpine says things in an ironical tone of voice and Mrs McAlpine pretends not to be keeping an eye on me. Maybe she thinks I am going to stick the pepper pot up my nose, or gob all over the table.

Mr and Mrs McAlpine are talking in the kitchen now.

I stand in the dining-room doorway looking at my boyfriend. 'Bye, Alan.' He is still sitting at the table, with his back hunched over it. He looks at me and his eyes look like they did that time in the bothy. Like he is bare and broken.

'Why won't you ever tell me anything?' he says. He is angry. He stands up. 'Why won't you talk to me?'

I don't know what to say. I am dumb. And he is exploding in this small dark room with the thick carpet. How can I stop it?

I go towards him and reach out to touch him.

He flinches away. 'D'you do that to him? Eh?'

'What?'

'Just don't touch me, Vanessa. You're a total fake.'

'What do you mean?'

'Does it matter? D'you care what I think?'

'Yeah.'

'Do you?'

'Yes.' My nails are hurting my palms. Deeper and deeper I dig them. Go in, go on, find the blood. It's in there somewhere. 'I love you.'

He grabs my arm. 'Do you? Do you?' As if he wants me to say no.

But I nod.

'And nobody else?'

I shake my head.

'Are you shure?'

I look him in the eye. 'Yeah.'

He isn't smiling. Perhaps I have done this wrong. I hang a happy look in my eyes. 'Nice try,' he says, putting his hand on my hip. 'Oh.' He sounds tired. 'You know I love you, don't you?'

I say yes, but it's a lie. I'm not sure of his love at all. How can you be?

Alan pushes past me, dashing into the kitchen. 'I'll walk Vanessa home,' he says.

But his mum points out that it is raining and says that they will take me in the car.

Morna's engine grinds still beside the house. I spy her unloading bags of Christmas shopping. I sneak fast towards Alan's bedroom but she is through the front door before I've made it. 'Ugh,' she says, looking at me. 'What are you doin here?'

'Nothing.'

She looks me over. 'Can't afford any clothes of your own, eh? Hi mum!' She goes into the kitchen. They are all in there, now. They are making happy loud noises at the sight of all the shopping bags. I stroke the bumpy wallpaper in the hall.

I change back into my own clothes, cleaned and dried by Mrs McAlpine. Alan and his dad take me home. When I get out, Alan says he will see me tomorrow. He seems happy. I wave at them from the doorstep and go inside.

Mum is not back yet. I go to my room and start reading chapter five of *The Spy Who Came in from the Cold.'*

I stay on my bed when I hear the car come home. My sisters' voices swing loudly round the house. My mother is laughing with them. The noise softens as the kitchen door closes behind them, rolling in undertones. I listen to it. They are not missing me. I go back to my book but it is hard to get into it again. Still, I manage nine more pages.

Feet patter up the staircase and the bedroom door opens. Bryony's face pops round it. 'Hi Vanessa!'

'Hi.' I smile and stay put.

She comes in, hesitating, and then she leans over and kisses me. Her lips are wet with apple juice. It is a bit unpleasant.

'Are you coming downstairs? Mum said to leave you if you were sulking. Are you sulking?'

'No. I'm reading.'

'Are you coming downstairs?'

'OK. In a minute.' I keep my book in my hand. 'How's school?'

'All right. Charlotte is being really annoying, so mainly I'm friends with Rosie Gunn now.' She bounces on to my bed. 'It's quite cool. We do loads of stuff together. The only thing is, she falls over a lot.' Bryony looks thoughtful. 'Our main things that we do are drawing, talking and fashion design. We have designed a really cool hockey team. I'll show you if you like. Where are all your pictures, Ness? What happened to all your drawings?'

'I decided I was too old for them.'

'But I really liked them.'

'Yeah, well.' I get up and go downstairs and Bryony chases her tail around me as I go, ducking and squealing like a mad thing.

Mum and dad come back from Edinburgh airport. They aren't saying much. I watch dad hugging my sisters. He comes to me the last and bends towards me. I notice that I have grown since I last saw him. I am nearly as tall as him now. He pulls my head into his shoulder and squeezes me in his arms. He smells of whisky and stones, like always. A big man's smell. My father is home.

'Hello, trouble,' he says.

I smile. 'Hi, Dad.'

No more Mr Crawford for a fortnight.

Celebratory roast beef comes prancing down the table on dinner plates. Everything is bright and starry, as if it's got a high temperature. Lucy and Bryony can't stop talking, and dad is laughing at everything they say. He laughs loudly and he keeps refilling mum's glass. Getting pissed together is my parents' favourite activity.

Mum has made a lemon pudding. She sits at the end of the table, spooning it out. It wobbles in the bowls as we pass them along. Lucy shakes her bowl in front of her to make the pudding wobble harder. She starts giggling. Mum looks at her wine-flushed face and says, 'How much have you had to drink, darling?'

Lucy tosses her hair. 'Not as much as you.'

Mum stares. Then she glances at dad and starts laughing. Lucy is laughing too. Everyone is laughing. 'Did you hear that!' says mum. 'Not as much as you!' She is nearly crying with laughter and relief.

Dad has given me a keyboard for Christmas. It is good, because I can sit in my room for hours playing tunes. You press buttons for different backing rhythms, like Calypso or Reggae or Jazz. I can play all the tunes in the book.

Finlay Salvesen comes to stay. He is mum's godson, he appears every winter like the holly and the figs around the house. I keep catching him looking at Lucy in a funny way.

There is a party going on downstairs. Mr and Mrs Crawford are here with their sons, Malcolm and James. And about twenty other people. Dad is giving people drinks and making jokes. He is really funny. Everyone always laughs and is glad when he is there. He teases people and they love it. Mum is being perfect, too. I don't know how she does it. She glides around like a graceful sheepdog, herding up lonely guests into the conversation and moving on to the next one once she has returned them to the flock of happy talkers. Sometimes they tell little stories about things that have happened. Mainly it is about skiing.

Francis broke his leg larst yar, ha, ha. He went round claiming it was a run-in with some moguls, but don't believe a word of it! Silly boy broke it climbing out of the chalet window to sneak awf to the pub!

Oh man. I wish Alan was here. I turn the page of the music book and start playing 'The Holly and the Ivy' with a calypso beat. It's pretty funky.

Lucy opens the door. 'Mum's going to kill you. Gillian Grant's got no one to talk to.'

The laughing is louder with the door open. Finlay is standing behind my sister. I look at him. 'Why do you come here?' I ask.

'Must be the friendly welcome,' he says.

The laughter gets louder still as I slide downstairs and move softly towards the drawing room. It is almost spooky. The guests are all talking and laughing, louder and louder. They have got something to laugh at which I don't understand. I don't understand it at all as I stand by the door lifting a glass of lemonade. I feel like a man in front of a herd of flamingos. The chandelier twinkles overhead.

'Vanessa! Darling, you remember Gillian? You went to her party last Christmas?'

Gillian is dark and glossy. Smartly dressed but somehow cool. She is wearing a black silk shirt and trousers. She looks more like my mother than I do. I hate her already. 'Hi!' she chirps, holding out her hand. 'It's nice to see you again.' She is just being polite. You can tell she is one of those people to whom social grace comes as easily as peeing. I shake her hand. 'I remember,' says Gillian, 'you were wearing that gorgeous gold dress.'

'Yeah.' Mum always buys us the best dresses. The shop girls in Droopy & Brown's swoon when she walks in.

'So, where are you at school again?'

'Crieff High.'

She frowns. 'I haven't heard of it.'

'It's a state school.'

'Oh. So. Did you have a good Christmas?'

'Yeah, yeah it was all right. How was yours?'

This is stupid. Neither of us cares in the slightest.

'Great! God, I can't wait to go skiing, though. My brother Francis broke his leg last year in Meribel so we thought we'd try somewhere else in case it's jinxed! Ha-ha-ha. We're going to Val d'Isère in Jan. I can't wait!' She wriggles excitedly. 'Do you ski?'

'No.'

'You should, it's brilliant. Oh, didn't you get expelled?'

'Yeah.'

'Sorry, that was so rude of me.'

'It's fine.'

'No, that was really rude of me. God, I can't believe I just said that.'

'It's fine.'

'God. How embarrassing!' She laughs. 'So, you don't ski?'

'No. But you do.'

'Yes.'

'Well. I'm glad we've got that sorted out.'

She looks at me as if I'm one of Satan's little elves.

'Would you like another drink?' I ask her.

'Yes!' She brightens. 'Thanks, Vanessa.'

I take her glass and don't come back.

Mum and dad are happy at parties. They always know just what to do and say. It is like they were designed for them. Their party smiles don't look false like others sometimes do, and their interest in small talk is genuine, because it makes sense to them and they understand the way it works. It is like a little universe, a better one, where it is possible to be perfect.

'I think that went rather well,' says dad, slipping his arms round mum's waist.

Mum smiles contentedly.

I wonder if the Crawfords had a nice time. I saw Lucy flirting with Malcolm and James in the hall. If only Mrs Crawford knew what the women of my family were doing to her men, I'm sure she would not have been quite so ready to pour out her drainage problems to my mother. Still, I like her. If it weren't for her, mum and Mr Crawford might run off together and leave all the rest of us behind. Or maybe they wouldn't. When I see mum and dad together, I can't imagine her leaving him for anyone. Nor can she, I don't think.

Malcolm Crawford visits my older sister in his second-hand Volkswagen. He comes and picks her up and they go to the pub in Methven. She says they are just good friends. Mum says she hopes they don't get busted for under-age drinking. I think the whole thing is weird. Finlay leaves early.

Alan comes walking through the muddy slush to visit me. Dad doesn't think he is suitable. He takes me aside and says, 'Nessie, don't you think you're a little young to be having boyfriends?'

'Oh, it's just the one, dad.'

'You know what I mean. There's plenty of time for that sort of thing when you're older, like Lucy is. I just want you to be happy. And I think you'd be a lot happier if you waited till you were a bit older and found someone who you've got a bit more in common with.' He looks at me meaningfully, with love.

I nod, and keep seeing Alan.

I tell Alan that I am going to be quite busy until the end of the holidays, so he can't come round to visit. Instead, I go and visit him when I can get away without dad noticing. Mum covers for me sometimes.

'What are you so busy with?' asks Alan.

'Just stuff. It's quite boring. You know, just helping my parents and stuff.'

He nods and squeezes me tighter. 'I hardly ever see you,' he complains.

I am not going to tell him about my father and his embarrassing ideas about people's backgrounds. It would be insulting, and also it would make Alan think my dad is a prat when really he is dead nice.

Dad thinks I am a keyboard-playing genius. He knocks on my bedroom door and makes special requests. His favourite one is 'Bridge over Troubled Water'. I say that he just likes that one because he is an engineer, and he roars with laughter. Dad always laughs at my jokes.

I stand on the gate and wave as hard as I can, watching him go. His strong arm waves back at me from the wound-down car window. Bryony is running down the wet road after him. 'Bye!' she screams. 'Bye, Daddy!'

Another car roars down the road and she hops into the verge, almost falling. Lucy sighs and jumps down from the gate. The bar shakes beneath my feet.

Bryony sits at the kitchen table with all her sweets. Dad always brings us back a selection of Middle Eastern delicacies. We get chewy sweets with nuts in, ones that are made of honey, yoghurt squares and Turkish Delight. I have eaten all of mine already. Lucy has eaten a handful and will take the rest back to school for her friends. This is not because she is particularly generous but because she likes to be careful with her calories.

Bryony hasn't eaten a single one. She sits and looks at them, grouping them into different categories and then rearranging them. She keeps counting them. As if me or Lucy might be stealing them in the night. She picks one up and licks it, then puts it back on the table.

'Bry!' exclaims Lucy. 'That's disgusting!'

'Why?'

'You can't lick it and put it back. It'll get covered in bacteria.'

'Oh.' Bryony looks solemn. She rearranges the sweets for the seventh time. Lucy does a very handsome exit. I think she may have been practising.

'I just wanted to taste it,' explains Bryony, looking at me.

I don't answer. I only smile, and she smiles back. Poor kid. I go to see Alan.

'My dad's gone,' I tell him.

He plays some more chords. 'Do you miss him?'

I shrug. 'Sometimes.'

Alan nods.

'Hey, maybe we could have a band. I've got a keyboard now.'

He grins. 'Gallus.'

'We could tour America.'

'In an acid bus.'

'Yeah.'

'That's what I want to be,' says Alan. 'A musician. Right, Vanessa. Listen to this.' He plays me a song about going underground, by The Jam. I have never heard him sing before. His voice is sweet and hard at the same time, like twigs in a glass jar. It is sad and it knows the tune. I like listening to it.

'Sing me another one,' I say. He plays to me for an hour. He tries to get me to sing with him but I won't. I am too embarrassed. It is nicer just listening to him. I lie back on his bed and close my eyes.

I pretend that I am cold and ask to borrow a jumper. Alan pulls his drawer open for me. I take a dark-blue woollen one, chunkily knit and a little fraying at the cuffs. I have kissed him wearing it. It prickled my skin.

I go home through the biting cold with the jumper on. Alan sometimes asks for it back, but I just keep forgetting to return it to him. I love having something of his to wear. I put it on when I come home from school and sit doing my homework in it. It is massive on me.

It is coming up for Easter now. The big nights that have been swallowing up all the daylight are thinning fast. It is light in the mornings and the sun comes streaming through my window and wakes me. Mum says she can't understand why I don't close my curtains. I don't like them, that's all. I like the sun to wake me.

I lie there and wish I didn't have to go to school. Siobhan is my friend, I suppose, but I don't really trust her. I don't actually like her very much at all, but her company is okay. Angie hates me. Every time I speak in the classroom she sniggers. The teachers don't say anything. I expect they don't hear, or maybe they think I'm a snobby cow as well. Laura just gives me looks. The two of them neigh at me in the corridor when the boys aren't looking. I don't know what that is all about.

Debbie watches me as if she is waiting for something. Alan says she is okay and that I just see a bad side to her. He says that she is nice. I know why he says that. I see her being nice to him, and her loveliness then is genuine. Alan says, 'It's a shame you two don't get on,' as if it is an equal situation. He says, 'I know she can be a wee bit moody, but Debbie's not a bitchy kind of lass. Don't take it personally, Vanessa.' And I can't explain, because he is never there when it happens. He is always somewhere else.

Mum has gone to pick up my sisters again, from school. I asked if I could come too but she said it would not be appropriate. It's a shame, because maybe I would have seen Alice. Alice was my good friend. We used to tell each other ghost stories. Also, Alice told me about sex. So I am quite indebted to her, really. Her parents didn't like me much. I am not very good at getting along with parents. Some kids have the knack and some don't.

One time, Alice's parents had friends coming round for lunch on our leave-out weekend. Me and Alice were playing naked commandos in the bushes. Alice's mum went mental when she saw us shooting her friends. It's not like we had real guns and actually killed them or anything. She just disapproved. Still, it was dead funny. But I didn't get invited again, even though the naked commandos had been a joint idea.

Alice did the drawing on the pavilion with me, the one I got expelled for. I didn't dob on her when they caught me, because that had been all my idea. Alice just helped me.

I didn't even know what I was going to draw until I got there, and then I just saw it, this big whale scene and all the little people. I don't know where it came from. It was probably lurking on the pavilion all along, and I just drew over it in paint that people could see. Alice found me when I was halfway through. She'd been looking for me all evening and she said she thought the drawing looked cool so I let her do some. Anyway, I expect she'll get expelled soon too, all by herself. She smokes like a chimney. On the other hand, her dad is on the school board. He is some big shot in Aberdeenshire. He's also got a big secret stash of porn magazines. Alice showed me them once. We practically killed ourselves laughing. They're full of these women with powdery faces and enormous breasts trying to be dead sexy. One of them had a hairbrush pushed up her bottom. It was funny.

Me and Alice used to do imitations of them, except for the hairbrush bit, and also we had our clothes on. We clutched our chests and threw our legs open in the air and sometimes we did the captions from the magazines as well. Oooh yes, fuck me, do it to me big boy. One of the pages had 'Give me your big banana', which was the best. We used to shriek it and then roll around laughing.

I really miss Alice. She wrote to me soon after I was expelled, but I didn't write back. I can't be bothered with writing, and I expect she just wrote out of politeness.

My sisters come home. Mum is smiling and breathless as she walks through the door in a short khaki mac. I love the way my mother dresses. It is always as if somebody worthwhile might be watching, and it's such a shame that they're not. Under the khaki mac is a dark khaki roll-neck jumper and a black skirt. Her hair is scraped up in a knotted thing and her lips are glossed the colour of poppies. She is beautiful.

'Hello, darling,' says mum.

'Hi,' says Lucy. She even smiles at me. Bryony gives me a hug and then goes into the fridge.

'Where's the rhubarb crumble?' asks mum.

Oh God, God, shit. The kitchen goes pale. I was supposed to be taking it out of the oven at half past five. Mum is looking at me like a little bird. Her red mouth glows in the middle of her face.

I grab the oven gloves and turn my back on her. My hand shakes as it yanks open the oven door. I can hear mum shouting behind me as I pull out the dish, 'What! You left it in! There's no point taking it out now, is there? You'll have ruined it!'

But I take it out anyway and put it on the trivet. It is black.

'Maybe it's okay underneath,' says Lucy.

'Don't be ridiculous! Look at it! Look!' Mum's face is shaking. She grabs my neck and pushes my head down. I am up close with the scorched pudding. It smells of burnt crustiness and badness. It is very hot. 'It's ruined, isn't it!'

She looses her grip and I straighten up. I just look at her. I am

83

focusing on my bones. Ribs are the best. You fill them up with all your feeling till you can't feel a thing.

'For God's sake!' says mum.

'It's only a pudding,' says Lucy. 'Please, mum.' She sounds very grown-up.

'It is not only a pudding,' says mum, exasperated. 'It's a rhubarb crumble which I made specially for your first supper back home. I wanted us all to have a nice meal together, but obviously Vanessa has other ideas.'

'I don't mind if we don't have pudding,' says Lucy.

'I don't bloody well care if you mind or not!'

I start sliding towards the door.

'Get back here!' Mum is coming towards me. She grips my wrist and pulls me past my sisters, across the room. It takes her a while to unlock the patio door one-handed. There is something faintly ridiculous about the situation and a laugh comes out my throat before I can stop it. She glares at me. It isn't human when she does that. It isn't mum. It's the stranger who you're told not to go with and it scares me stiff.

Mum has got me in the shed and pinned me up against the wall. Her hands are round my neck. 'Don't you ever laugh at me.' Her hands are squeezing, but never too hard. I know she is just trying to scare me, just doing it to make me pay attention. I am trying not to be scared. 'Don't you ever, ever laugh at me!' It is only a little bit tight in here. A little bit tight inside my body. I'd like to get out. 'Do you understand?' She knocks my head backwards, but nice and gently. It thuds quietly against the stone. 'Do you understand!'

I nod. I want more air. She lets go and her arms swing gently down to her side. She looks at me as if I am an evil arsonist. 'I don't know why you make me do this. Life would be so much easier if you would just behave like any normal child.' I nod again. I know she is right. 'I just get so angry, that's all. But you know I love you.' She hugs me tightly. 'You know I love you, all the time, even when I'm being angry.'

The bolt slides through the door.

And it is true. I know she loves me when she's being angry. I know she loves me when she's hurting me. That's the way love is.

Shit. It's going to be freezing tonight. I do star jumps. Then I sit on the wooden workbench. The door of the shed reopens. Mum is standing there like an angel, smiling. 'I tell you what,' she says. 'You can come back inside.'

I lean over the bathroom tap, swilling out toothpaste after supper. Bryony comes in. I stand up and dry my face in the fluffy yellow towel. Bryony is just hanging around. I look at her, wondering what she's up to.

'Ness,' says Bryony. 'Are you all right?'

'I'm fine.'

'What did mum do?'

'None of your business. She didn't do anything.'

'Ness.' She is reaching out towards me and I can't hear it.

I flap my arm. 'Get away!' I say. 'Get away!' She keeps fumbling towards me. I push her backwards. 'For fuck's sake!'

She stumbles sideways and clings to the wall with her big stupid eyes pointing at me. I grab her arm and then I don't know what to do with her. So I just shake it, hard, and slam the door behind me. Jesus.

We all go to church on Easter Sunday. Except dad, who couldn't make it back to Scotland. Mum tried not to look disappointed when she told us. I was glad to see her sadness. She couldn't really love Mr Crawford – although he has been visiting from January to March. Mum says dad is getting a full month off in the summer. I can't wait.

The church is full of daffodils. They fizz yellow in the alcoves and upon the windowsills. It is a beautiful day as we walk in. Sunlight streams through the stained-glass windows, lighting up Saint Sebastian. He is pierced with arrows all over his body. A hunting dog looks up at him, but he is busy looking at God. That is the most interesting window. The others are just full of ladies and gentlemen in medieval dress, saying, 'In Memoriam,' with the names of Lords, Ladies and wealthy common people. The dates of the deaths are mostly late 1800s, with a few 1900s as well. So I'm not sure why the people on the windows are dressed as if they come from the Middle Ages. It seems a bit silly.

The minister comes out in his robes and we all stand up. My view is largely obscured by Mrs Carrie-Scott's hat. We all call her Mrs Carricot. I used to think it was dead funny. I examine the service sheet to see how long we have got to go. Church always seems to go on for ever.

I don't know why we come to church at Easter. Christmas I can understand, because you get to sing carols, plus there is a crib. But there doesn't seem much point at Easter. Mum just thinks we ought to. She says, 'It's just a nice thing to do.' Is that what God is? A nice thing to do? I look at Saint Sebastian full of arrows and I think that can't really be it.

We stand and sit and we read things out from the sheet when we are supposed to. We listen to a boring sermon which consists of the minister relating an anecdote about an Easter chicken. But he only makes it last nine minutes, because he knows we all want to get away and enjoy our Easter Sunday. We sing a few songs.

Jesus Christ is risen today, Alleluia
Our triumphant holy day, Alleluia
Who did once upon the cross
Suffer to redeem our loss
Alleluia

Everyone is looking smart and looking forward to a nice family lunch, singing about a man being stabbed and nailed to a piece of wood and left to die. Singing about a man who came back from the dead and it sounds like they're singing the national anthem. Nobody is listening to the words. I look at Saint Sebastian and I feel sorry for him. God isn't here. This is just a load of bullshit.

The nearest thing I see to God is May. The air is warm and the light rolls over the glen like a lion rolling in grass.

Me and Alan go up to the lochan again. The warm weather brings hillwalkers to the bothy, so we can't go there any more. We lie in the heather and Alan has his tea beforehand. We sit on the rocks and talk. We make love and I can see all the insects in the heather, close up, between my eyelashes as we do it. There are little spiders there. They shake as I move back and forward with him. I always nearly get there. Then it is gone and I wait.

Alan's hands are either side of me, on the ground, propping him up as he thrusts. I love watching his face when he isn't looking, when he has his eyes closed. He looks so involved in it all. It is rather beautiful. His mouth opens, towards the end, and he gasps. As if it is always a surprise for him. I like that noise. 'Oh,' he says, but it isn't a word. 'Oh.' His arse pushes faster. I can glimpse it through a gap between his arm and ribcage, and its sudden stillness as he shudders inside me. He slumps down on top of me, breathing hard. 'Oh,' he says, laughing. I feel his breath against my neck. I circle him with my arms.

'Hey,' I say. 'You're not light.'

Alan rolls off me and on to his back beside me, pulling off the condom and tugging up his cut-off jeans. He grins at me. I smile and then I just lie still, with my eyes closed, enjoying the sunshine on my naked groin. I am still wearing my T-shirt, but my shorts are somewhere in the heather. The vegetation rustles scratchily under my bum. The world is hot. Alan leans over and licks the skin on my forearm. I start laughing.

An eagle is flying up above, floating on the thermals. It circles over us and soars still higher, a little black cross in the sky. It can see us, down below, and we are just a speck between the far-off mountains and the North Sea. Suddenly Alan seems very close. I look in his eyes dead straight, so that at least there is one little bit of truth. I hold his face in my hands and remember it.

'I love you,' says Alan.

'I know.' For a second, it is real.

The sun grows hotter, right into July. School is over for two months. Me and Alan spend our time outside, walking up into the hills and stopping where nobody can see us. We build shelters and lie down in them. Sometimes we take Alan's tent and stay the night.

In the daytime, we swim in the lochan or the pools in the burns. There is a waterfall high on one hillside where we stand under the speeding water and get drenched. Down below is the valley with the road to Crieff. We watch the cars and lorries burning along it and we feel like we belong to a different universe. We are like the birds and the early peoples. Thundering water rushes over our heads, spilling off our bodies. Alan laughs at the way it jets forward from my wet chest. I just like the way he takes his T-shirt off before going in. His bare chest gleams and sparkles and I know I never want anything else except the sunshine and this boy.

In the burns we build dams to make the pools deeper. In the lochan we wade right in with our trainers on. There is a sharp and rocky bottom. We splash each other with water and dive under. The water is soft and clean. You can swim underwater with your eyes wide open and it doesn't hurt a bit.

When we have swum, we lay ourselves down on the ground and dry off in the sun. Sometimes, we are skinny-dipping and so we sunbathe naked. Our bodies darken until we begin to look less nude.

Usually I take a book with me on our expeditions. I am into the Russians. I think there is something cool about them, probably because they had a revolution. I read some plays by Chekhov and novels by Dostoevsky. Alan teases me. He says, 'Ach, you're a bit of an intellectual, aren't you,' and he thinks it's funny that one of my books is called *The Idiot*.

Alan prefers real-life books. He usually reads biographies of musicians. He could tell you anything you wanted to know about the adolescence of Bob Dylan. He talks to me a lot about music. He tells me that his tastes have matured. He isn't into stadium rock but more independent music. His main influences are The Jam and The Ramones. You quite often hear him singing 'The KKK took my baby away' at low volume whilst tying a trout fly to his line.

'I think we should live together,' says Alan. 'We could get a wee chalet or something.'

I turn away and pick up my book. He is being daft. There is no way we could do that.

'Why not?' says Alan, when I don't speak.

'I'm fifteen. It's illegal.'

'Bollocks.'

'Anyway, I don't want to.'

'Why not?'

'I just don't.'

'It's your mum, isn't it. You're scared of what your mum would say.'

'I am not scared of her.'

He lets me read half a page of my book before he starts in again. 'Has she ever hit you again?'

For Christ's sake. 'No.'

'It's just – remember that time? I ken you said it was the only time, but—'

'Alan, just leave it. I'm not scared of my mum. She doesn't hit me. I just don't want to go and live on my own in a hut.'

'You wouldn't be on your own. I'd be there.'

'Right.'

Alan gets it into his head that my mum is some tyrannical queen, holding me against my will. I am the princess in the tower. He strokes my hair and says things like 'I know something's wrong. You've got to trust me.' I start feeling anxious about it. There really isn't anything wrong, and Alan is building up this big thing in his head. I feel guilty for the care it elicits. What's going to happen when he finds out that everything really is fine? It's like I'm tricking him. But I am not trying to and I keep telling him that he's wrong about mum. He doesn't understand. I am happy with her.

Alan blinks and scratches his neck, paused for a second. A hot fly skits past his ear. The wind is humming in the grass. I stare away across its stalks.

'I could take you out in Morna's car tomorrow,' he says. 'I could teach you to drive. It'd be good.'

'You haven't got your licence.'

'So?' he answers, almost cross.

And feeling sorry for him I say Okay then.

I don't want it to start, the driving lesson. I ask for a cup of tea and then try to spin it out for ever across the glass-topped coffee table in his lounge. The house is quiet. Alan sits beside me and drinks his sweet tea quickly. Minutes pass. He won't stop looking at me.

'So tell me again,' I start, 'the brake is on the left, or the right?'

'It's in the middle.'

'This is going to be a disaster. Can I have a biscuit?'

'No. Clutch, brake, accelerator. Okay? Let's go.'

He stands up.

'I don't know how to do it,' I plead.

'You'll be fine.'

'I think I should learn the theory.'

'Well, the best way to learn is to do it.'

I'm not so sure.

'Come on,' he says, walking out the door, and there is nothing else to do.

Alan straps me in. 'What about you?' I ask, and he says, 'I'll be fine. Right foot on the accelerator. Now turn the key away from you.'

'This one?'

'Aye. Okay. Do it again.'

Noisy air roars in the window at us.

'Ease off,' says Alan, loudly above the din. 'That's it, that's it,' as the noise hushes down to a trundling cough. 'Left foot on the clutch, down to the floor.'

He works the gears for me, and the handbrake. He tells me I should start by getting used to the pedals. And now he thinks I've got the hang of them, but I haven't really, and he leaves me doing the gears myself. I bring the car around the side of the house and stop it. Alan is ecstatic, you'd have thought I'd just sailed single-handedly across an ocean. I am crazy proud.

And scared. I've never liked cars, there's too much that can go wrong. Let the steering wheel slip and your neck goes with it. They're dangerous things, more animal than machine. Moving one by myself and not breaking anything, me and Alan included, is brilliant and wrong. I start laughing with the nerve of it. I can feel my legs trembling, veins fluttering like ribbons.

'See? You're fine,' says Alan, though I'm not. 'We'll do it again. We'll just keep practising till you build up your confidence.'

I bring the car back round the corner. Then we circle the house, slowly. One wheel humps up on the grass. My neck shakes when it comes back down again. Heart going furiously, pulsating muscle. It feels funny, cruising past the back doorstep, like his house is a big bus stop.

Alan gets me to drive down to the end of the track. 'That's it,' I say, when we get to the road, letting my leg off the pedal. It is aching and shaking. The engine splutters out, just as I am saying, 'That's me for today.' I open the door and get out. Standing tall, feeling dizzy. Smelling smoke and dust.

Alan is walking round the front of the bonnet. 'Well done. That was really good, Vee. Look. You didn't break anything.' He grins and kisses me, climbs in the driver's door. I walk round to the other side, lean my head and shoulders through the door hanging open for me. Alan looks comfortable behind the wheel, arms and legs loosely just right. He is moving the gearstick around. Has his hand on the key, face turned sideways towards me now, waiting.

'Mind if I walk?' I ask. 'I'd rather.'

Smiles. 'No. I'll see you up there.'

I smile back and swing the door shut. It slams, though I didn't mean it to. I watch him, but his head is turned over his shoulder, looking through the rear window as the car roars to life and speeds backwards, away from me, the way we came. He drives it so straight and even, it looks like the car is on an invisible string and just being reeled back in.

Anyway, after that he keeps trying to get me to go driving again. He says I'd be really good. I keep saying No. Last time was just beginner's luck. I would break the car if I tried it again, and it's not even mine or Alan's to break.

My sisters are at home for the summer holidays. They know about me and Alan. Bryony thinks it's really funny. I go to the loo and she says, 'Are you going to see your boyfriend?'

'No, I'm going for a piss.'

She just giggles.

Lucy has started coming into my bedroom for sisterly conversations. 'I don't know what to do,' she says. 'I don't know whether I should sleep with Malcolm.'

'Do you love him?' I try not to sound too incredulous.

'I don't know.' She is twiddling her dark hair. I have always been jealous of Lucy's hair. It is exactly identical to mum's – dark and shiny like molasses and smooth like glass.

'Does he love you?'

'I think so. Do you think you will lose your virginity with Alan?'

I don't know what to say. I shrug. 'Maybe.'

'Yeah, I guess you're a bit young. I don't know. I'm just worried that if I sleep with Malcolm then he might finish with me.'

'Why would he do that?'

''Cause he'd got what he wanted.'

'Nah, I don't think so.'

She doesn't know about mum and Malcolm's dad.

I came in from school in June and found them on the sofa together. I wouldn't have minded if they'd had their ankles round each other's necks. But they were curled up together and they looked happy, welded together into one piece. Mum had put her old James Taylor record on and they were enjoying listening to the same music. Mum had her eyes closed for once, and her head was leaned back against Mr Crawford's chest. Mr Crawford looked fiercely luminous with love. It was hard to believe that someone who was so normal and boring at parties could look like that. His arms were round her front and her bosom rested on top of them. Her thin gold necklace was trickling down between her breasts in a crisp black shirt with one too many buttons undone.

They didn't hear me come in. I stood in the doorway for ages but still they didn't see me there. Sunshine was pouring in the windows and particles of dust shone and fluttered in the air as if they were little gold angelfish.

blossom it's been much too long a day, seems my dreams have frozen

James Taylor was singing to the angelfish, but from mum's face it looked like she was part of the song too. I watched them sitting there and wondered what they were thinking. I never imagined adults sitting and listening to records together. There was something too young about it. And there was something too young about them, curled into each other so naturally. Something too open. The song came to an end and I held my breath. In the softly crackling silence I was sure she would feel me there, but the music started again and still nobody knew. I crept away.

Dad comes home for his summer month. I catch mum looking at him sadly. I want to rush up and cover those eyes with my hands.

It is surprising that dad doesn't notice something is wrong. But then, half of everything is fine. And the other half is very well pretended. They laugh just as much as usual and they still get pissed together at suppertime. They still tease each other about their hangovers and dad still chases mum around the kitchen and out on to the sunny terrace. He still kisses her in the garden and she still talks to him about her flowers.

'I thought I might put some mahonia in here, what do you think?' She is standing in skirt and sandals with her hand shading her eyes even though she is wearing sunglasses. The world is very bright behind her, the sunshine like camera flash. I know things are going to fall apart. I know because I can see the way she looks at him when no one is looking. As if she is asking for forgiveness in advance.

Chapter Four

I am nearly sixteen and she is still there. I see her drinking coffee on the garden bench. I watch her feed and prune her plants. She puts shit on them to make them grow. I hear her voice, singing songs in the kitchen. She stops when I walk in.

Mr Crawford comes. They wander around talking to each other. Mum has decided that she likes having me there with them. I think she needs a witness. We eat meals together and she tries to include me in the conversation.

She keeps coming into my bedroom. She loiters in the doorway, saying, 'What do you think of John? He's very amusing, isn't he. Wasn't it funny, that story he told about the girl in Frankfurt being killed by a giant cake? At the fête.'

'Yeah.'

'Well don't you think so?'

'Yes. Yes, I do.'

'You never had much of a sense of humour,' notes mum. Her eyes float over my wall. 'I like your pictures.'

I buy *The Face* because it's got the best photographs. My walls are scattered with their rectangles: singers who look like angels, icons trapped in black-and-white moments, bodies sleeping in sand dunes and swing parks, and some that I just like for the colours. I also have wild animals from *BBC Wildlife Magazine*.

'Thanks.'

'Yes,' says mum. And then she just stands there for a bit. And then she goes away.

Bryony and Lucy are away at a tennis camp in France. Mum asked me if I wanted to go and I said no.

Lucy's skin is like mahogany. Her eyes and teeth gleam white as if she might die of healthiness. She is going to be eighteen on Bonfire Night, but it's still the summer.

Malcolm Crawford comes round often to admire my sister's suntan. She gets into his car wearing white T-shirts and pedal-pushers and sunglasses like Jackie Onassis. I don't know what she sees in him. He has a wardrobe of interchangeable stripy shirts and is politely dull. Although now he's been seeing Lucy for a while, he's become daring enough to buy a pair of coloured jeans. You can always tell when he's feeling dashing because the red jeans come out. Lucy comes into my room and tells me that she thinks she loves him, and I try to take it seriously.

'I'm sleeping with him,' says Lucy.

What a horrible thought. I don't know why she's telling me, because I don't particularly want to know. 'Oh, right,' I say.

'Are you shocked?'

'No.'

'Have you slept with Alan?'

'It's none of your business!'

She looks surprised that I'm pissed off. 'But I just told you about me!'

'So? Do you think I want to know?'

'For fuck's sake!' Lucy is staring at me as if I've just committed some heinous crime. Just because I don't want to be tipped over and poured out. She lurches towards the door, picking up a book from off my desk and hurling it at me as she goes. The book hits the wall. Its pages splat openly and it flops on to the bed beside me, showing its words. Poor thing. I close it and replace it on the desk. My bedroom door has slammed.

Everyone is at home when the brown envelope comes, stamped by the Scottish Exam Board. Vanessa C. Gordon has got seven 1s in her Standard Grades, if you believe the piece of paper. How embarrassing. But mum is pleased. She says, 'Gosh, well done Nesspot!' and gives me a big hug. Bryony seems upset and starts clamouring, 'Mum! Mum! Look at my fashion design!' Not that she's got it with her. She runs upstairs to find it and brings it in for mum to see. Lucy doesn't say anything. She just looks at Bryony and walks out. I follow her. I think I might go and see Alan.

Lucy passes me brushing my hair in the hall and she says, 'Well done with your exams, Vanessa.' It sounds quite formal.

I say: 'Thanks,' and feel embarrassed again.

'You're cleverer than me.'

'No I'm not.'

She squints at the ceiling and walks away.

Maybe I won't go to see Alan. What if he's got worse grades than me? He might think I'm too clever as well. I said I'd go round, but now I think the thoughtful thing to do would be to wait for him to call me.

Alan doesn't call. I wait three days and then I can't wait any more. Why hasn't he rung? I build my face in sandstone as I pick up the receiver and dial.

'He's not in,' says Mrs McAlpine. So I wait for him to call me back, and he doesn't. So I cut my nails, stare out the window, and call him again.

'Where have you been?' I ask him.

'I went into Perth. Met up with Robbie and Debbie and everyone.'

'Oh.'

'It was a good laugh. We went to Pizza Hut.'

'Oh right. So. Who was all there?'

'Robbie, Debbie, Pete, Laura, Sarah Black. Angie. Pete's cousin, this guy called Lindsay. He's coming to Crieff High next term.'

'Cool.'

'Aye. I had a really nice day.'

The line is quiet. Just shallow breathing pegged on it. Mine.

'We were celebrating, getting our results.'

I don't say anything.

'You didn't come round.'

'No. I know.'

'Why not?'

'I don't know.'

'Don't you want to know what I got?'

'Yes! Yeah, I do.'

'Well, I'm not telling you now.'

I start laughing. It's like ice on a bright red swelling. Alan starts laughing as well, but with a rock in the bottom of it. 'I really don't understand you,' he says. Again. Neither of us is laughing any more.

'Well,' I say, and leave it at that. I'm hoping he'll ask me to come round.

'Bye, then,' says Alan.

'Bye,' I answer, and wait for him to hang up. He might invite me at the last minute. The line goes dead. I put down the phone. Me and Alan, we seem to be always trying to love each other in the wrong place. It is an ectopic affair.

Lucy comes into my bedroom again. She is wearing a silk headscarf, with her dark hair tied into a pair of loose bunches at the nape of her neck. She looks like a very glamorous pirate. I'm glad that one of us inherited mum's sense of style. I wish it was me. 'Vanessa,' she says. 'Is everything all right at home? When me and Bryony are away, I mean. Is mum alright with you?'

I shrug. 'Yeah.'

'Would you tell me if things were bad?'

I grin. 'Maybe.'

She smiles back at me and for a second she is really my sister and I love her. Then she says, 'I worry about you,' and it is all undone.

'There's no need to,' I say, looking back down at my book. It is called *The Book of Laughter and Forgetting*, by Milan Kundera. 'I can look after myself.'

'I know. But you shouldn't have to.'

'I'm really fine, Lucy.'

She examines my face. She won't find anything there, though, because I spring-cleaned it long ago.

'Okay,' she says. 'But ring me whenever you want.'

'Right.' I smile lightly to reassure her.

'I love you,' she says. Why does she say that? It makes me shiver.

Alan has stopped saying that he loves me. I miss it, from him. It really made sense when he said it. We go to meet each other in the lay-by and walk up the hills, but we don't make love any more. I try to climb on top of him but mostly he turns his head to the side and says, 'Vanessa, don't.' Sometimes there is wetness in his eyes. I am too scared to ask him what is wrong. Because I know it's me.

Alan says, 'You don't really love me, do you?'

I don't speak for a few seconds. Then I say: 'Yes, I do.' But it sounds unconvincing. The truth always sounds unconvincing from a liar. I'm just not used to telling it. He laughs in a cold manner and the laugh is like something physical that sits there with us afterwards, watching to make sure that we don't give ourselves away.

I am dreading school. It used to be bearable because of the evenings and weekends when I saw Alan, but now we are freezing over.

We share a lot of the same classes, because we are in the same sets for Higher English, and also we are both taking French and History. We usually sit next to each other in these classes. Our maths sets are different, and my other Higher is latin while Alan's is art. We go down the street for lunch together but we don't know what to say. I am scared to speak in case I start the landslide. I know he is going to tell me that he doesn't want to be with me. And I don't know what I will do when he says it. Nothing makes sense if you take him away. I sometimes think there is a perfect logic to life, like in maths, an underlying logarithm, if you can just find it. It flows along, making sense, and you can understand it. But the trouble with this maths is that every little part is essential. If you take away pi then circles just stop making sense. Alan's like pi, and I am both the geometrist and the circle. I need him so that I can make sense of the world and I need him so that I can be understood. There are infinitesimal millions of numbers in the universe, but only one of them is pi.

Me and Alan sit on the wall at the car park, eating our chips. 'Do you still want to live abroad?' I ask.

Alan laughs. 'In a hot country. Aye.' He smiles at me, and I think he is remembering that big house with the veranda and the black car and piano. But I don't think he still wants me to be there in that house in the hot country with him. Mum says she can't understand why anyone would want to go out with me. A cold fish like me, with those horrid little eyes. Fish-eyes, she says, over and over. Fish-eyes, fish-eyes. I looked in the mirror and thought she was right. Glassy and far away from me. I am a worse person than I used to be. Perhaps Alan is just staying with me out of pity. I don't care if that is the reason we're together, just as long as he will stay.

'D'you still want to?' he asks me.

'Want to do what?'

He looks at me and then he looks down at his empty chip wrapper. 'Nothing,' he says.

I know what he meant: still want to go out. Please not that. Don't start it. I swing my heels against the wall and look away.

My sisters are home for half-term. Bryony won't stop crying

because she has got her period for the first time. 'I don't want it!' she keeps saying. 'I don't want it!'

'Put a sock in it,' says mum, though putting a tampon in it would be more sensible.

Bryony's eyes carry on dribbling.

Lucy tries to comfort her. 'It's not so bad when you get used to it,' she says. 'Honestly, Bryony. Look at me, I've had it for five years and I'm fine.'

'You're different.'

'Just leave her,' says mum.

'I think you're being a bit harsh,' says Lucy. I stare at my shoe. I stare at the way my shoelace is twisted as it crosses between one eyelet and another.

'Oh,' says mum, 'do you?' She is murderously polite. 'I think you'd do well to remember who's paying your school fees. Unless you don't want to sit you're A-levels. Do you? Do you, darling?'

Lucy is staring at mum like she really hates her. I don't know how Lucy can look at our mother like that. It is horrible.

'Do you?' shouts mum.

'Yes, mother,' says Lucy. 'I would very much like to sit my A-levels. Thank you so very fucking much!'

Jesus. Jesus, Jesus, I can't believe this. How can she talk to mum like that?

Mum's lovely face is going pale pink, like a seashell. 'Go to your room!' she says, shaking. Lucy goes.

I can't believe it. I can't believe that all mum did was send her to her room. She probably loves Lucy more than me.

'Right,' says mum. 'Bryony, you can go to your room as well, I've had just about enough of you.' She sighs and then notices that I'm there as well. 'Oh God,' she says. 'You can go to your room as well. Bloody well stop looking at me like that!' So we all go to our bedrooms, except Lucy, who telephones Malcolm and invites him round.

Malcolm's car pulls up the track an hour later. I hear its engine stop and the driver's door slam. There are feet on the gravel and mum is at the door. 'Oh!' she says, her voice muffled through the walls. 'Malcolm! Hello. Come in.'

I can hear Malcolm saying, 'Hi, Mrs Gordon. I hope you haven't gone to any trouble.'

'Oh no,' says mum blithely, 'not at all.' I can't help laughing in my room. 'Lucy, darling! Malcolm's here!' And then I hear mum say, 'I don't know where they've all got to,' and that really sets me off.

Lucy is coming down the passage and I stand at the top of the stairs watching her pass me. 'Malcolm!' She flings her arms around him, in front of mum.

Malcolm looks really embarrassed. He is patting her back as if it's crawling with potentially poisonous spiders. Like he's trying to kill them or maybe just trying to fish something out from underneath them without getting bitten. 'Easy, girl.' He laughs.

'I thought I'd do seafood lasagne,' says mum, entering into the spirit of things with remarkable panache. 'Girls, why don't you take Malcolm through to the drawing room.' She smiles benignly, as if she has been looking forward to this all week, and glides off to the freezer to find her frozen squid. Lucy looks at me as if she thinks mum is barking mad. I ignore her.

'This is delicious,' says Malcolm in his deep voice. He always exaggerates the vowel sounds, so it becomes 'durliishus.'

'Oh, is it all right?' says mum. 'And when are you off to university?'

'St Andrews,' says Malcolm, answering a completely imaginary question. 'Not till next week. No, now I'm a student, it's long holidays for the next four years!'

'Lucky you,' says Lucy.

'And it's economics you're studying, isn't it? How interesting.'

'Yes. Yes, economics. Mary, this is delicious.'

'Any ideas what you want to do when you leave?'

'Oh, anything that pays!' Malcolm thinks this is really funny. 'I expect I'll go into the City.'

'Really?'

'Oh yes.'

'Is it easy?' I ask.

'Well, no, I wouldn't say it's easy,' says Malcolm. 'No.'

'But you think you'll get a job there?'

'Well,' says Malcolm modestly, 'I hope so.'

'Well, that's good.' I smile at him.

'To be honest, I'd far rather be creative like Lucy. It's such a wonderful gift. Much more interesting than boring old money.' He's not very convincing. Perhaps Lucy finds fraudulence attractive, or perhaps she doesn't notice. She keeps smiling at him. After supper she slips an arm round his waist. They go into the small sitting room and mum tells Bryony to leave them be, people need their privacy.

I think I'll take advantage of mum's sudden support for personal freedom. I stand in the hall and telephone Alan. 'It's me.'

'Vanessa?' Who else does he think I'm going to be? Another girl, maybe.

'Yeah.'

'How're you doin?' He sounds relieved, for some reason.

'I'm fine,' I say a little cagily. 'What's going on?'

'What do you mean?'

'Nothing.'

There's an awkward silence.

'So what have you been up to?' he asks me.

'Ppp. Nothing much. Malcolm's round for supper.'

Alan doesn't say anything.

'He's really nice,' I say, though I don't know why, considering I think he's a plonker.

103

'Good.'

'So how are you?'

'I'm fine, Vanessa.'

'Maybe we could meet up tomorrow.'

'Don't sound too enthusiastic.'

I don't say anything much after that. I'm too embarrassed.

'Well, bye then,' says Alan. 'Sleep well.'

I hold on to the mouthpiece, not saying anything. I'm trying to think what I want to say.

But he just sighs and hangs up. 'Sweet dreams,' I say, into the blank tone of the empty telephone. Nobody heard me. I put the phone back on the hook.

I go to my room in order to avoid Malcolm and I lie on my bed reading *A Story Like the Wind*, by Laurens van der Post. I like the descriptions of the African bush and the white farmer trying to do the right thing. I particularly like the child, the boy whose father wants him to act European although he has grown up in Africa.

Mum made me have a posh party for my sixteenth birthday back in August. She hired a hall in Crieff and invited all these people who I don't even like. She said she was doing it for me, because she wanted me to have fun and why was I such a hermit, it was peculiar, Lucy had *begged* for her sixteenth party, who would have thought we were sisters. The only person I wanted there was Alan and mum didn't invite him. She said it would be embarrassing for him because he wouldn't know any of the dances. My old friend Alice was also invited but she couldn't come. So I had this big party with food and loads of punch and a bunch of people I don't care about.

Gillian Grant was there, being polite again. 'It's so lovely of you to invite me. I'm actually really exhausted by all the other parties, but I just really wanted to come.' She smiled and flicked her hair.

'Parties, parties,' I said. 'It is rather a bore, isn't it?' I was copying myself out of a Nancy Mitford book.

Gillian wasn't sure if I was taking the piss or not. 'Ha-ha-ha. To-tally.' She floated off.

I went and danced the Reel of the 51st. Vaguely, I wondered why this was considered a reasonable way to celebrate your sixteenth birthday. At English parties, nobody goes round doing English waltzes. If you want to see English country dancing done in traditional dress, you'd probably have to go and watch some weird preservation society demonstration. I suppose that's what this is.

Alan doesn't know the dances. The people at the high school can't do any of them. It's like we've boxed it all up. We don't want the deep-fried food and funny accents, but we'll keep the dances and the kilts and the rugged scenery. They're ours, ta very much.

I tried to smile at my dancing partner. His name was Farquhar and he was pleasant enough as Farquhars go, but I wished that Alan was there. He would have hated it, I know. We piled out of the hall at three in the morning and everyone was going up to my mother saying, 'Thank you so much, Mrs Gordon, what a fantastic party!' Except for the ones who were vomiting trifle in the toilets or shagging against the wall outside. It doesn't matter too much because they'll all send thank you letters.

And then we stepped outside, all walking to our cars, and everyone was calling loudly down the pavement: 'Bye, Selma! Ah'll see you at Patrick's pahti!' and the like. And a group of teenagers over the road stared. They were the same age as us, but wearing baggy jeans and hooded tops instead of kilts and ball-dresses. I thought I recognised one of them from school. They started laughing and whistling. I wished I wasn't there.

'God,' said Lucy. 'Check out the plebs.'

Malcolm, walking with us to our car, said, 'Like a troupe of laughing baboons.' Lucy giggled. I started walking quickly so that I was ahead and at a distance from her and Malcolm.

So, that was my sixteenth birthday party. Alan kept asking me if I was drunk and if there were lots of blokes there. I said I was a wee bit pissed and that there were loads of blokes there but that they weren't really my type.

'What's your type?' said Alan.

'You,' I said, and laughed. But he didn't laugh back, just gave me this deep and questioning look. I'm not sure what it meant.

'Does it bother you' said Alan, 'that my family's different from yours?'

'No.'

He never believes anything I say.

Anyway. I am reading *A Story Like the Wind*, except I still haven't found out why it's any windier than the rest.

Another chapter, and Lucy opens my bedroom door. 'Ness,' she says quietly, 'can I talk to you?'

'Yeah.'

She comes in and sits down and her movements are as quiet as her voice. Something is wrong. She sits and plays with her thumbs, frowning. I wait, till she says, 'Malcolm's just dumped me.'

'What?'

'We just had this big conversation, and he said he was glad I'd asked him round because he'd been wanting to talk to me. And then he said he thought we should split up before he went to university.'

I wait for her to continue.

'He said it wouldn't work. I don't see why not!' She sounds indignant. 'St Andrews is not exactly the other side of the world from here. And it's not as if we see each other much in term-time at the moment. I don't see what's going to be so different, just because he's going to be at university.'

'What did he say?'

'He said he just wanted to go and start somewhere fresh. Like what am I! Some crappy old stale person, obviously.'

I can't help laughing.

'It's not funny, Vanessa.'

'I know.'

'He's really serious. Do you think he just wants to go to university and be able to sleep with other people?'

Well, obviously. 'No,' I say. 'Don't be silly. Anyway, no one there's going to be as pretty as you.'

She snorts. 'I can't be that pretty if Malcolm doesn't want me.'

'Malcolm isn't everyone.'

'I really love him. God!' She grabs me and starts hugging me really tight. I can feel her shaking against me. I think she's crying. Her hair is in my face. I really wish she wouldn't be so close to me but I would feel a bit rude asking her to get off. So I just wait till she's finished. She sits back, rubbing her eyes and snuffling into her cuff. I don't like this. 'Sorry,' she says. I don't say anything, just sit there feeling hideously awkward. 'Well, thanks,' she adds, smiling nicely at me. 'You're lucky. You've got Alan. What's he like?'

'You know him.'

'Yeah. God.'

We both sit. Would it be rude if I picked up my book again? I'm not sure. Poor Lucy.

'Well! Thanks.' She gets to her feet and examines her face in the mirror above my chest of drawers. She blinks very quickly and arranges her hair. 'I just can't understand it,' she says and walks out of the door.

I can understand it perfectly, but I wish it hadn't happened. It's like a bad omen. Maybe me and Alan will be next.

'If I ever leave you,' says mum, 'it won't be because I don't love you. You know that, don't you?'

I just look at her very carefully, gauging how soon she is planning on leaving me.

'If I leave,' says mum, 'it's because I've got no other options.'

I nod, but only very slightly, so that she knows I don't think it's a good idea.

I think she is planning on leaving quite soon. She has got a funny look in her eyes, like her mind has already gone to the place she wants to be. She wants to be somewhere else. Not here in our house with me or the absence of dad, but somewhere else with Mr Crawford. I know she really loves Mr Crawford now because the last time he was here I heard them talking about Malcolm and Lucy.

'I hope he hasn't upset her too much,' said Mr Crawford.

'No,' said mum. 'I think it was fairly mutual.' Maybe she just doesn't want Mr Crawford to feel guilty. But I think it's more likely that she doesn't want herself to look rejected by association with Lucy. So she pretends Lucy wasn't rejected. And the only reason she would be so afraid is because she is terribly keen to be desirable always in Mr Crawford's eyes. She must love him as intensely as I love Alan. Nothing else can make you so fearful.

There's a new boy at school, the one Alan was telling me about. His name is Lindsay Douglas. Considering he's Pete's cousin, he is very nice. He has become friends with Alan. He brings me messages, telling me if Alan is unable to meet me at the gates for lunch, which I appreciate because it prevents me from hanging around up there like a fool.

I think perhaps Alan is avoiding me, because he never used to be too busy to see me. Maybe he just wants to spend more time with his friends. Fair enough. If I had any half-decent friends, I'd probably want to spend time with them too. I don't want to get in the way of his life. And it's not like I'm left on my own, because I go for lunch with Lindsay and Siobhan instead.

Siobhan keeps giggling. Maybe she fancies Lindsay. I'm not surprised, because he's really nice, and funny, and quite good-looking, although not as handsome as Alan. I'm glad that me and Alan share a lot of our classes, because it's a chance to be in close proximity without wondering what we ought to say to each other. I love him so much.

One time, me and Siobhan go for lunch without Lindsay. He says he's got stuff to do. We sit in a café because it's pissing with winter rain. 'Ye ken Sarah Black,' says Siobhan.

'Yeah?'

'Well.' Siobhan starts moving around in her seat and generally looking awkward.

'What?'

'No! No, nothin.'

I stare at her, going red above her steaming baked potato.

'It's jist – something that Debbie told me to tell you.'

'About Sarah Black?'

'Aye. But I'm not goin tae dae it.'

I'm not really that interested, until me and Alan are walking down the street, together again. I reach out for his hand and he grabs mine, really grabs it, and squeezes it. He looks ahead really hard. I'm thinking that maybe he still loves me. And then a girl approaches, walking towards us, and I feel his hand tense up. I look at him. Alan is looking at the ground as the girl walks past. She is carefully ignoring us. It is Sarah Black. And suddenly it makes sense. I hate her fucking trendy little rucksack. I hate her stupid hair clips. I hate her jumper, and her shoes, and I hate her fucking pancreas. I pull my hand out of Alan's and I walk on ahead.

'Vanessa! Vee!' I ignore his voice. I can't bear this. I have to get away from him in case he sees my face because it is giving things away. I can feel it letting things through. The world is getting spattered with all the awful things inside me, bits of Sarah Black are swinging in the trees, and pain and Alan and buggered-up love are screaming from the pavement. It is all escaping, leaving my insides hollow.

Alan is running to catch up, but I'm quite fast myself. He has to chase me all the way down to the river before he can get me. I turn round. There is his face. And if I didn't know better, I would think he still loved me. Beautiful face, looking sad. I'm glad you feel bad about it too.

'Get away! I don't ever want to see you again, Alan.' He just stands there. 'Leave me alone! For Christ's sake, please will you just go away?'

'I don't understand. What have I done?' His arms are fanning out from the sides of his body. 'Vanessa,' he says. 'Jesus!'

'Just go away.'

'Why? What have I done?' I wish he wouldn't say that. I don't want to think about what he might have done with Sarah Black.

'Please, just fuck off.'

He grabs me. 'Vanessa!' As if he wants to prove that he knows my name. He has got a hold of my jacket.

'Get your hands off me, Alan.'

He looks in my eyes and sees me managing to hate him. He looks surprised and kind of scared. He drops his hand. 'Okay,' he says. 'Okay.' And he stands there looking at me.

I feel like a melting statue. My lips are frozen together, but they might drift apart if I don't hold on. He turns his back and walks slowly up the street. That walk. I love it so much. I watch him walking right up to the corner. He gets to the top and turns round. He is far away now and I cannot see his face, just a small pale shape under the spark of reddish-brown hair. He is looking towards me. I stand here, looking back. And then he disappears round the corner.

He has gone. I turn round and face the river. I climb over the wall and sit at the top of the steep river bank, leaning back against the stone. No one can see me here and I start to cry. I keep on until I can't cry any more. But I can't stop saying his name. And now I am cold.

Mr Crawford and mum are fighting. I can hear the voices plainly as I read my book and scratch my nails hard up and down my forearm. It is clear what is happening.

'But you don't love her!' shouts mum. 'I know you don't!'

No answer from Mr Crawford.

'Why are you doing this?'

A vague mumble.

'Then why?'

'For God's sake,' says Mr Crawford, finding his voice. 'This isn't easy. Please, Mary. You know I love you, but I've got my family to think of.' He is not very original. 'My sons mean a lot to me.'

'More than me?' She sounds pretty sarcastic.

'No! But I can't choose, I just can't.'

'Rubbish! You already have. You've chosen them.'

'Mary, Mary, it's not so simple. Darling.'

I can hear mum crying. He is such a bastard. He is talking to her now, trying to soothe her as if she is some kind of hysterical pony. 'Maybe in a few years, when they're older. We can move away together then. But James is only fifteen.'

Mum can't stop crying. I know how she feels. 'Your bloody children! I would have done anything for you,' she says. 'I had an abortion for you. You know I didn't want to.'

'It was the right thing to do. You did the right thing.' Jesus. I had no idea. I put down my book and stand near my door. I almost open it and go downstairs, because I want to go to her and be on her side, but then I don't go and I find myself just standing in the middle of my room not knowing what to do.

'Mary, please believe me.' God, he is starting to cry as well now. 'I didn't want that either, but it was the only thing to do. Please believe me, Mary. I love you.' I'd like to slap his stupid face. He has got my mother, the most amazing person in the world, and here he is saying that actually he doesn't want her. When she loved him even more than she loves me. Arrogant jerk. When she gave away one of me for him.

Mum starts crying again when Mr Crawford has left. I am too afraid to go to her. Anyway, it isn't me that she wants. I get under my duvet and think about Alan. I might not have him any more, but I have still got my feelings for him. I bring them out and try to wrap myself up in them. I remember all the things he said to me, how much he loved me, and wanted us to live together. I know it isn't true any more, but at one time it was. It still exists inside me. I bear it in my mind to protect me while I think of mum and Mr Crawford and her aborting their baby. Poor mum. No wonder she is upset. He has made her realise how unimportant all the rest of us are, made her want to leave us, only to leave her stuck with us. I hold on to my stomach very tightly.

'Vanessa!' Mum is standing in the doorway looking mad. 'I thought you should know. If you care! If anyone bloody cares! I've had enough. I'm going to kill myself. I've decided.' No. No, she hasn't. The duvet is clinging to my legs. By the time I'm free of it she has disappeared. I chase her down the passage to her bedroom but her bathroom door slams shut just as I get there. The lock clunks.

'Mum! Mum, don't.' I bang on the door.

'Bloody hell,' says mum. 'Leave me in peace.' She is snuffling.

'Please, mum! You'll regret it!'

'Don't be so stupid. I won't regret it at all, because I'll be dead. You can tell your father. Don't bother telling John.' She starts crying again.

'Mum!' I am really howling at her now, with lungs I never knew I had. 'Mum, for fuck's sake, please, please come out of the bathroom.'

There is no answer.

'Mum!'

There is silence. Shit.

'I'm calling an ambulance,' I yell.

'No!'

'I am!'

The bathroom door bursts open and mum comes flying out, her face a big red blotch from all the tears, her hair a big mess from scrabbling her hands through it. She is definitely alive. Is she okay? Has she done it? I dive past her into the bathroom. There is nothing here. No razor blades. No paracetamol bottle lying on its side. No nothing. I feel like an idiot. I don't understand. Mum glares at me angrily. She refuses to speak to me for autumn.

In late November she cuts her hair off. 'I'm too old for long hair now,' she says, walking into the kitchen with her sharp bob. I can't tell if she did it to spite me or herself, or Dad or Mr Crawford. Maybe it was for all of us. It is the only thing she says to me.

Dad comes home for Christmas and mum tries to look happy, but she always laughs just a second too late. It is quite peculiar, hearing her talking again. I had got quite used to only ever hearing my own voice in the house.

I don't really notice the beginning of the holidays because I have been taking so much time off school anyway. Skiving, because I can't bear seeing Alan. It is bad enough having to get on the same bus as him without spending my day near him as well. It picks at my heart. So I get off the bus and slip out of the school gates, pull a coloured jumper on and go and sit in one of the tourist cafés on the main street. I read books, so it's not as if I'm entirely derailing my education. And I go to some of my classes sometimes, when I feel like it.

After a while, the school telephoned mum to discuss the

situation. She went in and had a meeting with the deputy head, which I also had to attend. She was great with Mrs Blair. She made out like she was really concerned, and then when we left she didn't speak to me. So I just carried on.

Bryony and Lucy are home as well now. Bryony is distraught about mum's haircut, she goes and locks herself in her room for a couple of days. Mum is fed up with her.

I help mum with the Christmas preparations, peeling chestnuts and sifting flour.

Dad doesn't know anything about anything and is being his usual kind self. But I can't help feeling a little angry with him as I watch him carve the turkey. He could have stopped mum from loving someone else. He could have been bigger and better. He could have been here. If things were okay between mum and dad then things would have been okay between me and Alan. I read about contagious magic in a book.

I am glad I'm old enough to have wine poured into my glass, more and more of it, deep deep blood. But I stop drinking when I start feeling too pissed. I don't want to act like a fool. I don't want to act like Lucy, who is sticking turkey bones in her beautiful hair and saying, 'D'you think I look like a geisha girl?'

Dad says, 'What a lovely family I've got', and he isn't being sarcastic. He really means it, sitting pink of cheek at the head of the table. Lucy giggles. A rounded end of poultry bone is sticking up and shining like a bauble in her messed-up coiffure. Mum just stares at the sauce-boat. I wonder if she is thinking about the baby which she didn't have with Mr Crawford. Maybe it would have been better than us.

There is too much silver on the table. It is reflecting everything that is in the room. Nothing is spared. Our windows and doors and faces curve uncannily around the sides of the candlesticks, sauce-boats and cracker barrels, never ending. You can even see snatches of the view outside. The line of the hill curves down and inwards to meet us with paper hats on. And the silver things reflect each other, so you can see the face of my mother reflected twenty times over, if you care to look close enough.

'I do love you all,' says dad. Bryony runs to him and climbs on to his lap, although at fourteen she is really too old and too big. 'I love you too,' she says, throwing an arm round the back of his neck.

Dad pats her tummy uncertainly. 'Sweetheart,' he says. 'I've just eaten.'

Bryony looks embarrassed as she sits back down in her chair. Mum smiles at her in a funny superior way, as if for some reason she is glad to see dad hurting her.

Lucy's chair scrapes backwards on the stone floor. 'What a load of bollocks,' she says. She is staggering across the dining room but turns round halfway. 'You're all full of shit.'

'Lucy!' Dad is staring at her, but mum is trying not to laugh.

'What's so fucking funny, mum? Share the joke.'

My mother is still dead quick. She is out her chair and across the floor in a flash. There is a flurry of red clothes and purple clothes and mum's head whips down to Lucy's arm. She bites her very hard and fast. It reminds me exactly of watching someone snap a chicken's neck. In fact, one of Lucy's turkey bones clatters to the floor as she screams. Her scream is short, more of a yelp really. Bryony has started crying again. I don't know when she is going to grow up. I start to make a swan out of my napkin.

'You're mad!' Lucy is walking backwards to the door. 'Dad! Dad, she's a total fruitcake!'

'How dare you!' He sounds like a very gentle earthquake. But Lucy has already gone.

'Mary,' says dad in a voice that clatters along in a can behind a car. 'Why did you do that?'

'What do you mean?' says mum. 'Just a game. No harm done.'

'Mary—'

'Oh for God's sake, stop overreacting. Who wants pudding?'

'Me!' squeaks Bryony. And dad looks at Bryony, looking radiant with hair in bunches, smiling happily at mum, her tears smeared away, and he thinks he must have got confused about something because obviously everything is fine. You can see it in his eyes. The four of us eat plum pudding doused in brandy, and Lucy's chair stays empty. Dad seems happy again.

I continue my education alone in cafés. I am now reading *War and Peace* by Tolstoy. It's slow going, but I have got it split into separate volumes so that it is easy to carry in my bag.

There are women in the cafés. They come singly and in pairs and threes. Never four, you never see four women in cafés together.

One day a man comes in, that's what I think, and then I see it's Alan. I bend my head so that my hair falls in a yellow curtain to hide the side of my face. The tip of my hair is trailing in my cup of coffee but I leave it. I wonder what he's doing here, and then I remember that it's the last day of term before the Easter holidays. The school has a half-day. And Alan is here in the café with me. I can see his dark shape in the corner of my vision. I see it turn to go when it sees me here. I see a girl behind him, pushing him into the room against his wishes. I know it is a girl. I hear her voice.

Alan and Sarah sit down two tables away. I strain to hear their conversation, wishing I could stopper the other customers' gabbing mouths with sausage rolls. I can tell that Sarah has seen me now, because her voice has changed. She is wittering on about Kerril's party, which they will both be going to on Saturday night. 'D'you think I should wear my pink vest?'

Alan mumbles at her.

'Do you like it?'

He says yes.

Alan likes Sarah Black's vest. I bet they are sleeping together. I'm glad they can't see my face. He has put his dick inside her, and come and fallen down on top of her. I know it. I do not own a pink vest. My hair trails in my coffee and I watch the ends of it. Suddenly they are very dear to me, the ends of my hair. I pull my face taut and lift the hair from the coffee cup. I squeeze it in my hand and it drops circles of hot brown liquid on to the checkered paper tablecloth. They are not absorbed. They don't go in, but sit there on the surface. My wet strand of hair falls down against the grey cotton covering my upper body. I get up and pay for my drink and I leave.

Lucy and Bryony come home for Easter. Lucy doesn't come out of her room as she is busy studying for her A levels.

Mum comes into my room at night and tells me I am the only one who understands her. It's true, I think. I just wish that she still loved me. I wish she loved me as much as the dead baby. She tells me about her and dad. 'Men, Vanessa,' she says, fiddling with the edge of my shelf. 'I was so in love with your father. I gave up everything for him, you know. Everything.'

'Like what?'

She looks exasperated. 'Everything.'

Everything, and then he left her. He had affairs with other expatriates in Saudi Arabia and now he comes home twice a year. Everyone must be laughing at her. Everyone must think she's a fool. How could he have treated her like this, she asks me, and I don't have an answer. I just say that I don't think she's a fool, and she laughs and says that's because I'm like her and understand. I am so clever. I was always the cleverest. She asks me how things are going with Alan and I tell her that we split up.

'Oh, darling,' says mum, hugging me tight. 'I know you were very fond of him. Poor you.' And I almost start crying about it, even though it was six months ago. I am so glad I've still got mum. She strokes my back as I inhale her perfume of smoky roses and she says, 'Ssh. It's okay.' We could be years ago. 'You just can't trust men,' says mum and I know she is right.

She tells me that she wasn't really in love with Mr Crawford, but I know she is lying about that.

I make myself a mug of coffee in the kitchen. There is very loud music coming from Bryony's bedroom upstairs, someone should tell her to turn it down. I go to drop the empty milk carton in the bin, and find a mass of pale-brown hair. I look at it, long hunks of it bluntly cut, and then I push it down with my hand so that the milk carton will fit on top. Mum walks past the window with the secateurs in her hand.

I catch the normal bus into Perth, the one you have to pay for. It passes here at eleven in the morning and makes its return journey at six. There are only ever four other people on it, scattered among the foam headrests coming undone. Fag-butt and dead-dog odour sleeps in the stuffing. The air of Perth is always delightful at the end of my trip. I make sure to be the first one off the bus. I wander around the shops, looking at things.

Janet sees me before I've spotted her. I am in a china shop and she is looking younger, with a fringe, and she has said my name and now she is asking me how I am and I can't think what to do so I pick up a mug and say: 'Bryony's fine, I must pay for this.'

I look at it afterwards, the mug I bought. It has a puffin painted on the inside. I stop going into the shops. There isn't really anything I want, anyway. You'd have to be stupid and I'm not. I understand mum.

Now I just buy ice creams and take my book to the steps underneath the monument. It is a gorgeous day today, so I roll up my black trousers, peel off my jumper and put on my shades. Under my jumper I am wearing a little white T-shirt with a red vest over the top. I feel comfortable and just right. Plus I can watch people through my shades. I only watch them for a bit, because they are actually quite boring. Just pottering to and fro, more interested in the windows than anything else. People aren't interesting if they're all just staring at sheets of glass.

'Hi,' says someone. He is next to me, and then I realise that it is me he is speaking to. I don't answer. 'Hi,' he says again. I look round to see who it is. No one I know, with relief. A nice-looking stranger with fair hair. 'Can I sit here?' he asks. He has got a funny accent.

'Sure,' I say, picking up my book.

'What's your name?' asks the guy.

'Vanessa. What's yours?'

'Ethan. Hi. Pleased to meet you.' He is holding out his hand and so I shake it and smile. 'Do you live here?' he asks. I say yes and ask him where he's from, thinking he might say Finland.

'Cornwall,' says Ethan. He flashes me a grin and my heart sidles towards him. It reminds me of Alan. 'You're, er, black and white and red all over.'

We sit and chat, and then he asks me if I'll go for a drink with him. I say okay, but only after I've finished the chapter I'm on. 'Right,' says Ethan. 'Do you want me to leave you, then?'

I say, 'Yeah, cheers.'

Zipping the book in my bag, scratching my arm, I go to meet him in the Irish bar at the prearranged time. Ethan is glad I came. I'm glad too. We drink a lot of beer and now and again Ethan flashes that grin and pools of dust glimmer on the floor. After several pints we meander down a side street and climb into the back of Ethan's camper van. Sun copies the orange-flowered print of the van's curtains on to the bare skin of his body. I get him to use a condom. He is dead fit, with muscles in his stomach and a nice smell about him. It is good to feel so safe with someone. I know he can't hurt me and I just let go.

Ethan wants to take me out to the coast and teach me how to surf. I say no, and ask if he'll drive me home. He takes me on a detour. We pick up a Chinese takeaway in town and then we go out hours away to the beaches, like he wanted. We just sit for a while looking at the North Sea and Ethan says he thinks I'm cool.

I'm feeling relaxed, looking out at the waves, feeling elated and in control. I feel as if I am out on the horizon, out on that line where the sea meets the blue and gold sky. The line is dead straight, like a string hung with lead. It is true because it is far, far away from the beach, away from the human edge of things. The straightness of the line will last for ever.

'You like sailing?' asks Ethan.

'I probably would, if I tried it. But I don't live near the sea.'

'I can't imagine that,' says Ethan, and tells me about how much he loves the sea and wouldn't ever live too far away from it. He tells me how it's really cool in Cornwall in the summer, they have bonfires in these coves and get really stoned, and his mates play the guitar, everyone has a good time, and you go to sleep listening to the sound of the waves crashing on the sand. 'Get in touch if you're ever down,' he says. 'You'd love it.' And he writes down his phone number in red felt-tip on a torn-off snatch of paper. 'Thanks,' I say, and for a second I almost believe that I'll use it. He takes me home.

He says, 'Nice house,' but obviously I don't ask him in. I get him to drop me off at the bottom of the track and I kind of smile, then shut the passenger door. I hear him driving off as I walk up to the house.

'Where have you been?' asks mum, hands on hips in the hall. 'The bus went past half an hour ago. Where have you been?'

I stay very still. Maybe she'll think I'm a hatstand.

'Answer me!' shouts mum, and the mirror quivers behind her. She is holding me by the shoulders and shaking me, as if I am one of those games, a maze with a marble in. If she shakes me enough then maybe she can get the marble to come out. Shake shake. But I'm all locked in. She carries on screaming in my face and then the telephone rings and she lets me go.

120

I rub the stair post with my middle fingertip, wondering about Ethan.

I am not trying to eavesdrop on my mother, it is just that I am being very quiet because I'm thinking. So I can't help but hear her. It's not her words that I hear so much as the tone of her voice, and suddenly I know that somewhere in his big house Mr Crawford is also hiding behind a closed door, whispering down a line.

Lucy guessed it first. She comes to my room only half an hour after I have heard them and asks me if I think mum is seeing him again.

'I didn't know you knew,' I say.

'I found out.' Lucy stretches a long and silky arm up to the ledge above my door and dangles in the frame.

'I thought you were revising.'

'How did you know?' And I know Lucy is talking about mum's extramarital activities rather than study plans.

'Mum told me.' Yes, mum told me. Mum confided in me and not you, Lucy, nor anyone else. I flick my hair back over my shoulder.

'What?' Lucy steps into my bedroom very smartly. 'She told you about it? When? Why didn't you tell me?'

I don't say anything.

'I can't believe you knew all along!' She puts a hand out and nudges my shoulder. 'Vanessa!'

'What?'

'You do realise that Mum having this stupid affair with Malcolm's dad was the reason we split up?'

'No it wasn't.'

But she insists that it was, because surely the whole thing couldn't have been a coincidence? Lucy doesn't believe in coincidence. Just lots of lovely chains of reasons. Cause and effect toppling in domino lines, making pretty swirling patterns. Malcolm found out that his father was having it off with Lucy's mother, so he dumped her out of loyalty to his own mother. It looks a lot nicer like that.

The trouble is that truth has no pattern. People slide in and out and disappear because life is random like a cat. Anyway, I'm not listening to Lucy any more. She goes out and slams my bedroom door.

Mum and Mr Crawford, at it again. They try to hide it, this time.

Chapter Five

She greets me differently every morning. I walk the stairs wondering with a little cat's cradle in my gut. Mum stands by the range with a smile or a joke or a hug or a snarl or a grab or a plain blank face, or she isn't there at all and I must go looking for her. Where are you hiding? Hiding our life.

But today she is in a glad mood. She throws her arms around me, happily squid-like. 'Darling,' she says. And kisses my cheek. She puts the kettle on so that we can have a nice chat over some tea. My intestines calm down.

We talk about my sisters, about Lucy going off to York in the autumn to do a foundation year in fashion design.

'Won't it be great?'

'Yeah.' I smile.

'She can make us some of those floaty transparent catwalk dresses with feathers stuck round the neck and we can wear them down to the Co-Op. That would raise a few eyebrows, wouldn't it?' Mum starts laughing. Sun swims through the window, flooding the side of her arm and pooling on the pink linen tablecloth. It trembles and flutters like the clematis outside.

Mum expects Lucy's postcard will arrive next week. Lucy is away in Italy and mum has been saying this every day. 'And Bryony's doing well, isn't she? I know her teachers say she's a little distracted, but that's often a sign of brightness isn't it.'

'Where is Bryony?'

'Oh, didn't you hear the car? Last-minute thing. She's away visiting a friend in Stirling. The mum picked her up this morning.' Mum drinks her tea. 'I'm glad I've got you. I'm feeling a little deserted at the moment!' She laughs again when she says this. It's a very engaging laugh. I can't help but start laughing too.

123

'Morna McAlpine's quit her course at Edinburgh Uni,' I say casually. Just for the pleasure of saying his surname in public. 'Apparently she's got a really good job.'

'You could have gone there,' says mum. 'Everyone knows you could have gone to Oxford if you'd wanted to. If it hadn't been for your illness. Poor Nesspot.' She reaches out and strokes my arm. What illness? When did I become ill? 'You know, I'm not surprised Alan isn't staying on for sixth year. Some sort of art college, you said, didn't you. You were always cleverer than him. I expect that's why it didn't work.' I don't say anything, and after a deliberate pause she moves on to other people. 'Did you know Gillian Grant is taking a year out? She's planning to teach English to schoolchildren in Nepal. Isn't that wonderful?' I nod. 'Maybe you could do something like that.' I play with the teaspoon in the sugar bowl, swirling patterns and stirring them out. 'Rather morose this morning, aren't you, darling? Everything all right?'

'Oh yes.'

I stand on the terrace and it's pleasant the way the breeze catches my tea-soaked throat. Injecting oxygen from the far-off sea. I'm just being friendly, I tell myself. I'm just being mature. I feel stronger as I walk down the track to the gate. We've known each other so long, after all.

I turn round, halfway to the lay-by, and look back at my house. It is big, and filled with so many versions of me. There is a pale face at the window of the shed. I stare and take two steps closer. A pebble of a face, looming behind the murky glass. A little hand comes out of the gap in the window and waves at me. Little fingers, black against the sky. I must be going mad. I raise my hand in reply and immediately wish I hadn't. Because it's crazy. I turn and keep going on my way.

Alan's house, small and clean. A white home in fields of green.

I'm big, now. I'm strong. I can just call in, to be sociable. Sun plays around, somewhere ahead of my feet. The tarmac is quiet. The glen is holding its breath, like an audience as the snooker player takes his shot, like it doesn't want to put me off. And with the world being so amenable, I take the turning down Alan's track.

The doorbell rings. I hear it. I have pressed it. That's fine. Footsteps are treading down the hall. The white-painted door is caving inwards. It's dark inside, like that other time I came. I remember, we ate Wagon Wheels on the back step. Alan is taller now. It was two years ago, a long time ago, I think, looking at his face.

'Hi Alan,' I say, wondering if the voice is mine.

'Vanessa.' His eyes are just the same. So clear. But we are different, aren't we? Everything is different. 'Hi, look, come in.' He hasn't smiled. I follow him into the house. It is quiet except for some music playing somewhere.

'Sorry,' I say. 'Are you busy?'

'Nuh. Just came in to get something to eat. I've been fixing Morna's car. Not that there's much wrong, it was just the brake fluid.'

'Right.'

'Anyway. I've fixed it now.'

'Cool.' The house is quiet. I was wrong about the music, it wasn't in the house, it is coming from a radio sitting outside.

Silence is seeping out of the umbrella stand and filming the hairs on our backs. I wish it would bugger off.

'D'you want to go outside?' asks Alan, and I am relieved. I say yes and follow him down the passage to the back door. We pass his bedroom and I can't help glancing inside. The desk where he used to sit painting those funny figurines has been replaced by a table supporting electronic music equipment. He's got a new duvet cover, cream with navy squares. Very modern. Sarah and he have probably had sexual intercourse underneath it. I look away and follow Alan's back into the harsh sunlight.

'So what are you doin with yourself?' he asks me, as we sit ourselves down on the McAlpines' new garden bench. I don't like the bench. It's uncomfortable, because there isn't really a garden. I feel horribly self-conscious and wish that we could just sit on the doorstep like we used to.

'I'm working. For mum.'

'Aye, I know. I meant—' But he doesn't tell me what he meant. He just sits next to me on the bench, five hundred miles away although our thighs are nearly touching. He is staring at the fence as if it's way more interesting than I am.

'We've got a fair next week, actually.' His gaze doesn't even shift. I wonder what goes on inside the footpaths of his mind. 'I heard you got into art college.'

'Aye.'

'That's brilliant.'

He nods.

'What are you going to do?'

'Me? What do you mean?' But he doesn't explain.

'So,' I try. 'You're going to London. That'll be cool. The bright lights of the metropolis. All the best exhibitions are in London. You always read about them in the paper.'

'Do you?' He looks at me like I've said something meaningful. And then: 'What's your favourite paper?'

'The *Independent*.'

'I didn't know you read newspapers. I thought you just read books. Do you still read books?'

'Yeah.'

'What are you reading at the minute?'

'*Prisoner of Zenda*.'

'Is it good?'

'Yeah. It's excellent.'

'Maybe I'll read it. *The Prisoner of Zenda*.'

I nod.

'I saw you came and sat your English Higher,' says Alan.

'Thought I might as well.'

'What did you get?'

'D.'

'Oh. I thought you would have got an A.'

'No.' Pull at my cuff. 'I read the wrong books.'

We stop speaking. I look at the rose bush, its bright pink petals like air-dropped supplies from another country. The rest of the garden is still unmown grass and weeds, though there is less of that now that a stone patio has flattened three square metres into submission by the door.

'How's Sarah?' I ask, bravely. I have to detach my mouth from my brain in order to make it work.

'Fine,' says Alan, and the horizon slips. The world is spinning at a different tilt. I don't know why the daisies touch my feet.

'Is she going to art college too?'

'Sarah? Aye right. Sarah's about as artistic as Yogi Bear.'

I wish he hadn't said that, hadn't slapped me with her familiarity.

'She's trying to get in to Napier,' says Alan. 'To do Business.'

'Oh right.' I want to go now.

'It's good seeing you,' says Alan. 'Lindsay said you were on good form.'

'Right.' Lindsay has only seen me on one occasion, just after I officially left school. He turned up at the house when mum was out and I asked him in. He asked if he could see my room, so I said Yes and took him up there. He said he thought it was really nice and then he took off all his clothes and got into my bed. It wasn't even night-time. I started laughing, and so did he. We had sex and it was a good laugh, in the manner of a fairground ride. But he got peeved afterwards because I was asking after Alan. He came round a couple of other times, but I could see him out of the window so I didn't answer the bell.

Mum told him to go away. He rang me up. I don't understand why. I thought men were supposed to want sex without ties.

'He obviously likes you a lot. He says that flower stuff you do is really cool.'

'Who?'

'Lindsay.'

'Oh.' I didn't know Lindsay had ever seen the dried flower arrangements I do with mum. I am faintly embarrassed.

'It's a nice day, isn't it,' says Alan.

I smile and close my eyelids. 'Yeah,' I say. But I can feel him looking at me so I open them again and look at the fence, seeing as it's so interesting. 'Well.' I sigh, in the conventional style of a person about to leave.

I think I have done quite well. We have talked about Sarah and I haven't vomited. It's all okay. This is how it will be from now on, when we see each other. We are two adults having a conversation about each other's lives. I feel depressed but strangely satisfied. Kind of numb.

Alan starts talking very fast. 'Do you think you and Lindsay will really stay together?'

'What?'

'He was saying how you might get a place together.'

'But I'm not even going out with Lindsay.'

Alan flashes his floodlight eyes upon my face. There is no sound for a few seconds, except the hum of the radio on the other side of the house. Radio Tayside. It's as if he's going to reach out and touch me with his hand, but he decides to speak instead. 'He says you are.'

'Well, we're not.'

Alan exhales. 'He said you slept together.'

'We did.'

Alan keeps staring at me and I don't want to be here any more. I get to my feet. 'Bye,' I say, and turn away. I start to walk very quickly across Alan's garden. Down the track I go.

Eventually I reach the road. I look back. Alan is bent over the bonnet of his sister's car. I thought he said he'd finished. I stand and watch him for a bit, the way his naked arms move, the way he wipes his hands on the back pockets of his jeans. And then I carry on walking along the road, such a short way, back home.

Mum is in the kitchen, doing the flowers, sitting behind a row of cream earthenware jars. She ignores me. I take a jar, and cut a block of oasis to go inside it. I hate the feel of the blade cutting through the green polystyrene, like a blunt knife on a soapy thigh. I take some dried roses from the pile on the table.

'Oh, hello,' says mum. 'Did you have a fond parting?' Her words squirt out like the juice from a lemon. 'Such sweet sorrow.' She is smirking, and I don't answer. 'Well?' she insists, after a pause.

'How do you know I went to see Alan?'

'Because you're so predictable. I know you inside out.' She looks up from her flowers, and suddenly she smiles, gently. 'There's nothing new you can do.' She's holding my hand as I stumble into this, holding her eyes up to my face as I look away from her and slide another stalk into the block. I can tell she is still smiling, sadly, on my behalf.

I try to ignore her, as I slot the flowers into place.

'You've got too much red in one corner,' says mum. 'Here, darling. Put some of this in.'

It goes well, the fair the next day. Mum seems really proud of me. She keeps saying, 'This is Vanessa, my daughter. She helps me.' Over and over. I am her daughter, Vanessa. I help her. By one o'clock my smile is huge and the hall is crowded. People keep buzzing round our table, our honey jars filled with dried flowers. Mum has made summer wreaths, too.

'Why should a wreath be just for Christmas?' she said, drying apple slices in the bottom oven. I didn't have an answer but then I don't think I was supposed to. Mum pretended she had a dentist's appointment and went to meet Mr Crawford, and I sat in the kitchen threading the curled slices of apple around the twigs, fastening on the blue hydrangea blooms with creamy ribbon like she'd shown me. She was all in a rush when she showed me, trying to get away. She looked so excited. 'Have you got it darling?' I nodded and she kissed the side of my head so hard. 'Love you,' she said, and almost ran from the house.

The wreaths are selling well. Mum is glowing beside me, talking all day long, a charmer of business. I feel so happy sitting in the chair behind our table with her standing at my side, chatting away.

'Mary!' sighs a woman in a quilted waistcoat. 'How *do* you do it? Oh, now these are *really special*.' She is picking up one of the wreaths from off our damask tablecloth, holding it, fiddling with the bits of dried apple. She keeps turning it round in her hands, holding it up to the light as if she's checking for forgery. '*Really* lovely,' she says, looking mum intently in the eyes.

Mum smiles. 'Yes, they're rather popular.'

The woman puts the wreath back down. Brightly announces that she has lots to see, and waddles off into the crowd again.

'Who on earth was that?' asks mum, leaning towards me.

I giggle. 'I thought she was one of your friends.'

Mum smiles wryly. 'Oh no. If she'd been one of my friends she would have bought the effing wreath, instead of just molesting it with her greasy great fingers. Silly bisom. Oh, hello Kate. We were just discussing horrible customers. I do hope you're going to be a nice one.' She's off again, and I'm laughing to myself as I take the money and give the change.

And then I spot Alice. I didn't recognise her at first glance because she's dyed her hair blonde, like mine. It was just when she turned sideways, putting some money back in her purse as I was holding out my hand to someone else. It is definitely her.

Alice always had a distinctive face, kind of beautifully bovine, long and mournful. When she isn't smiling, she looks like a manically depressed Ancient Greek. You'd know her anywhere. I stop laughing and duck behind my hair. What if she sees me? I can't imagine.

A small hand is playing with the hydrangea blooms, stubby little fingers poking their papery petals. 'Stop it,' I say. The wee girl looks up at me. Her eyes are curious and stubborn. Where's her mother, anyway? 'They're fragile,' I say. 'They're not for playing with.' She stares at me, interested in me in a peculiarly bored kind of way. And then she makes a real grab for them, crushing some in her fist. Her giggle is raucous like a drunk's. Her mother, too late, is scooping her up and apologising, getting out her purse. The little girl starts bawling. 'Don't worry about it,' says mum, shooing away the mother's money. 'They're all like that at that age.' What an awful noise.

'I tried to stop her, mum.'

'Ssh.'

'I told her not to touch them.'

'It really doesn't matter,' says mum. 'Children do these things, darling.' Her face seems amused at my bother. I can't understand. I look round, but it's not even like there's anyone standing near to hear her. 'Vanessa?' Her voice is questioning and fond. I look at her but I just don't know what to think.

I take the jar with the broken hydrangea and turn it round in front of me. It looks like it was one of mum's rather than mine. Mum has an indefinable knack for the proportions of beauty. The arrangements we make are always her idea: orange Chinese lanterns nodding sculpturally in sprays of greenish alchemilla, red yarrow in bloody buttons poking through. The yarrow grows yellow, by nature, but it takes the dye up very well.

I pull out the broken hydrangea, but the arrangement doesn't look quite right any more. It seems unbalanced. Mum is watching me. 'Shall I put it under the table?' I ask.

She shrugs. 'Leave it out for a while, I would. Someone might take it.' She smiles this really nice smile.

'Vanessa?'

Oh shit. 'Oh, hi there.'

'God! You haven't changed a bit.' Alice's face dimples with happiness, and I wonder, where did she get it from? I stay in my chair so that I don't have to kiss her or anything, because I'm clumsy with that sort of thing. Undeterred, she crouches down so that she's level with me, her long face beaming at me over the flowers. Her hands rest on the tablecloth. 'So what are you doing?' she asks excitedly. Why does everyone keep asking me that?

'I'm working for mum, doing this, you know.'

'Cool,' says Alice. 'Which uni are you going to?' How can she be so familiar? We haven't seen each other for years, not since I got chucked out.

'I'm not going,' I say. Waiting for her embarrassment, but she just frowns and says: 'Why?'

'I didn't get my Highers.'

'But you were really brainy,' she whispers, puzzled, across the table.

I look at her. She really was my friend. I try to smile. 'Anyway. How about you? Where are you going?'

'Edinburgh. I got on to History of Art. I'm on my year out at the moment.'

'Gillian Grant's taking a year out.'

'Are you still in touch with her?'

'Kind of.' My mother is engrossed in her customers, so I lean forward and whisper, 'Mum thinks she's Diana Dors or something.' Alice chuckles.

'Vanessa,' says mum, and my head flicks round too quickly

132

on its stalk. 'Could you give this lady her change?' I don't know whether she heard me or not. My eyelids grow redder. She might have.

I count out the change and turn back to Alice, her face still waiting for me. 'Gillian's going to Nepal,' I say with enthusiasm, so mum can hear me. My nerves are running wild, synapses pulsing like deer. 'She's going to teach English to school-children.' Lovely Gillian, nice Gillian.

'Poor school-children,' says Alice, nearly wetting herself laughing.

I can hear mum pausing in her conversation somewhere up above me. 'Alice!' she says. 'How nice to see you. Are your parents here?' And so Alice stands up and talks to mum, defused, and I start filling the gaps on our table with new stock from the boxes behind me.

'Oh, Vanessa,' says Alice eventually. 'Look, it's really nice seeing you again. I'll give you a call. You haven't moved house or anything?'

'No.'

I am three feet back from the table with a wreath in my arms. Alice can't kiss me here. She just raises a hand and smiles, and goes. I didn't realise how much I missed her. Mum gives me a look and I shrug helplessly. I am putting out the new wreaths when my mother leans forward beside me. 'I'm rather glad you left that school,' she says, 'if that's how they turn out.' She seems to have forgotten that beloved Lucy went there too and that Bryony is still there. 'Don't you think?'

'Yes.' I wish Alice hadn't come here.

And then Alice comes back. 'I was going to buy something!' she says, breathlessly. 'I totally forgot. How much are the wreaths?'

I don't speak, because I am concentrating on rearranging the jars. 'Sixteen ninety-five,' says mum.

'Great.' Alice is opening her wallet and handing over her

money. 'Mum loves this sort of thing.' It is my job to give the change. I scrabble in the tin, feeling nervous about how I'm going to get it into her hand. In the end, I drop it from a few centimetres above her palm. It works fine. I look at her face for a split second, but she doesn't seem to know anything. I look back at her belt and then at the tin. 'Bye,' says Alice, smiling naughtily.

'Oh, bye,' I say, looking up. Her high-heeled boots click off across the floor, weaving through the people until she is gone.

Bryony is sulking again at supper, her face like a plot of cold stew. She picks at her food. Mum is tolerant. 'Vanessa and I made two hundred and sixty pounds today, Bryony. Not bad for pocket money.'

Bryony looks up, tired and startled at the same time. What on earth has she been up to? She looks so guilty. She stares at mum for a second or two, before turning her gaze on me. As if she is disappointed in me, somehow. 'Good,' she says quietly, looking right at me. Dropping her eyes to her food again, she murmurs, 'That's really good.' I think she might be about to burst into tears again. She's probably jealous that mum took me to the fair and not her, but hey, that's her problem for not being here this morning.

'Did you have a nice time in Stirling?' I ask, swallowing some water.

'What?'

'Did you have a nice time?'

But she just looks at me like I've said something stupid. She just sits there, staring at me with empty fork prongs gritted between her teeth, watching me as I try to take a mouthful. As if I'm dumb for eating.

'I wonder what Lucy's up to,' says mum. 'Vanessa, what do you think Lucy's up to?'

My mouth is full of food. I'm trying to swallow it all in one go but it won't go down. At last, at last, my mouth is clear, I can say what I like and I say, 'I don't know.' I wish Bryony would stop staring at me.

She's like that all week, Bryony is. Glaring at me from behind her skinny little face. Watching me as she stirs her food around her plate. Slamming her bedroom door behind her. This morning she wasn't down in time for breakfast and mum didn't even say anything. She didn't come down for lunch, either. I don't know why mum always picks on me. I went and asked mum if I should get the cheeses out for lunch, but she was too busy to answer me, so I had a toasted sandwich on my own.

Mum is on her hands and knees in the garden, digging away at something with her small fork. The sky is overcast, but the air is warm. It feels like a day for the insects.

'Hi,' I call, although she must have already seen me jumping down off the terrace. I landed with a thump. I called her name, two seconds ago. Maybe she doesn't hear, because she doesn't answer me. I walk towards her. 'Hi, mum,' I say and my voice sounds like it's coming from a next-door room. 'Hi there.' What if she's dead? Dead while moving. 'Mum.' I touch her shoulder.

Mum shrugs me away. 'Darling!' she says. 'You can't just come barging out here and start mauling me.'

'Sorry.'

'Well.' She leans back, resting on her haunches and pulling off her gardening gloves. She shakes her bare hands and says, 'It's alright, I suppose.' Rising to her feet, she smiles and hands the gloves to me, stiff and smelling of earth. I hold them in my hand. Then I put them on. I don't know why, but I'm glad I did. I think it was an acceptable thing to do because mum doesn't tell me to take them off.

'How are you today?' asks mum, as if I am a feverish patient prone to psychosis. But at the fairs I have been good. At the fairs I was helpful and I was her daughter, Vanessa.

'Fine!'

'Well, that's good.' She sighs and eyes her lupins. 'It's the second of July.' It is. The second, hot and dark and sticky. She rubs her arm as if she's annoyed with it. 'My life isn't easy, you know. I don't think you've really got any idea.' A baby slug is sliding through the grass towards my sandal. I do not want its almost transparent slimy greyness sneaking over my toes, so I bring the flat of my sandal sole down upon its head, squishing it away. When I look up, I see mum has taken a step sideways towards the flower bed. She is breaking the head off the tallest lupin in the clump, a fine tall bloom. I watch it go. She has to twist the stem hard in her fist to tear it away. She is gripping the spire of pouting pink petals in her hand. 'There!' she says, her pretty face electrified. 'Why don't you take this? Here!' It is nodding its tip in my direction, proffered by mum. 'Go on!' Her voice is big and angry. The lips of the flower are shaking.

'Mum,' I say. 'I'm sorry!' Although I don't know what for.

'Take it!'

My hands are in the dark. I can stretch one out in its thick green glove and it won't be any the wiser. I close the fingers round the lupin's stem.

'There!' says mum. 'Is that better? Are you happy now?'

'Yes.' I am holding the flower stretched out in front of me, like it's an Olympic torch. I stare at the cylinder of my arm disappearing into the opening of the glove. It is very dark in there. I wish I could fit the rest of my body in.

'Right!' says mum. 'Well, let's go inside then. I need a coffee.'

I follow her inside and stand holding the flower in my gloved hand, while she stands staring at the calendar on the wall. She runs a hand through her hair forlornly.

'What's wrong?'

'Ha! Nothing, Vanessa. My darling daughter. Sit down.' My mother would make a very good queen, and more stylish than most. I sit, clasping the lupin's pink spike, trying not to disperse

136

soil over the tablecloth as it dries into dainty clods on the green gloves. Mum goes out. One minute she is creaking round the kitchen and the next minute she's gone. I don't know where, and crane my neck to peer out of the windows. Everything is quiet. A door bangs overhead. I better not get up. Although, it can't be the breeze because there is no wind today. The door bangs again. It sounds like someone's slamming it. I sit and stare at the lupin. Made for bees to climb into. The door slams once more, this time insistently. I stand, and tread carefully up the stairs. It sounded like her bathroom door. I am nearly there when it starts slamming again, now in rapid succession. I can see her wrist, pale in the gap on the other side, and for a second I think she is Lindsay Douglas. Then I remember that it's my mum. Her shining round brown eye must have been there in the gap too, because she has seen me. I know, because the door remains tightly shut now. There is no sound from inside.

'It's no use,' cries mum from behind the door. 'There's no point saying anything.'

But I do. I say: 'Mum, what's wrong?'

'You wouldn't understand. You with your nice comfortable little life.' She is sobbing and spitting.

'Mum!'

There is silence on the other side of the wood. I can hear her rummaging around, and then: 'How would you feel if your nice little boyfriend went on holiday with his stupid fat wife and forgot to call you? Didn't call you on the second of July! On the second of July. Oh, he promised me.'

'I don't have a boyfriend!'

'Vanessa! Vanessa. You were supposed to be clever. Maybe you can tell me. Is two years a long time?'

'Yes.'

'No!' she screams. 'No, it is not!'

'No,' I say. 'No, no it's not. Mum, what are you talking about?'

She is muttering. I can hear her going 'Bastard, bastard, bastard'.

'Mum, just because he didn't call you, it doesn't mean—' The tap is running, loudly. 'It's just a phone call! And – maybe he'll ring you tonight. Mum! It's only two in the afternoon.'

'He knows what time it is!' she shrieks, sounding almost pleased. 'Oh, Vanessa, do you think this will be enough? You were supposed to be *clever*. Do you think this will be enough to make him remember the fucking date, like I do? Do you? Do you think we might even be able to make him feel the *guilt*? Do you think we can?' And her face is suddenly with me again, and the door torn open in triumph. She hands me an empty bottle for paracetamol and walks past.

'Mum! Jesus!' I look down. A lupin and a paracetamol jar. My hands are full. She is lying down on her bed, saying, 'Well, it's all over now.' Fuck, fuck, no.

'Mum! You can't do this!'

'I already have, darling. It's all right. I'll always love you. Is forever a long enough time for you?' And I just stand here looking at her, beautiful with her gentle lines, lying calmly on her back. Looking pleased with herself. Why can't I make sense of it? I run downstairs, dropping the lupin and the pill pot on the table, dialling for an ambulance, but clumsily, with the gardening gloves. She can't leave me alone. I won't let her. The numbers smudge. Nine nine nine. I am gasping.

I turn round to run back to her and I see my little sister. Just standing there, so peculiar, not crying. Just standing on the other side of the kitchen, watching me. Useless little lump. I turn and pelt up the stairs.

They took her away with sickness on her shirt. I didn't go with her. I was afraid of what she'd say. Mum has had enough. She wants revenge on all of us.

*

Lucy says, 'She never meant it.' Lucy with her Italian suntan who doesn't know mum at all. 'Vanessa, honestly, she would never have done it if you hadn't been there.'

'It wasn't my fault!' Silly cow. You never even sent her a postcard.

'God, I didn't say it was. I'm just saying, she was only doing it for, you know, dramatic effect.'

'Fairly extreme for a dramatic effect. There's a bit of a difference between dry ice and suicide, Lucy.'

'She only did it because she knew you'd call an ambulance. I'm quite sure mum never intended to actually die. Okay? It's just not in her character.' Lucy is just trying to make herself feel better for not being here when mum needed her. 'Vanessa, you've got to be really careful not to let her manipulate you.'

'Yeah, I suppose if you'd been here you would have just left her on the bed.'

'She wouldn't have tried it with me.'

I can't believe the way she talks about mum. 'Lucy, don't you think mum must be pretty unhappy to try and top herself? Aren't you the slightest bit concerned?'

'Mum can look after herself. The only reason she's unhappy is she thinks she's not getting enough attention.'

That's what Lucy says, standing right here in front of me while mum sleeps upstairs. I shove her away from me. 'You are fucking twisted.'

Lucy doesn't answer me, for once. She just stands there, looking at me. I don't like it and I leave the room.

I came downstairs to cook supper. I was going to do it. But look, here she is, my big sister, steam rising from her as she leans over the sink. Pan water goes rushing down the pipes. Pasta drained. Everything ready. Everything done.

'I was going to cook.'

'Were you?' Uninterested, she turns and puts the colander down on the worktop.

'It'll drip.'

'I'll wipe it up.'

I feel so small and pathetic, a mouse on a catwalk, and no one can even see me. Mum can't see. Lucy is taking her supper up to her on a tray, and mum will think that Lucy loves her more than I do, but it's not true.

I say: 'I'll take it up, if you like.'

'No. It's fine, Vanessa.'

It's not fine at all. She is conning mum with tagliatelle and fried chicken. I watch her go and want to kick her backside really hard. I would hope she tripped on the stairs, but then mum might feel sorry for her.

Bryony is sitting at the kitchen table, spinning her glass round and round, upside down on its rim.

'I was going to cook dinner,' I say.

Bryony stops spinning and looks up at me. 'What,' she says, 'beans on toast?' She glares at me and then goes back to the beaker. It isn't quite like her.

I don't know what to say, so I just say 'Fuck off,' and sit down opposite her.

She is still ignoring me when Lucy comes back. 'What are you two doing?' asks Lucy, sounding all puzzled and amused. 'Look at the pair of you!' I don't see what's so funny. We're just sitting down at the table, waiting like we're supposed to.

'We're just waiting for supper,' I say.

'What, am I supposed to be mum or something?' Lucy spoons pasta on to her plate, standing separate from us two. She carries it towards the door.

'Where are you going?' calls Bryony, holding her glass tightly in her fist.

'To watch some telly,' says Lucy, standing calm like an

hourglass, immobile as the sand runs through it. Made for the job. 'Are you coming?'

'We have to eat supper at the table. You know we do.'

'Mum won't mind.'

'Yes she will.'

'She won't even know.'

'She will, Lucy. She will know.' I don't see why Bryony is so desperate to have Lucy sit with us anyway.

I can almost hear the smile in Lucy's voice as she answers, 'I promise you. I promise you she won't know. Just this once, we can all go and eat supper on the sofa.'

'To celebrate,' I mutter. She doesn't even hear me.

'Ness, are you coming?'

'No. I prefer sitting at the table. It's better for the digestion.'

She sighs and treads off down the hall. So I serve up for me and Bryony, and we sit and eat our food quietly. Bryony is very slow.

'Something wrong with your mouth?' I ask.

She shakes her head.

'You've chewed that mouthful forty-two times.'

'What, are you counting?'

'Yeah.'

She hangs her head forward over her plate and the mouthful drops out, its colour chewed off. It looks like a ball of bleached dry tuna meat. God knows what her point is. I finish my meal, taking care to look thoughtfully out of the window behind Bryony's head. The sky is dark deep blue. Dark deep summer, and mum is tucked up like a frail autumn leaf, thin in the covers upstairs.

Days, it's been. Maybe dad will come home now that mum's tried to kill herself. He could take early retirement and stay at the house, looking after mum. I am sure she would mend if he was there. If she could stop needing Mr Crawford then she would soon get over it all. She could get pregnant again, but with dad. Like she should have done in the first place. Maybe I'll write dad a letter.

I roll on to my front, returning to my book. Except I can't be bothered with it any more. It doesn't seem real. Not compared to mum. I put it down and just lie with my chin resting comfortably on the back of my hand, watching the insects. They scuttle across the stone slabs of our terrace. But you can tell that the real action is going on where you can't quite see it. You can hear the feverish solemnity of their life rising up from the cracks between the stone. Busy spiders. I can hear it, I know they're there. I just can't see it, that's all. I close my eyes and listen and don't think anything at all, just circles of little red spiders going round and round and the sun on the backs of my legs until the air cools and I'm chilly so I go inside.

She is sleeping. The window is open and a soft breeze blows the scent of her flowers around her hair. Little mum. I have to walk slowly, like I'm wearing a Chinese dress, so as not to spill the mug of tea. You wouldn't want to stain her bedroom carpet. As quietly as I can, I put it down on the mat beside her bed. She does not stir.

I have bought writing paper and envelopes especially for dad. I lie on my bed and think what I should write.

Dear Dad,

How's things in sunny Saudi Arabia? I hope you're well. Things aren't very good here. I don't know if you know, but mum tried to overdose on paracetamol last weekend. I am really worried about her. I think she really misses you. I don't want to put pressure on you or anything, but I think it would really help if you were at home. I know it's between you and mum, but I'm just really worried about her. I thought you

should know, in case she hadn't told you. Anyway, I'm fine.
Just sorry you couldn't make it home this summer. Maybe we'll
see you in autumn. Anyway, hope you're well.
  Lots of Love,
    Vanessa

Is that alright? I read it over and over. I was never very good at
writing, but I think it will do. I write dad's address on the front.

I'm awake at six o'clock. Sunlight is already petering in through
my window. I put on my denim shorts and flowery bikini top
and black jumper. I am going to steal a few sunny hours from
my sisters. I shall have them all to myself. I open the door of my
room and slide down to the kitchen to enjoy drinking coffee
and eating cornflakes on my own.

Mum was going to die. Mum was going to leave me. And she
was the only one I had. I pour milk in the bowl and eat. I could
not make her want to stay.

The river is black and slow. I stand at the pool where you can't
see the bottom, just the sunlight skating over the surface. I sit
on the rocks and watch it.

The garden is fresh, each hair of it picked out by dew: the fur
on the daisy stems, the spores on the mosses, the soft down on
every blade of grass. The sun is still drowsy sweet and mild. I
saw how peaceful she looked last night, and dad will come home
soon, I'm sure of it. I step through the sun and the long
shadows, cutting flowers for her bedside. It makes me feel like
part of the planet again. I cutting flowers for her.

I creak her bedroom door open. Her voice, agitated, croaks,
'Who's that?'

'Me,' I say. 'Vanessa.' And I round the edge of the door
holding the vase of flowers. Is this okay? I wonder. She looks at

me, confused. I'm standing at the end of her bedroom. And I need to know, is this okay? It's so important.

'Oh. Vanessa. Are those for me?'

'Yeah, of course they are.' Are they okay?

'Bring them over here, darling. Oh. They smell lovely.' She looks up at me and smiles. 'How sweet of you. You're such a nice girl. Give me a hug.' Her neck still smells the same, of musk roses and green shampoo. Her nightdress is sacred. I am giddy with her closeness.

I stand up, so as not to spoil it. Mum looks at me and smiles again. Then she picks up the travel brochure lying spread on the covers, 'Real Africa' it says, and I leave her alone.

I make scrambled eggs and I can't help feeling excited. Everything might be all right. Mum and dad must be planning a holiday in Kenya. They went there on their honeymoon, see, on safari. There are photos of mum in a safari jacket, twenty years old and looking like a model. She is laughing in most of the photos, and in most of them dad is staring at her, smiling. They are in an open-topped jeep, bumping through the bush at sunset. They are on the white sand beach at Mombasa with drinks by their hands. They are suntanned in the restaurant. I have seen them. In the past.

Perhaps I don't need to send the letter after all.

My sisters are out on the terrace, sunbathing, when the telephone rings. I sit at the table and let it. The answer machine clicks on. 'Hi Vanessa,' says Alice's happy voice. 'It's Alice here. Great seeing you again, look, do you want to meet up over the weekend? I'm coming into Perth anyway on Saturday, tomorrow I mean, if you'd like to go for lunch or something. It'd be lovely to chat properly. Give me a ring!' I go into the hall and replay the message. Then I replay the beginning bit again, and then once again, the bit where she says 'Hi Vanessa,' and then I delete it from the telephone's memory.

*

Mum sits outside. She seems fragile, like a Chinese lantern. She still insists on taking Lucy to her driving lesson, though. Lucy is learning in a shiny purple Vauxhall Corsa, which she thinks is a stupid car. Mum has to spend a whole hour in Perth while Lucy drives around. A whole hour, in the town where Mr Crawford lives. I hate it.

They come home, and Lucy keeps talking about driving when everyone else is trying to relax. 'You just have to find the biting point, it's like *feeling* for the car, like mind over matter. I'm quite lucky, Mr Purdy says my clutch control is perfect. He thinks I'm going to pass first time.'

'So you keep saying.'

'Oh, grow up, Vanessa,' says mum. I get up off the terrace, dried moss clinging to the backs of my thighs. I brush it off but my hands sting the skin. I'm going inside. 'Oh, for God's sake!' cries mum. 'Do you have to go off in a sulk about *every little thing*? At least Lucy's *learning* to drive. At least she's not still trailing around my apron strings. You can't even find a job of your own. Oh, go inside, if you want to.' She waves her hand at me. Mosquito daughter. Shoo. Sticky yellow fly-paper catches at my wings, and it doesn't smell nice. I tear myself away.

Bryony is giggling and Lucy is saying, 'Shut up, Bryony.' I hate them both. I hate everything except my bedroom. My face burns with my stupidity.

The four of us sit round the table and it could be years ago. Everything smells just like it always did, we are eating off the same plates, eating the same food, it's just that we've grown in our chairs.

'How was Florence?' asks mum. 'Full of tourists?'

'No. It was fine. I liked it.' Lucy passes me the salad.

'Italian men are dreadful, aren't they?' drawls mum in a

conspiratorial kind of way. Like me and Bryony aren't even here.

'Yes,' says Lucy. I don't see why mum has to care so much about what Lucy thinks.

'Have you spoken to dad recently?' I ask.

'No,' says mum, as if I am tedious. 'Why? Should I have done?'

I shrug. 'No. I was just wondering.'

'When's daddy coming home?' asks Bryony.

Mum breathes out like a fire eater.

'I'm sorry!' squeals Bryony. 'I'm sorry! I'm sorry!'

'Good Lord,' says mum. 'What on earth is the matter with you?'

Bryony's face starts wrinkling up. It looks like she's going to cry again, but she manages to stop herself and eat a piece of cold chicken instead. Lucy watches her as if it's really interesting. I look at mum. 'Has Gillian Grant gone to Nepal yet?' I ask her.

'No,' says mum. 'She's saving up. Doing a bit of secretarial work in Andrew's office.' Andrew is Gillian's dad. I bet he pays her well. Mum smiles at me. So it was worth asking. I smile back.

Mum touches me in the hall as I go up to bed. She holds my arm, tightly, and tells me that despite everything she loves me. I tell her that I love her too. I smell the smell of her soft dark hair. 'Dear Vanessa,' she says, like it's the beginning of a letter. Lucy is drumming her fingers on the door frame.

I lie in the bath for hours, watching the patterns of the water and the dusk flutter on the ceiling. Until the window is black and the water is cold, and then it is time to go.

Chapter Six

Lucy has passed her test and goes bombing round the roads like she's on her way to Goodwood, wearing shades. She makes tapes for driving to, in her room. I lie in mine, trying to get to sleep.

Someone is knocking on my door. 'Come in,' I call. The knocking pauses.

'Can I come in?' a little voice begs.

The handle turns. Mum's head pokes round the edge of my door. It turns my stomach, because the voice was small and pathetic like Bryony's. 'Am I interrupting?' she asks with timid eyebrows.

'No.' I frown. Because I am just lying in bed with the light off, doing nothing, and it is obvious. Because this is not like mum and she is scaring me now.

'Are you sure? I feel I'm interrupting.'

'I'm not doing anything.'

She comes and sits on the edge of my bed then, which she hasn't done for ages. 'I'm so tired,' she says, yawning. 'I've just been doing the washing up.' She stops, as if she's waiting for me to challenge the truth of this. I stay quiet. 'I don't get enough help from you girls,' she goes on. 'I can't do everything. I can't do it all on my own.' She stops and runs a hand through her hair. 'And now you're getting a job, you'll be out all day and I expect you'll be using our home as if it's free lodging.' Her voice is damp and whiny. 'You won't like Tighnacraig.' She sighs. 'I've heard things about that hostel. It's full of travellers. Nobody knows where they come from, these people who pass through there, they could be absolutely anyone. I don't think you'll be very good there.' Her voice is so soft, I can't bear it. It flops around the room, limply slapping at my face, and it is cold

147

and wet and pitiable. What has happened to mum? She never talks like this.

I lie still against my pillows. 'I thought you wanted me to get a job,' I whisper.

'Don't twist my words!' Thank God. She is off, back to normal, burning again, dry and bright. Standing up and waving her hands around, saying, 'Oh, you think you're so clever, Vanessa. You don't need my advice, do you. Little miss clever clogs. Fine.' She stops, into that dead car crash stillness. 'Fine,' she whispers, staring at me. 'Do what you like.'

After she's gone, I get out of bed to close the door after her. The light was coming in off the passage.

She doesn't say anything in the morning, though, hasn't objected since. In fact, she went and found me some oil for my bike, from the garden shed.

I like cycling along the glen in the morning, it's one of my favourite things about working here. Cycling west, with the sun coming up behind me, like I'm riding a wave. Cycling further into the hills, further away from Perth, in the opposite direction from the rest of the world. Right up and out through the pursed lips of the valley I ride, and take the forestry track through knitted sitka. Midges fuzz out of the trees in the morning sun. I'd never been down here before, but the track brings you out at the tip of Loch Tay and you can see Tighnacraig at the other end of the water, a long white cottage with enormous lean-to sheds. Eight miles from home and it feels like more.

Cleaning is not such bad work. It might be menial but at least you don't have to be servile like a waitress would, or even talk to anyone at all, if you don't want to. I am happy here as I sweep the linoleum floors with my big soft broom, puffing up dust. There is a nice rhythm to it, swooshing the broom under the bunks, collecting my dirt into a neat little pile for the dustpan. I open the windows in the empty dorm and look out. The backpackers are congregating at the lochside, a clump of hairy buttercups in their white or yellow T-shirts and cargo shorts. They start tramping off down the road as I watch, talking loudly, bowling their Antipodean vowels like cricket balls through the warm air. I go downstairs to fetch my bleach-reeking bucket.

One of the hostellers calls 'Hoi' as I pass the open back door. I glance over my shoulder. Jeff introduced himself on Tuesday. Now him and his friend are sitting at the picnic bench outside with the accoutrements of sandwich spreading laid out before them.

'Hi,' I answer, and carry on towards the wash room where buckets are kept.

'Cam and sit with us,' says Jeff, as I pass them on my way back.

I smile and say, 'Work to do.'

'Oi'll give you a cheese sand-wich!' Jeff yells after me, and I laugh, halfway up the stairs by now.

They're nice, foreigners. I like their generosity, the way they always think the best of things. I like the way they love my country, the way they think it's all just for fun and I am to be part of it. My toes sing, wriggling bare inside my tennis shoes as my mop splashes over the lino. The floors sparkle. The Australian boys are laughing outside.

They have gone by the time I come back down. The sky has clouded over a little and I pull my jumper back on as I go to sit at the picnic table with my tinfoil sandwiches. I make them every morning, my supplies. I know it's only a packed lunch, but when you're riding your bike up the glen with food in your bag you sometimes feel like you could just go anywhere. Like you could go right past Tighnacraig and straight on up through the mountains till you got to the end of Scotland and were stood facing north right into the Arctic. You sometimes feel like that.

'Hi there,' says Meriel, plonking down a mug. **I ❤ BONAR BRIDGE**. It is steaming with reconstituted tomato soup. She swings her leg under the opposite side of the bench, settles herself, picks up the mug and starts slurping.

I used to feel afraid of Meriel, when I started. She always seems dead certain, of everything, right down to where she wants to sit. 'Hi,' I say. I pick up my sandwich and carry on eating. Meriel's older brother Stuart owns the place. It was him who gave me the job. We both just sit here and it feels all right, her company. I glance up at her but she is just scrunching up her eye and wiping a midge out of it.

'Why don't you have real soup for your lunch?' I ask, 'seeing as you live here.'

'I like packet soup better.'

'Really?'

'Yeah.' Slurp. 'I like the wee croutons.' She looks at me. 'Do you want some?'

'Nah. Ta.' I lean backwards, chewing, letting my eyes circle the tall hills, the tarmac and the loch. The air smells sweetly of warm grass and sheep droppings. I glance at the back door of the hostel, creaking open. No one is there, though. It is just the breeze.

'Jeff been cracking on to you?'

I shrug.

Meriel blows on her soup. 'I saw him topless in the washroom this morning.' Slurp. She looks up at me again, with a friendly glimmer in her eye. 'Fitty McVitie,' she whispers. 'Nice one.' She starts laughing and I don't know what to do. Am I supposed to join in? Is this communal?

'I like Stanislas,' says Meriel.

'Who?'

'Stanislas. You know, Jeff's friend.'

'Oh right.'

'Might pull him at the hut on Friday.'

150

The hut is at the bottom of the woods behind the hostel and it stinks of stale tobacco, but it's quite neat all the same: the seats are all sawn-off tree stumps and the tables too, except obviously cut off at a different height. I go in there with my mop, soaking up the spilled beer. Stuart runs it like a very miniature pub, with a cassette player and everything. He may as well take advantage of his captive market, seeing there's nowhere else selling beer for ten miles. He's just making the most of it while he can. The whole place closes up on the first of October, dead until Easter when the tourists rise with the Lord.

I have a vague idea of the backpackers wintering in their homelands, sitting cross-legged eating sausages on their various sandy beaches, wearing incongruous woolly hats.

'Yeah,' sighs Meriel, and flicks a midge off her arm. 'How come you're not getting bitten?'

'Because I wear Jungle Juice.'

'Huh.' She swats the air above her head. 'How old are you?' she asks.

'Eighteen,' I lie. Well, more than seventeen now. The sun breaks out from behind the drifting cloud and I have to put my hand up over my eyes. It's bloody bright.

'Eighteen? No way. I thought you were the same age as me.'

'Why. How old are you?'

'Twenty-two.'

I gaze at the walls of the hostel, because they are the only cool place for my eyes to rest. The whitewashed stone is soothingly blue in the shadow.

'Well!' says Meriel. 'Better go and see where Stuart is. Check in with the boss. Let him know I'm off tomorrow. I'm going into Perth.' She is disentangling herself from the picnic table. 'Do you want to come with me? You're not working tomorrow, are you? I'm going shopping for kit.' She is rubbing the backs of her thighs.

'No,' I say. 'No thanks. I'm doing something with my mum tomorrow.'

Meriel shrugs. 'Okay.' I watch her gangling over to the door with the Bonar Bridge mug dangling from her pinkie.

My sisters are out when I get back home. They're out a lot at the moment. I don't know where they go.

Mum is enjoying a cup of afternoon tea on the terrace, her legs slung up on the bench beside her, skirt hitched up around her knees. 'Can I do anything?' I ask, looking at her.

'Mm? Like what?' asks mum. She is reading a magazine.

'I don't know. Is there anything that needs doing in the garden?'

'You could weed the rose bed.' Her mouth is curled up too, as if she finds me amusing.

'Okay.' I want to shake her. I shake my hands instead and go find myself a gardening fork.

The dirt gets under my nails in little crescent-shaped cakes, black and soft. I do not turn round when I hear the car coming up the drive.

My sisters' voices bounce off the drainpipes and then dissolve in the softness of the house, eaten by the rugs and papered walls. Maybe they didn't see me. Where do they go, anyway? Sometimes I think they were just waiting until I was out the road. When I get up, there are dirty patches on my knees. I carry my pile of weeds to the bonfire patch, over by the compost heap.

The stench of puffy black tomatoes and runny peelings hangs lazily over this corner of the garden. Heavy delphiniums rustle behind my back. Turning round, I see mum, still reading, small, carried away on their blue heads.

I stand on the terrace for a minute, wondering whether I really ought to interrupt her. I'd been hoping she would notice me and look up. She is still reading her magazine. She is my mother. 'Mum.' A bouncy ball thwacks against the inside of the kitchen window. I hate it, for it makes me look stupid. Bloody Bryony. I carry on angrily. 'Mum!'

She looks up, sternly enquiring, like a bird cast in bronze.

'I just wondered – I just. Would you like to do something tomorrow? With me, I mean.'

That ball, again. Bang, against the window. 'Stop it, Bryony,' I yell.

Mum is looking at me. 'Don't shout at your sister,' she says. And then: 'What were you thinking?'

'We could see a film. Or go shopping, or something.' She is looking unimpressed by my suggestions. 'We could go and have lunch somewhere.'

'Actually, I'm busy tomorrow.'

'Why? What are you doing?'

She tilts the shiny pages of her magazine back to a comfortable reading angle and sighs.

Nothing more, so I go inside. Bryony laughs at me. She sticks her tongue into her lower lip, making her chin bulge. She is flapping her scrawny wrists at me and the grotesquerie is absurdly effective. I can't get away from her fast enough.

'Did you have a nice time with your mum?' asks Meriel, flipping her short hair away from her face.

'Yeah. Yeah, it was nice.'

'What did you do?'

'Oh, just stuff. Went into Crieff. Had a coffee, looked round that gallery. Mum bought a – vase.'

'You get on really well with your mum.'

'Yes.' I curl a bit of hair round the tip of my finger, turning the skin plum-coloured. 'We're very close,' I say and let go of the hair. I pick up my mug of hot chocolate. I'm taking my tea break indoors this morning. 'Listen to the rain.'

'It'll stop by this evening,' says Meriel. I don't know how she can be so sure, even of the rain.

153

*

I close my thumb over the jet of cold water, making it run harder, like a knife. I'm hosing down the minibus – mine are catholic cleaning duties – in a borrowed hostel cagoule, and my lunchtime sandwich is sitting small in my belly. Rain patters down on the lid of my head, and I feel little and look forward to going home. I wish mum was there more often. She spends a lot of time away at the moment, and my sisters too, separately from mum. It is as if everyone else knows the house is sinking and I am the only one who stays. But I want to, I want to stay there and curl up on my bed with photographs of men. With dad, and Alan. I wish I had taken more photographs of Alan. I always felt too embarrassed about wanting his picture, like it made me too obvious, silhouetted me against the sky. I only have three photographs of him. Three photographs, for a year and a half.

I have to go into the hostel to ask Stuart to move the minibus into the vehicle shed, and there are people everywhere. I push my hood down, and the room smells of wet heather and steaming skin. Everyone is talking. A girl is sitting in front of the stove in her vest and pants, laughing. One of the boys has his bare foot behind his ear. It's Stanislas. And Stuart is over there, on the other side of the common room, with a clipboard on his knee. People are standing around him and he is writing down their names for the next excursion. I shouldn't interrupt. So I just pick my way towards him and stand in the queue. I am hot. My neck sweats against the plasticky cagoule fabric. I can feel my cheeks turning pink.

Stuart takes control. I hand my words over to him and he turns them into something of importance, in the way he nods seriously, the way he thanks me and rises to his feet. He is crossing the room and people move their limbs to let him pass. I follow in his wake, as if I'm part of him.

I get into the front passenger seat of the minibus. I realise as soon as I've got in that it was stupid, seeing as we are only going ten feet. But Stuart acts as if it was a perfectly sensible thing to do. He plugs the key in the ignition and turns to look at me. 'How are you finding things, Vanessa?'

'Fine,' I say. And then we're there. I open my door and climb out.

'You don't have to do this just now,' says Stuart, as I go looking for the hoover. 'Don't catch cold,' he says. 'If you're cold, come in and dry off first, and do this later.'

'I'm fine.' I smile and nod. 'Honestly.'

'Are you staying for beers in the hut this evening?'

'I don't know.'

'You should. It's fun.'

'Oh well. Maybe I will.'

There is heaps of crap in the minibus: sweet wrappers and scrunched-up tissues, but mainly big dried clods of mud from the backpackers' boots. I pull the hoover as far as its cord will let it and start to suck it away. It is noisy work, crawling across the seats with my nozzle, making things disappear. I do not hear the rain slowing to a drip. By the time I switch the machine off, the sun is dabbling down again. Meriel was right.

The loch is glimmering outside the skewed window of the hut. It feels funny, being among so many people in here, nine or ten of them, when usually it is just me and my mop. But I like it in here, with the wooden walls and wooden floors. It reminds me of being in Alice's treehouse, when we used to hide up there, spying on her brothers and pretending to be fairies or assassins. I lift the green glass bottle of lager to my lips. I'm glad I stayed. Stuart was right, it's fun. Everyone is having fun and I am here and I don't mean anything except my face.

Nobody even minds me not saying anything. I can just sit here, quietly, in the corner, and that is allowed. I watch Meriel, teasing Stanislas about something, the abseiling, I think. Stuart presides over everyone subtly. You can tell it from the faint smile on his face as he chats. I drink my beer, sucking at its cool woody stream.

One of the girls starts skinning up. Stuart tells her she can't smoke indoors, Mandy.

'Come on, Stu. The ground's wet.'

He shakes his head. Mandy goes outside, wafting expensive perfume from her green batik T-shirt. Stuart watches her, and smiles, as if he is deeply pleased. Then his head turns and catches me looking at him. I look away, leaning my head against the wooden wall of the hut. You can still smell the sap.

I'm quite drunk, I suppose, by the time Jeff comes over and sits himself down beside me. 'You aren't sighing much,' he says. 'Mar quiet than a did dog. Go orn, Vanessa. Sigh something.'

I'm feeling so relaxed that I smile. 'I don't really have anything to say.'

'Doesn't stop most chicks.' He smiles and clinks his bottle against mine. 'Cheers.'

'Cheers.'

I don't protest when after a while he slides his hand down the back of my jeans. I'm feeling kind of staggered as I stray down to the loch. The dark hills shudder around me, like stage scenery, shifting when you look at them. I'm puffed. Jeff's there already.

I like the way Jeff looks at me. His back is pressed against the side of the boathouse, pressed into the shadow. And I'm on top of him, either side of him, head giddy. My jeans are round one ankle and the grass is sodden beneath my knees. I stuff him inside me and start to rock. Jeff gazes up at me like I'm a mad strong lion. Admiring me, as if I could be anyone. I grip tighter, digging my thighs in, winding it up, gathering pace, rocking away. Into nothingness. Rubbing myself out on the end of him. All that exists and ever has is the splintery wood under my outstretched palms. A curve of muscle, a red dot behind my head. Nothing else.

'What happened to you?' Mum nods toward the clean and empty cereal bowl in front of me. Bryony watches me suspiciously, as if I am trying to steal the crown for faddy eating.

'I just don't feel well.'

'You didn't get drunk and ride your bike into a ditch, then,' carps Lucy. 'You're not hung over. You just happen to look as wrecked as your handlebars outside? Well, that's good.' As if it's her business. I wait for mum to tell her off, but she doesn't. Lucy stands up, clattering the breakfast plates into a pile and carrying them over to the dishwasher.

'Perhaps you could learn to retch more quietly,' suggests mum, looking at me in a faintly interested way. 'Vomit pianissimo. Other people live in this house besides you.'

'Sorry.'

'Sorry! Oh, I should think you would be.' She lapses into silence. I wish Lucy could be a bit more noisy in her stacking of the dishes. She seems to be merely playing with them now, chiming their china gently. I push my chair out. Mum flares up. 'Did I say you could get down? Did I? Did you hear me say that?'

I stay where I am.

'Answer me!'

'No.'

'No.' She stops again, clasping her hands in her lap and gazing meekly at them. I dare not move. We both just sit here, and Lucy carries on clinking the china. Minutes pass. Bryony is still at the table too, trapped in her chair for no reason. I am sure she could get down if she wanted to, but she looks frightened of something, the way her eyes flicker round the walls, as if she's praying for Jesus to appear. Jesus or dad. I look at mum, but she is still gazing into her lap. Her shoulders are taut, though, you know she's waiting for you to move. Lucy slams the dishwasher shut and stands looking at us. I am dreading my sister's voice, but she just shakes her head and leaves the room.

The telephone rings. We all just sit here.

'Bryony, could you answer that?' says mum in the voice of a psychiatric counsellor, words detached from her humanity. Bryony gets up and leaves the room.

It's just me and mum. Until Bryony comes back and tells mum that the call is for her, that it is Mr Crawford. Mum forgets me then, rises quickly looking glad, and I am left cheated in my seat.

I go outside to check on my bike.

It's turning out to be quite a good summer, in general. I should have got a job earlier. At least I have something to do. The work makes me happy. Meriel treats me as if I were her friend, and sometimes I have sex with the backpackers. I'm in the swing of it now. I like the way they take my mind away, obliterate me quite entirely, if only for a second or two. It's a relief. So easy, and then they leave. No awkward expectations. Because we're young and it's all for fun, and there's nothing strange in that, is there.

We make a good team. Me and Meriel share the boys, while Stuart takes his pick of the girls, and it works out fine. I think the backpackers like it too, sleeping with natives. It's all part of the experience.

The only thing that surprises me is how many of them take my photograph, for souvenirs, and I feel ashamed again when I think of my three wee snaps of Alan. I wish I'd known it was allowed.

The wood polish smells good, waxy and high in my nostrils. I smear it into the counter where the telephone and directories sit. Stuart ambles through the front door. If he was a gunman, I'd be dead.

I attend to my polishing. Stuart pulls out the telephone book from near my wrist. He is flicking its pages. 'What are your plans?' he asks me, without looking up.

'How do you mean?'

'What are your plans after this? In October. Your ambitions.' He still isn't looking at me. He is running his finger down the page.

'I hadn't thought about it.'

He is writing a number in biro on the back of his hand. 'Attractive girls usually have plans,' he says, and walks back out the door. I stand still for a bit and then I put his biro back in the pencil pot. I shift, and the row of keys behind me catches the sunlight, sending it shooting on to the low ceiling where it spins and hangs from the beams. The book of bookings is sellotaped together along its spine. I move it delicately like a wounded patient, holding it carefully in my hands.

Lucy chooses this moment to appear. 'Hi,' she drawls. She walks further in, there is nothing to stop her. She is leaning heavily on the counter, but this is not her place. She leans her head against her hand. Her hair curls on to the polished wood disgustingly. I want to brush it away. It's like having pubes on your coffee table. Gently I lay the bookings book aside. 'What do you want?'

'Nice to see you too.'

'I saw you at breakfast.'

She stands up. 'I need to talk to you,' she says, and her voice has changed. Like everything is play-acting, everything except this voice I've never heard before. As if my sister could be a whole other person. It shocks me into looking at her properly for a second. 'It's important,' she says.

And then Bryony shambles in, casually straggling from the doorway. Standing beside Lucy, and I hate the way she does that.

'You can talk to me at home,' I say.

'That's the thing. I can't.' Lucy gives me this funny look, like words are supposed to pole-vault over the rim of her eyes and I'm supposed to catch them. I step sideways, pulling out the drawer full of postcards for sale. They've all got jumbled up, the different views. They need sorting out.

'I don't see why not,' I say. Carefully slotting the pictures back into their groups.

'Do you like working here?' she asks, and her voice is back to normal now.

I look up. 'Yeah, it's all right,' I say. I smile, and she smiles back.

'Right,' she says. 'See you tonight.' And they go. Bryony keeps turning round and staring at me, all the way to the door. I wish she would have stayed.

I sit down in the chair with its frayed rush seat. The chair is so low that when you're sitting on it you can't see over the top of the counter. I put the correctly ordered postcards back in the drawer and I sit down here some more, harboured by dead wood freshly oiled. I stay very still. It smells good.

When I get home, Lucy's car is gone, its place taken by Mr Crawford's silver saloon. I go and sit in front of the television with a pile of toast. I wonder what dad will say when he comes back. I wonder if he'll punch Mr Crawford, or just cut him up with words. Ha-*cha*.

I try and concentrate on the programme, but the television presenter keeps reminding me of Lucy. She has that patronising prettiness down pat, and the same discrepant desperation. The more beautiful women are, the more power they have, the more eager they are to find someone to give it away to. I don't understand it. Lucy, embarrassing herself with Malcolm, and mum, giving everything away to Mr Crawford in the bedroom upstairs. I might be a bit of a slut, but at least none of them gets a hold of me. I switch channels and watch the news but it doesn't seem terribly relevant.

'Ah, Vanessa,' booms Mr Crawford, as if he's pleased to see me.

He takes up the whole of the doorway, taller than my father. 'How are you bearing up?' he asks, ignoring the television. 'Enjoying the new job? Sounds awful, I must say.'

'Actually, I really like it.'

He rocks on his heels for a moment, hands in beige corduroy pockets. 'Yes,' he says. 'Loot is loot.' I wonder why he came in here. He's like the bank robber getting his alibi. 'Right,' he says. 'I'll be off then.'

'Okay.'

He doesn't waste any time, either. That's his car, growling down the drive all of thirty seconds later.

I watch the end of the news, then take my plate back through to the kitchen. Mum comes in almost right behind me. 'Hello, Vanessa,' she says, sceptically. Her eyes are pink. Her face is all scratched-up and blotchy.

'Hi mum.'

'Did you have a nice day?'

'Yes.'

She sniffs. 'Did John come and talk to you?'

'Yes.'

'What did he say?'

'Nothing. He just asked me how my job was.'

She looks at me as if I am annoying her and trudges off to open the window. I watch her and tell myself that truly I did come out of her belly.

This afternoon I am disinfecting the toilets and the washroom. There is always a cigarette butt in one of the urinals and I always have to fish it out with my yellow rubber finger. I wear my Walkman when I'm doing the toilets. It makes it more fun. I sing along while I scoosh, a song about a runaway train going the wrong way on a one-way track. The tune rakes loudly out my throat.

'Hi there.'

I swing my head round and I get the feeling that the new backpacker has been standing there for a while. I nearly take my headphones off before remembering that my hands are wearing gloves spattered with piss. The song is still going full volume in my ears as I remove the gloves. I pull the headphones down round my neck. 'Hi,' I say. I think he's going to be this week's boy.

'Hi,' replies the backpacker. 'Where do I check in?' Unusual – he sounds like he's from Scotland. That's an Edinburgh accent.

'At the desk.'

'There's nobody there.'

'That's because it's lunchtime.'

'So what should I do?'

'Wait.'

He laughs, I smile.

'Leave your bags in the hall,' I say. 'Stuart'll be back at four.'

'Ta,' says the backpacker. I put my headphones back on. Hell, I feel like a grown-up.

Meriel is talking to someone called Hodge, and Stuart is sitting with last night's Brazilian. I am beside Meriel on the grassy bank, laughing because she is funny. The beer tastes all right, but I wish my hands didn't smell of toilet cleaner. And my boy hasn't come to join us yet.

The pee is really hot coming out of my body. I must have been desperate. I wipe myself and go to wash my hands. The loud flushing and the rumblings from the cistern are disconcerting. The kind of noise that something sinister could hide behind. I glance in the mirror but there is nothing behind me.

Stupid me. Paranoid spider head. I go into the kitchen to get myself a glass of water. The backpacker is sitting there, eating spaghetti at the table.

'Oh. I didn't realise you were in here,' I say. 'Everyone else is outside.'

He glances at me and says, 'Nothing to apologise for,' although I wasn't apologising.

I fill my glass at the tap. 'What's your name?'

'Gregor. What's yours?'

'Vanessa.'

'Oh, same as my sister. Nice name. It's made up, isn't it?'

'How do you mean?'

'Some writer guy made it up for a story.'

I frown. 'Really?'

'Yeah.'

I sit down with my glass at the other end of the table. Neither of us speaks for a bit. I'm a made-up person.

Gregor eats his spaghetti. I finish my water.

'What are you doing up here?' I ask.

'I like hillwalking, getting out of Edinburgh, you know.' He is winding his spaghetti round his fork, not looking at me. 'Thought I'd climb Schiehallion tomorrow morning.' He takes a mouthful of food and eats it slowly.

'Oh right.'

Neither of us says anything else, so I get up and push my chair in. Rinse my glass and set it on the rack. 'You don't fancy a beer outside?' I say.

'No,' says Gregor, and I dislike him now. His face was misleading. He looked like he might have wanted me, I wouldn't have asked otherwise.

Meriel welcomes me back. Stuart reaches up and squeezes my hand, which makes me feel better. I see the way the Brazilian girl looks at me, fearfully disdainful, wondering if I am about to try and mug her. I like it. It makes me feel like I really have a knife. I sit down beside Stuart and half smile. He hands me a bottle of lager and smiles right back.

'When I was at university,' says Stuart, and I realise I never knew he'd been, 'we read this book, which said that if games didn't have rules then there could only be one game.'

'Ever?' I ask.

'Ever. If you don't have rules.' He flips his eyes away from me.

'What is it?' asks the Brazilian. 'What is *it*?'

Stuart drinks his beer. 'Doesn't matter,' he says, loudly. 'Com-pli-cated.' But it's not really. Stuart just can't be arsed repeating himself. He glances at me, like we're hiding something from the Brazilian. Like he's checking to see I've still got it. Like we're playing the only game.

I am in my bra and pants, under the covers. The duvet is cold. I shiver. 'You don't like them, do you?'

Stuart looks over at me. 'Like who?'

'The backpackers.'

'Doesn't matter whether I like them or not,' he says. I turn my face away as he steps out of his jeans, crosses to the bed and pulls the cover aside to get in. Transition is always so embarrassing. But he's here now. The table is set. I turn my face to him and do not smile.

He starts to kiss me, like I knew he would. 'You're lovely,' he says, as I close my fingers round him.

I wake up first, and check my watch. Seven o'clock. The sun is high in the sky. White light cuts through a gap at the edge of the window blind. I climb out of bed, looking for my pants. The sun splashes in my eye, making me wince. My breathing is heavy and a little sticky as I roll the dirty knickers over my toes. My skirt is crumpled, but I'm feeling good. I'm feeling clever and strong. One up on the Brazilian. One up on me. I fasten my bra and wriggle into my vest, smoothing the orange birds down over my torso.

'Where are you going?' asks Stuart. His voice is dusty and his eyes are screwed up in my direction. There is something serious about his question.

'Home. You know.'

'What's the big rush?'

'I've just got stuff to do.'

'Come back to bed.' He smiles his wreck of a smile. It's very attractive.

'No. I'm really sorry, I've just got to get back to my house.'

He doesn't say anything. It feels rude to leave, so I wait until he says, 'Fine' and then I say, 'Okay. Well look, it was really nice.' I mean it.

'Right.'

'Bye.'

Everyone will be up soon. I'm afraid of meeting Meriel early on the stairs, but there's nothing, not even a cough. The house is silent except for the creaking of wood in the sunlight. I close the front door quietly behind me.

The air is cool as I pedal through the trees, spinning my tyres over the dropped needles. Sunshine seeps weakly from behind the drifting clouds, but not enough to warm me yet. Harder than wood, it's lucky I'm riding fast.

The sky opens out over my glen, cloud stretching out into a rippling cottony sheet, spreading beyond me. You wouldn't know how shadowy the land was beneath, if it weren't for the patch of slope in sunshine further up. The grass seems spotlit, absurdly green, then the light upon it dapples and disintegrates. I sway into the lay-by to let a lorry pass.

I lean my bike against the wall.

Water is heavenly, even in the downstairs shower. I didn't dare go upstairs where falling water might have woken them. Sparkling rosemary shampoos my goldy locks. The scent splits up my nostrils with such cleanness that it's odd to open up my eyes and find myself indoors. I soap my pubic hair, cleaning out Stuart's sperm with my hand. I'm fine. I start to sing.

Clean me. Big, strong, clever me. My legs are light as I move round the kitchen, smiling and scrambling my eggs. I got Stuart and got away. Toast pops up, just asking to be buttered by me. The kitchen seems to be built around my body, on purpose, as if I were actually supposed to be here. I spread mayonnaise on the toast, top it with tomatoes, and slot it on the plate next to the yellow and satisfactorily eggy mound of egg. I am so happy.

'Good morning,' says mum's voice. I don't turn round. I know that I shouldn't, just from the sound of it. 'So you decided to come home. Have a nice night, did we?'

'Yes.' I stand by the open cutlery drawer.

'Glad you enjoyed yourself.' She is leaning against the cupboards in the corner of my eye, her arms folded like garden trellis across her chest. I wonder what mum would look like in a column of climbing roses? Doubtless they would suit her. She would drag them like a heavy dress, pained but never undressing, and the pink blooms would match her pale lips.

'Having breakfast on your own? Couldn't wait for the rest of us? Are we not good enough for you any more, Vanessa? So let me see. Have you made scrambled egg for everyone? Oh, no. Just enough for you. Just looking after number one.' There are bubbles bursting in her voice. She paints her words over my face like hot varnish, sealing me in. 'I wonder who you're fucking now. I wouldn't mind if you were a genuine slut, Vanessa, but that implies a certain generosity. Being a slut. There's nothing generous about you, is there? No, you're faking it. Not fooling me, though, are you? I know what you're like.' She laughs and pulls out a chair for herself at the kitchen table. I can hear her sitting down. I don't know what to do. I'm still stuck by the open cutlery drawer, my plate of egg nesting innocently on the worktop. I can't very well eat it now. I leave it, and go upstairs to my room, to wait until nine o'clock when I can start again.

A fine rain falls in the afternoon, like a lank mop sweeping over the grass and rock. You can hear it dripping into puddles as it flops on the terrace below. The light is dimmed, the outline of the hills weeping into the sky. Having a good cry. But you can see the pool of sunlight in the west, travelling down the glen. You know the rain won't last long. It's just a midsummer tantrum, because the heat has been getting too much for itself. Not too much for Lucy, though. She's been lapping up the sunshine all morning, tanning herself a darker shade of brown in the garden. Shining like a diamond. Trying to be better than mum. It will never work.

I switch on the radio in my room and sit on my bed. I feel snug in here, with the summer rain falling against the window and a kind of happy tiredness seeping through my joints. I am safe.

The sun is fallen in the sky by the time I wake, a low gold light filling the room. The rain has stopped. Music swells out from my radio as if it were coming from another room. I am far away, and glad.

It was the chill of early evening that woke me, scratching at my bare legs. I tuck them under the duvet and lie watching the sky outside my window. Imagining that a version of Alan is lying here beside me, resting its calm and heavy head on my breast. I would like to feel its weight.

But I was right to be careful, in the end. He never knew how weak I was, never had that satisfaction. Nobody will ever know they've hurt me. I am the independent daughter, the one with the cold hard fish-eyes who didn't feel a thing. I'm not like my sisters. I can walk away.

*

Lucy opens my door. 'Can I speak to you?' she says. I'm not in the mood for Lucy's pale and gloopy thoughts. I don't answer. She comes and perches on the windowsill, legs concertinaed against the wall. 'I'm glad you're enjoying your job,' she says. 'But look, Vanessa. Look at me. Are you listening? I never know if you're listening or not, it's very disconcerting.' She sighs. 'You've got to think further ahead. You can't stay here with mum for ever. She'll drive you mad if you don't keep your detachment from her. You've got to hold its length.' It's farcical, the way Lucy talks during these sessions. Her words blunder around like couples in the dark, amiable noses colliding with misplaced chins. 'Bryony's had the damage,' she says. 'I don't want to watch the same thing happening to you. Not like I think you're about to become anorexic, but something else, I don't know what.'

'Bryony isn't anorexic.'

Lucy doesn't say anything.

'She isn't. So, she has this weird thing with eating, but Bryony's always been like that. She's never liked food. She's just a bit scraggy.'

Lucy sits there, looking down at me from the window. After a while she says, 'Okay, forget Bryony. Leave Bryony out of it. I still think you need to sort something out.'

'Really.'

'Yes, really. You need to speak to dad.'

'I do speak to dad.'

She looks genuinely surprised, then. 'Oh. I didn't know.'

Ha ha.

'Oh. Okay then. I'm glad about that.' She is getting off my windowsill, brushing down her bottom and leaving my room, saying quietly to herself, 'How funny he never said.' She is frowning lightly as she closes my door.

Lucy, speaking to dad. She must be. I don't feel quite so clever now, lying under the roof. Lucy is speaking to dad. No joy in my little fib now. Lucy has really got him while I must just pretend. Why her, I wonder. I always thought he liked me the best. It looks like I was wrong about him too. I pick up the jar of face cream next to my bed and hurl it at the wall. It claps as it hits the paint. Bastard dad. She can't even speak properly.

Still, there are others. There are a lot, I remind myself, an awful lot of others. I have a fine number of men in my collection these days. There is dad, who must go in brackets now. So, so (dad), Alan. Ethan, Lindsay, Jeff, James. Luke, Brad, Rohan, Kevin, Mortimer, Stuart. Stuart is a good one to have on the end there. He makes a convincing bookend. But still, I wish mum was a man.

I'm supposed to be going to work tomorrow morning.

There is nobody in the hostel by the time I turn up. I was late on purpose, because I didn't know what to say when I saw him again. I go and get my broom. The bunks are littered with personal possessions. I try not to look at all the hairbrushes and T-shirts, the postcards and the tattered paperbacks. I just take away the dust from underneath them.

'You've got a nerve,' says Meriel, her voice breaking over the softness of my sweeping.

I straighten my back. 'What?'

'Shagging my brother. Turning up late.'

I don't know what to say, so I don't say anything. Maybe she'll forget I'm here.

'Bollocks,' she says. 'Bollocks.' She is walking towards the door. 'I wish you hadn't,' she says, and disappears. I look round to where she was standing as her feet clatter down the wooden stairs.

I finish sweeping the floor, and then I have to go and fetch my mop. I have to walk through the kitchen, where Meriel is sitting at the table smoking a cigarette with her copy of *The Great Outdoors*. She doesn't look up and I don't speak.

I leave, and the water sloshes in my bucket as I move off up the stairwell.

I go outside to have my ham sandwich. Meriel stays indoors. My skin is quite brown. The hairs on my arms are silvery white, like my limbs have been licked with salt. I don't see why I shouldn't have slept with Stuart. My new period and Lucy and dad twang against each other in my womb. Veins of pain suck at the waistband of my cut-off shorts. I get up, scrunching the crumb-scattered tinfoil in my fist.

She hasn't moved. I swallow. It takes me a minute or so to manage it. I say: 'Stuart knew what he was doing.'

Meriel looks at me pityingly. She stubs out the end of her cigarette in the saucer of ash beside her arm.

My knees are trembling. 'Why is it such a big deal?'

She looks up at me again, sharply. Then: 'Oh. I suppose you're just being young,' she says. 'I thought we were friends, when you were just another girl who was trying to sleep with my brother. That's all.'

I stand here, breathing, for a minute. Wondering if I really was her friend. An immense liking for Meriel flares and scratches in my ears.

I don't turn up at Tighnacraig the following morning, or the Friday after that. Nobody calls to complain or ask why. I am relieved, and I fantasise about Stuart for a short while.

Only Lucy seems to notice that I am not biking off to work any more. She asks me questions and I say Oh, I slept with the boss. She gives me a funny look and says she hopes I'm joking. Sometimes she can be quite a prude.

Mum takes longer. Three weeks or so, and then we pass in the passage upstairs and she has almost walked past me when she says Aren't you hanging around the house more than usual? I say yes. But that's it, she doesn't want to know anything else, she just nods and walks heavily down the stairs. The heaviness is peculiar for one whose body is generally acceded to be full of grace. It's one of the things people always comment upon, my mother's poise and grace. When I was small, I mistook her for the mother of Jesus. In some ways she is: immaculately conceived, at least. But there were always two Marys.

'I'm getting old,' she says, hulling the end of the strawberries on the kitchen worktop. The blue and white china in the glass-fronted cabinet looms darkly above her.

'Your hair still shines.'

She looses a mocking laugh, but I think it is not aimed at me. I watch while she picks her voice back up. She swallows it, mulling it in her cheeks, and opens. 'I feel I haven't done anything, Vanessa. It dawns on you one day, that if you haven't done anything by now the chances are you never will. There isn't time to start.' Strawberries pass through her hands, from plastic punnet to china dish. 'It's a terrible thing. To understand you're going to disappear.' I think it sounds quite nice and look at my hands. 'Do you think people will remember me?' asks mum.

'Yes.'

'Yes. Maybe you will remember me, and maybe your children will remember me. But after that I doubt it. Isn't it strange? People will come across my photograph and they won't know who I was.'

'You're not that old, mum. You're only going to be forty-one.'

'No,' she nods. She carries on with the strawberries until the whole punnet is done. 'You are the only thing I've done, really. You and your sisters.' She looks at me, with a mix of horror and pride. Then she smiles, less proficiently than usual.

*

The day of the birthday dinner falls open, fearsomely empty. A hollow ewe's belly to be stuffed with preparations. We have our instructions.

I'm deft, going round the toilet bowls. It must be my professional training. Scoosh, scrub, flush. I even clean the toothpaste specks from off the bathroom mirror.

In the warm kitchen, Lucy puffs a strand of dark hair away from her eyes. I watch it falling back again. She pushes it away with the back of her hand. Wet pastry clings in clods to her fingers, webbing her hands.

'Hello,' I say, friendly and pleased with myself though my knees are a little sore from the kneeling bends. I pick up a grape from the shelf and roll it between my finger and thumb. It feels lovely and cool and soft. Dusty and round. I pop it in my mouth.

'Do you want to chop some mushrooms?' She isn't looking at me. She is giving her all to the pastry as she rolls it out on the shelf next to me.

'Sure.' I am on my way to the larder when mum walks in. I raise my head with a smile.

'For God's sake!' she sings. 'Bloody well pull your finger out, Vanessa! The others have been helping me all morning. Where have you been?'

'Cleaning the bathrooms.'

Mum stares at me. Pearl globules gleam in her ear lobes. She is disgusted.

Lucy looks up at me as I come to stand beside her, chopping my mushrooms very slowly. 'Mum told me to clean the bathrooms.' I tell it to the chopping knife, knowing that Lucy is listening.

Lucy looks back at her pastry, nicely laid into a flan dish. She pats it down with her fingerpads, nipping off the over-spill expertly between finger and thumb. I expect she learnt it on her cookery course in Tuscany. 'Mum's in one of her moods,' she says. 'Just humour her.' And she sniffs and blinks and carries the flan case away. 'Those mushrooms need to be fried,' she calls over her shoulder. She thinks she's so clever. Mum is just something to be handled. And I am to fry the mushrooms.

Bryony is sitting at the table, carefully chopping apples. She is crying. She looks up at me. 'Hi there,' I say. She looks at me as if I've done something awful to her. Then she carries on chopping her apples, like she's obsessed with them. The mushrooms are sticking to the pan. I pour in more oil and give it all a good scrape.

Mum tears around us, pulling things noisily from the cupboards, slamming and banging. Then gradually the banging of doors becomes less violent. She is calming down. She actually runs her hand through her hair and smiles. I smile back at her.

'Sorry, Nesspot.'

'Don't worry.'

And we all work happily for an hour or so, even Bryony, who still has tears slithering down her cheeks.

By the time we stop for a late lunch, I am feeling quite elated. Lucy has thrown a quick soup together, served with casual crostini, and I don't even mind her face as she dishes it up. I butter my bread.

We are clearing away the soup bowls when mum slams her palm into her forehead. 'Christ!' she cries. 'We've forgotten the blinking pheasant! It's nearly five o'clock Bryony, I told you to remind me, that was your job. Why didn't you remind me?' She is whirling away from me into a rage, blurring round the kitchen and out of my head. Her voice escalates, higher and higher until you think it's going to fall off the edge, but it never does. There is always further to go. And the pitch of her penetrates the walls, curling round me, squeezing me out. She stands with her back to me, leaning over the table, leaning into

Bryony on the other side. Her narrow shoulders are steady and only her arms quiver as she shouts.

I step towards the door as Lucy passes me, stinking of determination. Don't do it, Lucy, please don't. Clumsily, Lucy rounds the end of the table and starts dragging Bryony out from behind it. She is moving her towards the door, taking her hostage. I get told to humour mum; Bryony gets rescued. Mum starts screaming louder. It's none of Lucy's bloody business, she shouts.

'Shut up!' yells Lucy.

Why does she have to do this? Lucy the big sister, saving everyone. It really annoys me. Mum slaps her. It serves her right. 'You can't do this,' says Lucy. 'You can't treat us like this.'

'How dare you have the nerve to tell me how to bring up my children. I'm your mother. How dare you be so arrogant?' She is moving even closer. I sneak towards the exit and glance round. Bryony is squeezed between Lucy and the wall, like a sheep in a pen. She is staring past me, fixated on my doorway. She edges half out from behind Lucy's body. Her face falls away from her wide, scared eyes, like walking out the door is something difficult and dangerous, a long leap down instead of common sense. Bryony is moving towards the door, and mum and Lucy are too busy shouting at each other to notice. But then she goes and ruins her escape. She panics, and her arms are in the air and she's running full-tilt, screaming.

Mum and Lucy stop. Everyone is staring at Bryony, running screaming to the door, tugging at the handle, lurching away, thudding down the hall. Her hair was in the air. Mad little kelpie. She's gone.

Mum is the first to speak. 'Right!' she says. 'Let's get cracking.' Lucy glowers at her, but already mum is turning her back, striding off to the shed where the dead birds are stored, plucked yesterday. The room feels sickeningly empty.

Lucy looks at me. 'Well, say something.'

'No.' I turn round and start getting forks out from the drawer.

'What's your problem?' I think I might go and look for some paper napkins. 'Why won't you talk to me, Vanessa? Stop pretending you can't hear me. It's really sad.'

'I'm not pretending.'

'So answer me.'

'I don't think there's anything to talk about.'

'You were lying, weren't you. About speaking to dad. I asked him.' The way she is watching me is making my skin hot and itchy. She is angry with me. 'Don't you want to know? Don't you want to know what dad and I have been talking about? Don't you want to speak to him too?'

Desperately, I shrug.

'Fucking hell, suit yourself. You always do.'

'Oh, please, girls. No arguing. You know I can't stand it.' Mum thumps the bald pheasants down on the table. They stink. Mum puts a fist to her chest. 'It makes me feel all tight inside.' Lucy flounces out. Mum sighs. 'Just you and me, Nesspot.' She shrugs and sticks her fist up the pheasant's arse.

They came in spurts, the guests. Parents who remembered not to mention my father and offspring who talked about schools and universities I don't go to. Mum wore black. Mrs Crawford wore red and yellow and purple flowers, looking like a tongue twister. Watching her husband not speaking to my mother. You could tell she knew mum was looking at him every time her head was turned. Bravely, she discussed the installation of central heating in her cottage in the Cairngorms with a woman in a wine-red top and a massive lizard brooch. I never knew anyone get so much conversational mileage out of domestic pipes. Fire and shit.

I caught her, though, just after we'd brought the plates of

food into the dining room. My hands were freezing from carrying the ice bowls. My mother makes them by pouring water between two cut-glass bowls and leaving them in the freezer. She waits till the water is starting to frost, and then she slides these little flowers in and closes the lid again. To get the ice bowl out, all you have to do is flash it under the hot tap and gently tap the glass bowls away. Then all you are left with is the impression in ice, a coldly moulded perfect replica of the pair with flowers suspended right inside it. So pretty, and very clever. It doesn't last long, though. You have to use it within a couple of hours, because then it begins to blur around the edges and slowly slides away down the table.

Mrs Crawford's face had slipped sideways. Misery glistened on her skin like the cold sweat in my knuckle bones, wiped over her with a pastry brush. Clammy. She was watching my mother laughing at something someone else had said. And then she must have noticed she was letting on, because she bolted the other face back on top. It stayed put all evening, held in place by the refrigerated egg white underneath. Pastry caking and smiling. Her sons hawed and nodded like good boys, enquiring after the hobbies of their parents' friends. Complimenting my mother on her flowers, opening doors and fetching forgotten napkins. They smiled and put on serious listening faces as required, watching everything with small eyes and remembering to sympathise in the right places.

My mother had had a lot of wine. Flushed with her own unassailability and smiling generously, she approached Mr Crawford's wife and asked, 'Diane, how *are* you?'

I strained to hear Mrs Crawford's reply. 'Super!' She looked jolly in a strained sort of way, like a cat in a tutu. 'Happy birthday!'

'Oh,' said mum, 'I'm sure I shouldn't be celebrating them any more, but what the hell.' She laughed again, and it sounded like a victory: happy little bits of sparkling quartz raining down on Mrs Crawford's head. Mrs Crawford tried to look like she didn't mind. She even tried to join in the laughing.

'Mary's a bloody good cook,' said someone to somebody else, from a low dell in the noisy conversation. For a second I thought Mrs Crawford was going to cry. I don't know why she came. Surely Mr Crawford wasn't worth all this? Standing under the Dutch painting, waving his wineglass around to emphasise some point, studiously ignoring his wife and his lover. Coward. I kept seeing the way he looked at mum, the times when she was looking somewhere else. Like he owned her, but was afraid someone was going to run their keys down her side. Or afraid that she might spin out of control. His eyes were doubtful.

I slipped in and out of all the rooms, watching from behind plates of smoked salmon and bowls of nuts, holding them out, taking them back, carrying empty dinner plates and refilling glasses. Helpfulness is the best resort for anti-socially minded persons. I moved between the angular bottoms of underweight daughters and the broader arses of confident sons just back from shagging their way round Australia.

I felt glad that I'd been giving something back to our Antipodean cousins, redressing the balance a little, quietly undermining the conquest. And I didn't have to stop and talk to anyone.

Lucy talked. Lucy talked like a ping-pong ball, her chatter going up and down, bouncing between bats. Where did she learn how to do that? She never missed, not once.

She only faltered when she tried to talk to Malcolm. I passed them in the hall, Lucy giggling at Malcolm's jokes. 'Yur, St Andrews, it's a bit like a beach resort without the resort!' Ha-ha-ha-ha went Lucy. 'Golf and sheep instead of dodgems! Great ice cream, though.' Oh, ha-ha-ha, went Lucy. And flicked her hair. I wonder if perhaps she actually is stupid.

'I love ice cream,' she confided.

'Great stuff,' agreed Malcolm. It's a shame they split up, really. So much in common.

'Do you remember those knickerbocker glories we had at Littlejohns?'

'Er, yur, yur.' Malcolm looked anxiously around. And then he just said, 'Excuse me' and walked away.

Lucy looked round desperately, smiling. Relieved that only I was there. 'What are you staring at?' she demanded, but I was already turning away. I heard her shoes patter down the rug and then her hand was on my elbow. Lucy and her big thing about touching people. She coughed. Such a little cough, you'd think it belonged to a rabbit. Brightly caught my eye and she started talking away as if everything was fine and I just went along with it.

'Ah, the beautiful Gordon girls!' Mr Dibden was wielding a camera. I think he'd had a little too much to drink. 'Gorgeous girls,' he slurred. 'may I photograph you?'

'Oh, okay,' said Lucy, throwing her arm round my shoulder and jutting out her hip. I felt hideous as the flash went off in my eyes.

'Like models,' said Mr Dibden. 'My wife used to be a model, you know. In the sixties. I don't think—' He stopped and stared at me very intently. 'They were . . . so discerning then.' And then I was glad I was with Lucy, because I just let her end the awkward pause with a polite laugh I've never mastered. Mr Dibden looked at her with surprise. 'Ha! Yes!' he exclaimed. Inexplicably, but Lucy understood, because her face was relaxed and her laugh was genuine now.

She touched Mr Dibden's arm. I don't know how she can do that, the thought of it makes me shudder. 'You're so funny,' she said. I had somehow entirely missed the joke. I didn't care, though, because Lucy was taking me through now, holding my hand, leading me away from there, away from the man and the look of foreign language.

I saw mum's hand, straight away. It was resting on the base of Mr Crawford's back, naturally, like a bird. Her fingers glowed appallingly, obvious pale against his dark-blue shirt. Why couldn't he have worn a flesh-coloured shirt? I watched as Mr Crawford stepped sideways, away from mum. Her hand fell lightly through the air, through space, drifting down to her side. I tried to look at her face and caught a glimpse of it, the fierce lostness, as she spun and left the room. Her shoulder almost brushed me.

I watched and watched her go. The blood in my head began to swirl into soothing patterns. I could hear it dragging its leg through my veins. Bump bump across the ridges in the runway. Someone was holding their hand out for me. Run, Vanessa, run. I'm trying! My hand slid into the wall. The patterned paper coagulated around it, filling the gap. Then the wall slid against me and toppled sideways.

Bump bump across the ridges in the runway. I was in, but it never took off. Black wall solidified uncertainly under my palm. Pushing me outwards, inflating my lungs. Precariously. As if the wall could let go of me at any moment and all the air would come whooshing back out and send me soaring through the air like a dying balloon. But it didn't. There was just Finlay crouching in front of me with an almost sexual expression of concern.

There was Mr Dibden saying, 'Good God someone's drunk aren't they' and mum saying, 'Oh bugger off thank you Finlay have you got her?' Mum, coming back and making sure I was all right.

Sloshes of the usual talk amplify into a big river, a great loud murmuring hurting my head as I lie upstairs. Glad of the excuse. They all flow out the plughole, glugging as they go. I creep back downstairs, flop down into an armchair and pull a bowl of pistachio nuts on to my lap. There's only five left. The shell of number one cracks between my teeth. I tip my head back and admire the pattern of light on the ceiling, hurled-out twinkles from the hanging crystal. The room is filled with fifty different perfumes and colognes, all still having a conversation. The smell of wine and empty squished-down sofa cushions. Flames flicker in the large fireplace.

'Are you okay?' asks Finlay, sprawling on the rug with his arms propped out behind him.

'Yeah. Totally.'

'What are you up to these days anyway?'

'Not a lot.' I crunch another nut between my teeth. 'How about you?'

'Nuh.'

'Nothing?'

'Ach, uni, same as everyone else. Beer and parties. Driving around, thinking I'm cool. Same as usual.'

I laugh, although I didn't mean to.

'What's the score with Malcolm and your sister?'

'Fuck knows.'

'She still in love with him?'

'Why?'

'Looks like it.' Finlay watches the cushion beside me for a second or two, gets bored, watches my face instead. 'Tell me, Vanessa. How do you think she hasn't noticed that he's a complete wanker?'

'Well, he does have beautiful manners.'

'Yes, that's true.'

'I don't.'

'No, you don't, do you. But that's why we like you.'

I sort out the tassel on the cushion, straightening its threads, and then I get up and go to the kitchen.

'Where's my godson?' asks mum, disengaging from a hug with Bryony. She is drunk.

'In the drawing room.'

'Bring him through!'

I don't want to. I don't argue. I cross the flagstone floor of the hall and open the drawing-room door. 'Mum wants to see you, for some reason. She's in the kitchen.' Finlay sighs and stands up.

I can hear them as I go upstairs. Mum's voice saying, 'Darling! Was it hideous? All those boring people. The awful thing is, they're my *friends*.' And Finlay says something else back and mum starts laughing. My bedroom is so neat that I even fold my clothes as I take them off and stack them in a little pile on the windowsill, because I don't want to spoil it. But then I have to put my jumper back on, because I am cold.

I look out of the window, at Alan's bungalow tight and glowing faintly white under the dark sky. They will be warm inside. The McAlpines' house is always warm. They will be sitting in the lounge without jumpers, having celebratory drinks because Alan is going away to learn how to be good at something. Yellow light bleeds through the curtain. I wish I could sit behind their sofa.

Stars shine like grit in the eye of the sky, blinked away behind straggly clouds. The fields look soft under moonlight, like water or satin, washing away to the road. They flow easily around the blackness that is the conifer plot. Sheep are sleeping. No cars. It is not a human world just now. It calms me to look at it. There is knocking on my door, and I say:

'Who is it?'

'Finlay,' says Finlay, opening the door. 'Can I come in?'

'You already have.'

'Oh. So I have.'

'Just – hang on and let me get under the covers. God, it's cold.'

'At least you guys have got central heating. My parents are walking around the house in polar fleeces.' He has his back to me, gentlemanly, as I clamber into my bed.

'So, what's up?'

'Oh.' He looks around, half attractive. Finlay was a beautiful child, only his nose just kept on growing. 'You been redecorating?'

'Mum,' I explain.

He sits down on the end of my bed. 'Something going on between her and Mr Crawford?'

I am disappointed and don't speak. 'Right. Because Malcolm and James were being rather rude about her and I wondered why, seeing as they were enjoying your bubbly wine at the time.'

'What were they saying?'

'That she was a tart, that she was flirting with their dad. Didn't know what he saw in her. Cheap and nasty, mutton dressed as lamb.'

'Yeah, well.' It's hardly surprising. Them with their pointy politeness, padding it up and showing it off to everyone as if it were breasts. When really it's made of rubber. Anyway, my mother is many things, but cheap and nasty she's not. 'They're just jealous. Their mother looks like frigging mutton dressed as trout.'

'Easy, tiger.' Finlay smiles. 'I did point out that it's not generally considered polite to slag off one's hostess.'

'Good.'

'You're not going to tell me what's going on, then?'

'No. I'm too tired.'

'Ah!' squeaks Lucy, as she bursts through the door. 'Sorry! I didn't realise you two were – I didn't – I.'

'Don't be silly!' cries Finlay, jumping away from me, away from my bed, eyes like fireworks. 'You're not interrupting anything at all.'

'Oh – no,' says Lucy, kind of smiling. She disappears, pulling the door behind her.

Finlay falls back down.

Neither of us says anything for a while. Then he pats my knee through the duvet. 'Well, old girl,' he says. 'I'm going to bed.' To sleep, perchance to dream: Lucy's hair flicking over his closed eyelids. 'Good night,' he says, standing over me.

'Sweet dreams,' I say.

He gives me a funny look. 'Do you want me to switch your light off?' he asks, standing by the door. I don't. But I pretend that I do. There is blackness. 'Night, then,' says Finlay's voice through it, as light from the passage swills through the opened door. It closes with a gentle turn of the catch. His footsteps are fading through the house. I fall back against my pillows, feeling looked-after, and gaze out of my window at the stars. I can't get a hold on the sadness.

My mother and Finlay are hunched over the corner of the kitchen table when I come downstairs. Bryony sits poker-straight, at the other end. My mother giggles. 'No! No, I really don't think so, Finlay.'

'Oh, go on Mrs G, it'll sort you out. You look awful.'

'Nesspot, darling, this dreadful boy is trying to make me drink Irn-Bru and egg yolk! Would you tell him to stop?'

I shrug. 'Yeah.'

'Oh, honestly.'

'When are you going home?' It is something to say, after all. I just want to ask him something I haven't been told to say.

'Me?' says Finlay.

'No, Bryony.'

'I live here!' squawks Bryony, shaken out of her stillness.

'Yes, I was being sarcastic. Oh, never mind.' I pull a plate out of the cupboard and then I get embarrassed and start towards the door.

'I was planning on leaving tomorrow morning, if that's all right,' says Finlay, but I'm already halfway out the room.

'I will not tolerate that sort of rudeness!' She is in the hall, behind me, grabbing my elbow. 'Do you hear me? Do you hear?' The walls turn round, pulling moonies, and it's her cheeks. She holds my nose closed and spits into my opened mouth. The spit is warm and dirty. 'There! See how you like it!' Her hands let go and her shirt hisses away through the shadows.

I sit through lunch not speaking but listening to all the words they say. Finlay ignoring me and Lucy laughing and telling endless boring anecdotes from her social life. Mum acting like a girl and Bryony scraping her food into patterns. Nobody even notices that I'm not speaking.

I haven't been into Bryony's room for years. Five years, it must be, since I was in here last. It hasn't changed at all. The same horse and pony posters adorn her wardrobe door. There is no reason why I should feel guilty, though. It's not as if Bryony wants me here, now that I've come. She doesn't look up. She just kneels there, hunched over on the floor, nodding. The nodding doesn't stop. It's creepy. 'Bryony?'

She is busy, rapt in her painting and glueing. Bryony makes things. It's what she does. She writes and draws. Above her head, her desk is smothered with paintings and poems and cut-out politicians from newspapers modelling her paper dress designs. I don't know what it is that she's so scared of, scrambling away up the wall with pens and pencils as her crampons. You can always smell the sickly scent of agitation on her.

'What are you making?'

'A house.'

'Can I see?' No answer is a good answer and so I bend over her shoulder. She is glueing a white staircase into its heart. The whole thing is made of card painted white, little boxes slotting against each other. It is a kind of fairy tale modernist hacienda.

'It's not a doll's house,' says Bryony. 'It's not for dolls. It's not for playing with. It's just a house, by itself, okay?'

'Yeah, yeah, okay.'

'Like an architectural model.'

'Yeah. It's good.'

'I've written a story. I'm sending it to Penguin.' I want to tell her to stop, to stop her relentless making, to go and lie down somewhere soft. I want to push her backwards and watch her fall. 'It's about me!' she says, defiantly. Her head swivels owl-like over her shoulder to find my eye. 'I'd like to be a writer, you know.' The head swings back.

'I thought you wanted to be an artist.'

She shrugs. 'Either.'

'Kind of like Lucy. With her pots.'

'No! No, not like Lucy with her pots.' She says this in a mocking sing-song voice. 'Lucy's pots are just a hobby. She doesn't *mean* it. It's hardly the same thing, is it? Making something just for fun, just because it's a nice hobby, just to make something that *looks* nice. It's not the same as making something because you *mean* it and you *need* to make it.' Bryony looks at me accusingly. What a nutter.

'I'm going out now,' I say, although I'm not. Bryony turns back to her architectural model. 'Bye,' I say, but she doesn't look up. I know she can hear me, though, because her cheeks have stiffened into thin pink taffeta under her pale brown hair. It grew back. I close the door and leave her be.

I decide to go out after all, as a mark of respect. I climb the hill behind the house and go and sit on the fishing rock at the lochan's edge. Having a face feels miraculous out here. I hug my knees to be warm and watch for bubbles on the surface of the water.

Alan rang while I was out. I called him back and he asked me to meet him. It was his idea. At Green's, he said, the restaurant in Perth, by the river. Lunch, not dinner. I suppose there is less chance of us leaking backwards during the daytime. At night you could be anywhere. You wouldn't know, in the dark, if you didn't have the date on your watch. All nights can be the same in a way that days cannot.

Mum and Lucy have been advising me on what to wear, as if I am their joint project. 'What a shame it's only Alan,' says Lucy. Still, they are very thorough in their advice.

'Don't let him kiss you, darling. Just show your legs. And don't eat the bread.' [Mum]

'No, don't eat the bread. It's terribly fattening.' [Lucy]

'It looks greedy. How about this one?' [Mum]

I try to ignore them. They are making me feel left out, acting as if they are sisters. I don't like it. I don't know why they are behaving like this with each other. I tell them I'd rather get ready on my own but mum dismisses this as nonsense, assuring me of their pleasure in assisting. At least I dissuade Lucy from daubing me with lipstick. On my big mouth it always looks ridiculous.

Mum holds me tenderly and strokes my hair. Oh, it's just like the old days. 'Very pretty,' she says. So are you, I think. Only you're growing older. All that drinking. All those pills. There's always an edge of panic in the light behind her eyes. I wish I could make it go away. But she doesn't want me; she wants a big man to take care of her, someone to hold her and be bigger than her and choose her over everyone else. Not a daughter who's only hers because she made her. A kind of sad, grudging love as she holds me and tells me that she loves me. Crusty old placenta.

And I cling on to it for a second too long, because she pushes me away. She gives me twenty quid, crisp lilac paper like a dead leaf in the clear bright air. 'Drive well,' she calls to Lucy, who is already climbing into the car. Lucy raises a hand in acknowledgement and slams the door shut. I open the passenger door. Mum never says *Drive Carefully*. It's always *Drive Well*.

*

I wish Lucy and mum hadn't made such a big deal out of my date. Now tweaked weeds are curling into a fat hairball in my gut. It's just lunch. It's just my first proper date, and at least I have the advantage of knowing beforehand that nothing will happen.

I was concerned that Lucy might use this opportunity to lecture me again, but she doesn't. She just chatters away in that melodious voice of hers, telling me about this man she met in Italy. Thirty-six, married and fantastic in bed. Had a tongue like a spatula. She gurgles and glances across at me.

'How pleasurable,' I comment.

Lucy smiles at the road ahead. 'That's the third person I've slept with. You think I'm naughty, don't you.'

'No.'

'Have you slept with anyone?'

'Yes.'

'I knew it! With Alan.'

I don't answer.

'Just with Alan. Just one. I was probably the same at your age. Just one?'

'No.'

'No? Oh. How many, then? Someone else? Go on. Tell me.'

'Eleven.'

Lucy doesn't say anything after that. She tries to drive as if she's not concentrating, like that will prove something to me. She lets her hand float airily over the steering wheel and gazes around serenely at the hills.

After a while I turn the radio on. Lucy says, 'I slept with Malcolm at mum's birthday party. We had sex in the upstairs bathroom.' I don't say anything. 'We'd just had *sex* when you came over to talk to us. And Mr Dibden took my photograph.'

I turn the radio off.

'I wonder if I can get a copy of the photograph.' Lucy turns the radio back on and pushes the volume up. She smiles pointedly, tapping her fingers on the wheel.

Lucy drops me outside Green's, executes a three-point turn, and points her nose to the shops in the town centre. I wait until her car is out of sight and then I think about crossing the road.

In the end, I decided to wear my little red sleeveless top and the black low-slung trousers. I want Alan to see where he kissed me, in the navel where I got cut off. But Alan isn't here. The man is asking if I have a reservation and I don't know whether I do or not.

So crowded. It's the sunny weather, I suppose. Everyone is making the most of themselves before the cold drips in. I wish Alan could have been here when I arrived. The glassy room is humming with words, with fork against china, the scent of lamb and black chocolate. I have to squeeze between the backs of the wooden chairs. The restaurant must have got them from a church for they have empty slots where the hymn books should go. The waiter pulls one out for me at the tiny empty table in the corner. It has a thin seat pad tied on with ribbon. I order a bottle of red wine and wait.

I see Alan before he sees me. Swinging through the door, searching round the room. I look away, reading the blackboard, knowing he is walking towards me now.

'Vanessa. I'm sorry I'm late.'

'Oh, hi. No problem.'

He is still standing up. I wonder if I am supposed to stand up and kiss his cheek. I stay in my chair and just smile up at him. He touches my hand briefly. 'Hi there,' he says.

I order mushroom soup and pheasant. Alan orders mushroom soup and roast lamb. I pour wine into our glasses. We talk about people from school. Alan keeps mentioning

Sarah Black and I try to ignore it. I don't know why we are here. I can only presume this is what people do. I eat the bread.

He starts asking me about what I want to do, over and over. 'What do you want out of life?' he asks, and it's odd the way Alan can ask questions like that and not look the least bit embarrassed.

There is nothing that I really want out of life. Once, all I wanted was Alan. And here he is, and I feel a lot happier than usual, having him here. It's just a shame he's free to not want me back. 'Nothing,' I tell him.

'What, there's nothing at all that you want? Nowhere you want to go?'

'Not really. I leave that kind of thing to Lucy.'

'Nothing you want to do?'

'Like making the world a better place.' I let Alan refill my glass. 'Or making money. No. Can't say I particularly want either. It's only worth making the world a better place if you think people are worth it, and it's only worth making money if you think there are things you want to buy. I can live without following some fashion hack's diktats. I am not enchanted by things, and anyway, I've got loads of money already.'

'It's people that matter,' says Alan. 'Your friends and your family.' He sounds like a brownie leader. I don't say anything. 'You've got friends,' says Alan.

'I know.' Patronising git. Anyway, I don't. 'So, what did you want to see me for?'

'Jist.' He shrugs. 'Jist – I don't know, really. See how you were getting on.'

'Yeah. Good luck down south.' I try to smile like I mean it and it almost comes off. Because he smiles back at me, and eats his soup very deliberately. The pheasant comes, and the roast lamb, which is pinky in the middle, and a white dish of vegetables to share. Parsnips and green beans, steam rising as I spoon them on to my plate. I sit back. The wine tastes good inside my mouth, dark red swirling through the hazy aroma of laundered napkins.

We walked past here a couple of times back when we were together. I said it looked like a nice place, and Alan said he would take me here for my birthday. He never did. I suppose he has forgotten.

'It's funny, isn't it,' I say.

'What?'

'This. You and me sitting here being friends.'

'Why is it funny?'

'Because I used to think I loved you.'

Alan dips his head sideways and wipes a piece of bread through the juices on his plate. He doesn't say anything.

'It's just sad, that's all,' I go on. 'It's sad to realise that what went on between us was never real. Don't you think so?'

'I don't know.' He won't even look at me.

'I think it's a bit of a let-down. Personally.' I take another drink of wine.

We are relieved when the waiter comes to ask if we would like to see the dessert menu. We both say no simultaneously. We start talking about abstract things, like the state of contemporary music. Alan says he thinks that the current obsession with retro is unhealthy. It means nothing new is happening. It means our musical culture is stagnating. I twiddle the stem of my wineglass and say it's because nobody wants to take risks. The past is safe and dull. It belongs to other people, like a war on television. Alan says I am right. Our agreement depresses me.

Saying goodbye is easy after that. I can kiss his cheek with confidence and I wave as I walk away, pulling out my phone to call Lucy.

Mum is like a daddy-long-legs on a mirror, a proud energy lighting up her clothes. She seems pleased to see me home again. 'Hello darling. Did you have a nice time? You know Gillian's plate looks smashing on the mantelpiece. You must go and have a look and tell me what you think. I'm sure Lucy could do something like that if she tried, don't you think so? Gillian says it's an Oriental glazing technique she uses. I'm sure Lucy could do it. She's so creative, isn't she? Very popular with the boys. I think men like a girl who makes things. Fertility.'

Her slender hand picks up the half-eaten doughnut from the side plate at her elbow. Jade glows from the ring on her littlest finger.

'Mmm. Such a shame she split up with Malcolm Crawford. Such a nice lad. I rather think she broke his heart, but that's Lucy isn't it. I always said she'd be a heartbreaker. Had the boys wrapped round her little finger in nursery, do you remember Nessie, she had Harry Robertson shampooing her Sindy dolls for her. Do you remember?'

'No.'

'Oh! Well. I have a very good memory. I always assume everyone else does too, but I suppose it's a bit unfair of me. How *are* you, darling?'

'Fine.'

'Oh *good*.' She pops the last piece of doughnut in her mouth and goes to wash her hands before picking up her embroidery.

Mum hears his car before I do, a silver wing gliding past the window. She rises smoothly, brushing sugar crumbs from her chest.

I glimpse the green silk of her jumper through the window. My mother on the doorstep, old and for Mr Crawford, but I see her on the doorstep of the cottage on Mull, young in a flowered shirt dress, smiling through her long hair. Laughing at me, and I am very small. There's a man behind her. His hand is on her round belly and it ought to be.

Chapter Seven

Lucy's car is revving on the gravel. I can hear her laughing. The car sweeps out from behind the house, and I can see Bryony is wearing shades, even though the sky is overcast. She rides with her window wound right down, her forearm casually leaning along the frame. She probably thinks she looks cool. Her mouth is immobile as they swing out of the turning, and then all I can see is Lucy's smile, and then they are gone. The music thumps after them.

Mum glances at the road from underneath her bush hat. 'Why didn't you go with them?'

'It's not my thing.'

'What isn't?'

'Driving around, just for the sake of it.' I'm older than them. I'm older than my older sister. I am adult, like mum – I choose to stay here, with her.

But she just looks at me and says, 'How peculiar you are.' The darkness of her eyes is faint in the deep shadow of her hat. Where the light strikes her cheek, the skin seems thinner than it should be. 'Oh well.' She sighs, and looks out across the glen as if she's expecting someone to appear. Dad and Mr Crawford, jogging down the slope, waving banners for her.

I am right here, next to her on the bench.

I pull my leg up closer to my face and carry on working on the braid, hooked through a safety pin to the knee of my jeans. I pull knots in the coloured threads, making diagonal lines. Purple, green and white.

'How d'you have the patience for that?' asks mum, suddenly and very fast, in that way she sometimes has. 'Friendship bracelets, aren't they called. You give them to friends?' Scorn chars the edges of her voice, curling it black and dry like burnt potato skin, thin and brittle. 'Who you going to give that to? Eh?' She flicks at it with her fingernail. I just carry on tying the knots, thickening the colour.

After a bit, I say, 'You can have it, if you like.' It makes her laugh. She gets up and I watch her disappearing round the corner of the house.

I stand up when I hear the engine in the garage. The car doesn't notice me trying not to run towards the drive, walking as quickly as I possibly can, on jerky bird's legs. I cannot read her expression, exalted, above me, high in the pulpit of the Range Rover's driving seat. The car is massive and I am the wrong side of it. It lumbers down the track towards me, brushing me aside. And then it stops and her window winds down. She leans her face out into the clean air. *Come with me,* I think. I dare not let my face move, not one inch. She looks me up and down. She opens her mouth. 'Mind your bracelet, darling.'

The engine revs again, but I am looking down and I see how the stupid thing is flapping round my knee still, clinging by the safety pin. I am fiddling with the wretched pin, still bent fumbling as she turns out into the road. She is roaring out of sight as I stand. If only I'd gone with my sisters. If only I hadn't stayed behind. Now I am a fool.

Stupid bloody bracelet. Pathetic string. I scrabble a hole in the flower bed and push it in. Dirt falls over the colours. I kick the pile of soil over them, stamping the earth flat again under my trainer. I jump up and down on it. If I can just push it down, just push it right, right away, then — what? Maybe she'll come back? I kick the sides of my own legs now, hating myself. And then I sit on the terrace, picking the earth off my skin. I am alone as a vole under the sky. Listening for the silent wingbeat, as if I will know when it comes. Turning my face sideways and closing my eyes.

When I go inside, and my eyes have become accustomed to

the darkness, I find that one of my cheeks is singed bright pink by the sun. The clouds shifted while I was looking the other way. My other cheek is soft and white like a baby's, where it sheltered in the shadow by the wall. Lopsided face. I look at it in the speckled glass and then I walk around the house, wondering what I can do.

The suds are pleasingly angelic, glancing rainbows through their froth as I swoosh the cloth through the bucket again. How weak my arms are, skidding out across the glass. Rubbing and rubbing, until I can see my face in it, until I have turned the window into a dark mirror. The green of the hills is greener in the glass, surreally green, an underwater fantasy shimmering over the kitchen's insides. A filmy painting strung across the empty chairs. I peer into the room, leaning close against the glass to see past my face, because if you look close enough at yourself then you just disappear. It is glowering, the emptiness of the kitchen. So I stand back now, and admire the twinkle of my handiwork. Sun so bright, but the air is cold. It's the wind. My hair stings my cheek. The telephone rings and I let it.

I pick up my bucket and slop across to my next window. I have just got my arm in the water when the phone rings again. Oh well. I shake my hands over the stones and go inside.

'Vanessa? Vanessa, is that you?' demands the voice on the line.

Of course it's me, mum. You didn't leave anyone else behind. 'Yes, it's me.' I curl the telephone cord round my finger, staring at the list of phone numbers tacked on to the wall.

Lydia –
Gordy & Pru –
Mr Beesley (electrician) –
Alec –
butchers –

Salvesens –
Oz –

'Oh, thank goodness. Darling, has anyone rung? Anyone apart from me?'
'No.'
'Oh.'
'Why?'
'Oh, no reason. Nessie, don't answer the phone, okay? I'm coming right back. I'll be back in twenty minutes. Don't answer the phone, will you?'

I look at Lucy's subheading, which runs:

<u>Lucy</u>

Malcolm –	Jamie T –	Selma –
Cameron –	Elspeth –	Grandpa –
Katie B-D –	Johnny –	Jamie B –
Ta –	Georgie –	
Samantha –	Fee –	

'No, I won't answer the phone.'
The line goes dead.

<u>Vanessa</u>
Alan McAlpine – 241 982

That is my list of phone numbers.

Still, Bryony doesn't have any at all. Her name is scrawled at the bottom of the page, but there is nothing underneath it.

I shrug and go back to my window-washing outdoors. I've been at it all of five minutes when the phone sets off again. It rings solid, on and on, the automaton bleat. When at last it stops, it is only in order to start again. What if it's mum? With something she forgot to say. Maybe she got cut off, didn't hang up. I'm afraid. I concentrate very hard on the rubbing of the glass. Polishing. Wishing the ringing would stop. Rubbing my cloth in circles. I'm feeling light, a lick of lighter paper, flipping over at the bottom of the sky.

Ages and ages the phone rings on for. I hear her coming, slowing after the lay-by, braking behind my back. The car rolls faster than usual up the track. Door slams on the sliced-off engine. Hurried footsteps in the gravel. She must be just round the corner. 'Good girl,' she calls to me, and she's in the house somewhere, and I am good, so relieved, trying to smile as I pick my intestines back out of the bucket. Smoothing them out as the ringing stops, at last. I can hear her voice, raised. 'She doesn't want to see you!' shouts mum. 'Leave it!' And then there is silence again.

I drop my cloth into the water and come inside off the terrace. The kitchen is empty, telephone sitting quietly before me on the hook. I close the door behind me. 'Mum?' I wipe my soapy hands on the back of my jeans as I walk over the flag-stones, past the staircase, I am sure she is in the drawing room.

Curled up in the window seat, half-hidden in the curtains, the hem of her skirt trails out towards the floor.

'Mum, was it someone for me?' She looks round. Looks at me blankly, as if she's trying to remember who I am. 'It wasn't Alan, was it?'

She starts laughing then. 'Oh dear. No, darling.' What a silly, hysterical notion. 'No.' Stops laughing again, quite suddenly. Looks at me in that same peculiar way and looks away again. 'No, it wasn't Alan.' She's gone, out the window.

'But was it someone for me?'

I wait, and then just when I think she's not going to answer me, just when I'm turning to leave her, she says, 'I just want to be left alone for a bit, darling.'

'I was going anyway.'

'Lovely view, this.'

'Yeah.' I thought I was supposed to be leaving her.

'No place to bring up three children on your own, though. You would have gone mad with it, Vanessa. Fine for your father, though, coming back here after a day in Edinburgh. Quite nice from that perspective, I suppose. What he really needed was a nice little grateful wife to keep everything nice for him. Do you think I'm a good wife, Vanessa?' I don't know if I'm supposed to answer. I say 'yes' just as she starts speaking again, saying, 'Awfully difficult, being on your own. I don't have the *solitary personality*. Not like you. You like being on your own, don't you Vanessa? You're always taking yourself off, away from the rest of us.'

'Not really.'

'We're quite different, you and I. I need to be around other people. Did you ever know how scared I am at night? With your father away. I hate having to go round locking the doors every night, it's a man's job, that. I don't suppose you're scared, though. Terribly modern, really, aren't you.'

'Sometimes I'm scared. Sometimes, in the dark –

'You would probably kick-box them, wouldn't you?' I don't say anything. 'Intruders. You're quite strong. In some ways. But it takes a kind of strength to sit alone in the middle of nowhere with three small children at your ankles.'

'What about Janet?'

'Yes. Yes, course Janet helped.' She sniffs. 'Certainly would have gone mad if it hadn't been for Janet. But you can't really talk to people like that. So it's not quite the same after all. Hardly even noticed when Janet was here. Which is what's good about her, but on the other hand. Why? Did you like Janet?'

'She was all right. I never really talked to her that much.'

'No. She had a soft spot for Bryony. It was Bryony, wasn't it.'

'Yes.'

'God knows why.' She sits quiet for a moment, and I wonder

if she wants me to go now. Her voice stirs. 'Always in your hair, girls are. You know, I was sure Bryony was going to be a boy. Positive. Mothers are supposed to know these things. Do you think your father ever loved me?'

'Yes.'

'No he didn't. I just wondered what you thought, that's all. He was my first boyfriend, you know. I don't think we were ever in love, though. Too young. At least, I was. We were just – impressed with each other. That's what it was.' She is staring down into the flower bed under the window. 'We were just impressed with each other.'

'Are you going on holiday together?'

'On holiday? With your father? Now?'

'Whenever. Yeah.'

'Of course I'm not going on holiday with your father!' She stares at me with a funny face, like she thinks I am dead stupid but is also pleased with me for some reason. She fiddles with the hem of her skirt. 'Why did you ask that? Why did you think that?'

'I don't know.'

She smiles to herself and looks out the window again. Then her face changes, smeared with her thoughts, sad as she says, 'No use expecting things. No use believing the things people lead you to believe.' She just sits there, as if she has forgotten I'm here.

'Did you want to be on your own?'

'Oh. Yes, if you don't mind.'

So I leave her there, forlorn in the window, waiting for one of them to come. Her grandmother smiles enigmatically down on her from the painting on the wall. I leave them both as I bring the bucket in and cook supper.

I go to tell her the food's ready, and I can hardly make her out in the dark twilit room. I get a strange irrational fear that it's not her, that the shadowy woman in the window is not my mother at all but someone quite different. 'Supper's ready,' I say, quickly.

When she turns to face me the paucity of light has rubbed her loose from her lines. Vague eyes look up at me from a face soft with shadows. And then she sighs, sharply, and I feel the relief of familiarity, the shape and the nub of it quite exactly right under my groping hands in the darkness as she says, 'Turn the light on, God's sakes, I can't see a thing.'

I made it all for four. But there's no sign of my sisters as I dish out the food, fried pepper skin shining so nicely among the sausages. 'Lucy and Bryony aren't back,' I say, putting her plate on the table.

'Yes, I can see that, thank you,' she snaps. So we don't mention them again. We just sit down together and I try to enjoy my mother's company without straining too hard to hear Lucy's tyres on the road outside. I don't want her to return, ever. I ask mum leading questions about her flowers, about her friends, about anything except my father and the disappointing lover. Something about my sisters being out, something about the whole day and this evening makes me bold and happy, like I'm her friend and not her daughter, like it's possible she could love me more than Lucy, and there is nothing to be afraid of because I didn't pick up the phone. I can be trusted. And I say, 'Mum, what do you think you would have done? If you hadn't married dad and had us, what would you have done?'

'Will you bloody stop with these questions! I mean, what *is* this? Are you trying to interview me? Are you trying to marry me?'

'I just wondered—'

'Well don't,' she shouts. 'Don't. Don't sit there *just wondering* about me, don't you wonder anything about me, ever. Leave me the hell alone.' She thumps the table so hard it jumps. 'Do you hear?'

*

'Where's mum?' asks Lucy, all breathless.

I shrug. 'Don't know.'

'Her car's still here.'

Of course it is. I stare at my thick sister and say, 'She's probably in the drawing room.' Lucy makes to leave – 'She's not in a very good mood. Lucy. She wants to be on her own.'

Lucy snorts, and charges off anyway. I shouldn't have told her where mum was. Why did I have to show off like that? I can hear a faint voice carrying down the hall through the open door. I get up and close it. I am on mum's side.

Bryony hums to herself, leaving the door gaping wide again as she wanders in. 'Close the door,' I tell her. She twirls round very, very slowly as if she hasn't heard me, but closes the door all the same, in a superior ironic ballerina kind of way. I don't know if I can stand this, the smug happy version of my sister. She floats around in such an aura of hideous satisfaction that you long to break the salt cellar over her head. 'What's up with you?' I ask. Her nasty little smile makes me wish I hadn't.

'Oh!' Oh! The gloriously pretended lightness of it. 'But!' she gasps, and rights herself. 'You probably wouldn't want to know.'

'Whatever,' I say, hoping she can't hear my crossness as I leave her and go up to my room. I can hear her singing extra loudly, somewhere behind me, songs from *Oklahoma!* I close my bedroom door. Footsteps are gathering like crows in the hall below.

'Shut *up!*' screams mum, half sobbing. 'Shut *up*, would you!' And the crows flap into the kitchen, subdued now.

I curl up under the duvet and hear the tug and pull in their voices, Lucy and mum, digging their heels in, fighting over their length of rope. This way and that it goes. I wait for one of them to fall, but the voices just go on and on.

A car comes. Everything is quiet for a while. Footsteps in the hall again, hesitating around each other, softly. My mother is murmuring to someone, quietly agitated. I hear his voice now, rising above hers, wrapping around it. They are standing by the bottom of the stairs. She has called him to her and now he is saying, 'Mary, Mary, everything seems different in the morning. Wait till tomorrow.'

'But he's coming *tonight*! I can't wait until tomorrow, tomorrow is too late. He wants her tonight. He's on his way, right now. Lucy, bloody Lucy did this.'

'No one can make Bryony – Mary, look at me – no one can make Bryony do anything she doesn't want to. Do you understand?'

'You don't get it, do you?' Her voice is rising again. Higher and higher, faster and faster. 'You really don't get it, John. She *wants* to go! She *wants* to leave me, do you see? My own shitty daughter!'

'I'm sure that's not true.' He doesn't sound very sure.

There is a second where he could say something else, something more. I can hear mum holding herself back, listening for it, and then it is too late. She begins to scream, '*I hate her, I hate her.*' Over and over again.

She charges into the kitchen. I get out of bed and stand at the top of the stairs. I can see her reflected in the dark window at the landing, the slender back of her in the open kitchen doorway. 'Don't you dare do this to me!' she screams. 'Don't you bloody dare!'

And then Mr Crawford, still standing in the hall, somehow knows that I am here and looks up at me from down below. We just look each other in the eye while she screams, and I think how odd a choice he was and how now he will never come back again.

My father walks in. He does it very simply, and he does not

know I am here. No supernatural glance, but then we have never shared a secret. He walks through the door into the hallway, and the way he does it is so familiar, the rhythm and the measure of it. I almost lose my breath at how well I've known him as he stands there, not seeing me up here, only Mr Crawford and the open kitchen door.

He stands still for a moment. His hair has thinned around the crown of his head. The small circle of polished freckled scalp gleams wholesome like a hardboiled egg, and I wish he had come sooner. He is looking at Mr Crawford. Dad is home. I wonder what he will do.

'Excuse me,' my father says. He steps sideways into the kitchen.

I never felt so alone.

'Where's her bag?' he is saying. 'Bryony, get your bag.'

Mum is breaking things. She is taking her favourite things and breaking them one by one, smashing them methodically on the shelf. 'Why don't you just take everything,' she cries. 'Why don't you just take everything I have. Why don't I save you the bother. Here's the plate you gave me.' *Smash.* 'Here – here's the pot Lucy made me for Christmas.' *Smash.* 'What else? What else?' She is scurrying round the kitchen, frantically opening cupboards. 'Must be, there must be something else. Water beakers. Not special enough. You only want to take away the good stuff, don't you. You only want the things I love.' Matter-of-fact, as if she's helping him with a shopping list. 'Tea set, wedding present.' *Smash. Smash.*

'Lucy, get in the car.'

'I'm fine.'

'Get in the car.'

She almost seems sulky as she slinks across the hall to the back door. 'You're supposed to be getting your bag, Bryony,' she says. 'Go on. Get your bag.'

'Where's yours?'

'My dad's decanters.' *Smash.*

'I'm coming back, aren't I.'

Bryony is hauling herself up the banister and now her little face is level with mine. I hadn't realised she'd grown the same height as me, still thought she was smaller somehow. She looks strange, like she's been electrified in her sleep. Her eyes are brighter than I've ever seen and she's looking straight at me. She turns past me and I can smell the fear on her, like the smell of snake, lingering as she marches to her door. I watch her going in.

Dad is shuffling around in the hall below. I bend over the banister and watch him turn. He sighs and starts towards the stairs. I pull back and watch him come. Slow heavy steps, and he is looking at where to put his feet, not at me. Turning the corner at the landing, and still he doesn't look up. I move my feet to catch his eye and he raises his head then. It is lucky I wear shiny trainers.

'Nessa.'

'Hi dad.'

He climbs the last stair, standing on the edge of the rug I float on.

'Is Bryony getting her bag?'

Bastard. 'Yes.'

'Are you coming too?'

'No.'

'Are you sure?'

'Yes.'

And that's it. He turns round and thumps back down the stairs as slowly as he came. I watch him all the way, and I watch Bryony too, passing me a few seconds later. It is as if I am invisible. 'Bye Bryony,' I call.

She stops on the step and looks at the reflection of me behind her in the stair window, in a black mirror in the night. Then she streaks away. Vanishes in a flutter of pale-brown hair, a quiet patter on the carpet.

That is my sister, leaving. That was her, with my father, the man who is in the driving seat taking her and Lucy away and I am here, turning away from the window so I don't have to watch them go. Light from their headlamps swings over my ceiling, gutting my walls. They are gone. The house is silent. My father came and went. He rooted her out from behind me.

His visit seems unreal now, not really him, like mum being someone else in the window earlier this evening. Wind rattles through the reeds in the field outside. No noise within.

Mum screams. Howling with grief, like an angry wolf mother. Her anger bleeds into the walls, hitting them so hard they seem to cower behind the paintings. I put my hands over my ears and look out of the window. The sky is deep grey instead of black. Bright shreds of moonlight gleam, locked in the rocks and fence posts. Hard to know if morning will come. She howls harder, as if she wants Dad and Bryony to hear her, a mile or two down the road by now. I wish I could just tell her to stop. To give up. They are gone.

I freeze as the stairs shake under her thudding feet. Breathlessly wailing now, not so loud, but purposeful, I hear her come. I stand with my back against the door. She is not coming in. I won't let her. My heart goes crazy as she canters over the top of the stairs. She is coming, she is coming, she is past. She is past.

Man's steps follow her. 'Mary!' cries Mr Crawford, angrily. 'Mary!' Let him deal with her. I hear her bedroom door slamming behind the pair of them, and I push my chair against the inside of my door. I get into bed with all my clothes on and gaze out of my window at the grey dog-skin sky.

*

I must have fallen asleep. Because it wakes me, the rattling of the door handle against the back of the chair. Knock knock. A cough. It rattles again.

'Vanessa,' says his voice, sounding embarrassed about my name. 'Vanessa!'

'What?' I call.

'Open the bloody door!' I roll over and face the wall. But Mr Crawford won't stop rattling at the handle and saying my name. I am scared the chair will let him in, the way it is thumping around now. I have to move it. I have to open the door a crack and see his face there, and how it is leached of every other day, deprived of every other night. 'Help me,' says Mr Crawford. 'Please help me.'

'What's she done?'

'I don't know, oh God. I don't know.' He is just standing here, staring at me. I start to run then, run towards her bedroom, and the walls stand back and leave me. The bedroom door is open. Her bathroom door is closed. I turn the handle and push hard, expecting it to be locked, but it's not. The door gives way too easily and I almost fall into the room.

I don't see her for a second. She is too quiet. Crumpled and still, moulded to fit another space. She sits on the carpet, leaning against the side of the bath. Her head leans too far over and her legs are jumbled over the floor, her body like an accordion with a hole in it. She is broken, you can tell just by looking. Oh mother.

Mr Crawford is standing in the doorway behind me. 'Have you called an ambulance?' I ask.

'Yes,' he says.

'Help me. We need to move her.' And so we lift her, Mr Crawford taking her under the arms and me gathering up her knees. 'Put her on the bed,' I say, 'and lean her sideways, like over the edge.' And we do. She is heavy, though, heavier than she looks.

'Hup, hup,' says Mr Crawford as we lift her on to the bedcover. As if she is a sack of dog meal. I glare at him over her gold-flowered blouse.

Mr Crawford wipes his hand over his hair. I am arranging her legs, tilting her hips, making her face the right way. 'I don't know any first aid,' says Mr Crawford. I ignore him.

I run downstairs. 'Where are you going?' he calls, panicky, after me. 'Don't leave me with her!' I don't answer.

Cupboard, second on left. The floor is covered in broken china. I skip over it, ridiculously merry like. Nothing is left in the cupboard. All the bowls are broken. I grab the plastic washing-up bowl from the sink and tear upstairs, snatching at the banister. The passage is so long, and she is at the end of it, poisoned by herself. Mr Crawford stands there uselessly, not even looking at her.

Her body is moving, though, thank God. Her chest judders, trying to retch. It's okay, mum. I am here. I kneel beside the bed and draw her head towards me. I slide my fingers down her throat.

She is trembling now in my arms. 'Hold her,' I say. Mr Crawford looks at me uncertainly, as if I might be a trap. 'Hold her,' I say again. 'I'm tired.' Not true, but he should be the one holding her, he really should. And he comes and sits behind her head, putting his hands under her armpits, holding her as little as he can. It's almost obscene, the way he cannot do it. When he looks down at her labouring face, his eyes flicker awkwardly, then fall away to the button on her cuff.

It's been so long. I hope she puked enough. It was thin, watery stuff.

'The ambulance should be here soon, mum,' I say. She

moves her head, trying to nod. I go burrowing in the tunnels of my brain, desperate to think of something else we can do until they come. But all I find are envelopes stuffed with memories and characters from books and how to skin tomatoes.

I walk around the room again. I stoop over her and put my hand on her stomach, thinking maybe I can soothe her a little, but her whole body flinches away from me. She is moaning. I move away, lean against the wall, hating the ambulance drivers. 'I don't understand it,' I say. 'The ambulance should be here by now.' I wasn't really talking to anyone, but I happened to be looking at Mr Crawford as I spoke. So I see his face, and the way he swallows, the way he looks at me. I see it dripping behind his eyes before he looks away.

I cannot take my eyes off him as I leave the room, glancing over my shoulder at him. Running downstairs now to the telephone in the hall. Nine. Nine. Nine. Pathetic bastard.

The waiting is worse this time. I hold her hand and she grips me hard with her corkscrew fingers, into the cork of my palm. Her face is twisting round and her breathing is worse. I start talking, stupidly. 'It's okay, mum,' I say, 'it'll be okay. You'll be fine.' She opens her eyes then, and they grab out from her face, desperately fearful like arms in the sea. And I have nothing to throw her but words. 'I love you, mum,' I say.

Despair fills her face as it disappears again beneath the pain. 'Don't leave me,' she whimpers.

My heart overflows with happiness in the pain. 'Oh mum.' I smile. 'It's going to be all right.'

She puffs her cheeks, breathing as if breathing is something that has to be done on purpose.

The smile disappears from my face. 'Mum! Mum! You're fine!'

'Where are they, darling?' she asks, and it is still her voice. 'Where.'

'They're on their way, mum. They're nearly here.'

'You called them?'

'Yes, yes of course I did.'

But she looks at me as if she is terrified of something, and then she pulls her hand away from me. She is shaking. 'Oh no,' she moans, quietly.

I watch her lying there, and I don't know what to do. Mr Crawford trembles. He pulls mum further towards him with his wobbling hands. 'There,' he says. 'There.'

'I want Lucy,' she whimpers.

I hear them come, although there is no siren. No need, I suppose, in an empty glen before dawn. I know it by its speed and the screech of its brakes. I go to meet them, the ambulance men with faces like hot Scotch pies.

'Are you all right?' asks one of them, the one I remember from before. I nod, and watch them lift her on to the stretcher. She is faint as they bear her away down the stairwell. Be careful with her. The cracks in her are meeting.

I want to throw myself on top of her but I just follow them down the stairs, my legs curiously twitching. Mr Crawford is directing the men, as if this is not their job. His treacherous voice barks and rumbles.

They are going outside now, into the paling sky. The ambulance doors are open. Mum goes sliding in, like a warrior already dead in a boat. I stand near the open doors. I see her face, the wrong colour, twisted up. One of the men holds out a hand to pull Mr Crawford in. He's in there now, holding her hand. They turn to me.

'No,' I say. Mr Crawford looks up. I look back at him. 'No. I'm staying here.' And I walk back into the house and close the door behind me, hearing their doors slam.

I see them through the french window over the terrace, carrying mum away, going as fast as they can but still it looks too slow.

208

So hopeful, such a confident stripe, little ambulance. I think the sun must be rising in front of you. The grass on the hillside bristles blue, turning bronze.

Chapter Eight

The china and glass shards of her are strewn across the kitchen floor. It is still dark inside as I walk around, and sit, on the floor among the pieces. Chairs will not do, no, nothing normal will do now.

I am here and they are all gone. Everyone is gone. She is not coming back, I know it. Watery sun leaks through the glass and makes a pattern on the wall. It doesn't make sense, how the pattern of sunlight and the broken night china can be in the same room at once. Hung-over dread blackens my eyes and I stumble upright and outside, my dumb heart quivering with horror at the whole world.

Keys are in the ignition. She's always careless like that. It roars frighteningly loud when I turn the key. Less pressure on the pedal. Now. Where is Reverse. Reverse. No. Shit. Only a car, it's only a car. She'll kill me. I wish my knees wouldn't shake. Got it. I'm out of the garage. Stop. Why does it go so fast? I can't seem to get the direction right. Bits of wall lurch violently past the windscreen. Swinging around here, over and over, trying to find the right angle to turn and let myself out. I wish I'd let Alan teach me properly after all. Oh God, okay, ready. The gearstick is stiff in its socket but I've got the right pedal now and I'm off down the track, too fast again towards the road, jerking the wheel round as the open gates fly by me.

A bitter sick taste rises in my mouth as I steer too hard around the corners. The engine rasps, as if it's struggling against something. I get it into third gear and then I leave it there because I do not want to keep changing, you know, it is too difficult. I wish my seat was not so high up above the road. It feels like I'm about to fall out, forwards over the bonnet as I stare at the tarmac blurring away in front of me. The car clock glows red, 06:59.

I should have gone sooner. I should have gone straight away. What was I thinking? Nothing, just nothing. A coward chewing in the corner, that's me. A paper hat of shadows on my head. I let her go. With him, and what might he not have done? The man who was allowed to see her naked. What is she wearing? I must remember so I can find her again, floating across the end of a supermarket aisle. The gold-flowered blouse, and black moccasins on her feet. They will help me catch her. You just have to remember, don't you, what it is you're looking for. The pattern of the sleeve.

It's taking me so long. The fields grow lighter at every turn, the hedges greener, the road paler, and now the whole sun itself is shining through the windscreen, blinding me. Just one day, mum. It is just one day. You can do it. But my hands are trembling on the wheel. A pheasant flaps out from the grassy verge and I swerve, ducking my head. A mass of feathers covers my eyes, beating rust. It disappears, soaring upwards. Colour bright, above the field. Into the trees. It's gone. It got away. I must focus, on the road. It has white lines and everything, the road, to stop you from straying. From killing yourself, or other people. Cat's eyes run under my tyres as I cut the bend.

A gap in the hedge and I can't help looking. Raking my eyes across the silver wet grass, but nothing is there. Not the bird, that's for sure. The bird has gone away. It flew into the trees. My heart shakes, full of beads.

Two lips are stiff and stuck together. They puff drily when I open my mouth. *Da Da Da Da Da*, I chant, to drown the noises in my blood. *Da Da Da Da Da*. This is what speaking is for. *DA DA*.

*

They took Bryony. That's what set it off. Dad, coming in the night. Bryony, sky high and frozen, like bird breath. Shattering on our heads.

I am behind the wheel and I shouldn't be. Oh mum. I was never meant to be in charge. This isn't right, none of it is right.

We belong together, mum, with you in the driver's seat. Just the two of us. I'm the one you can trust. I will carry your bags. I'll never leave you, not in the heat or the ice. In the melt-water flood I will find the phone. I will save you with magic numbers and practical skills, I will learn them off by heart and I will know what to do, every time, every time, you can count it. Are you counting? On your hand. Or count on mine, use my fingers if you like. I'm on a straight stretch anyway.

Here come my hands towards you. Up in the air, look at them. Crappy hands, white hands, they stick it for a second before they twitch and drop. Back, on to the wheel. Look at me. The big coward. I never rode no-hands upon my bike.

Lucy did, showing off. Freewheeling down the hill with her arms in the air, hands raking through the sky. Have you loved her more than me? Bryony tried to follow suit, behind, but her arms hung wing-like half decided from her side. She kept falling off, and trying again. I sat with a book and a visor to keep the sun out of my eyes. Tennis players were wearing them at Wimbledon, on the television indoors, and you were watching them, *remember*? You must remember.

I sat on the grass by the hedge, listening to Lucy on the other side of the thick green leaves telling Bryony that she doesn't know how she does it, it just comes naturally. Their voices faded as they rode back up the road, tyres clicking on the tarmac. Lucy whooped as she took off. Never cared about keeping quiet so you could watch your programmes in peace. Streaked a line that hissed louder and passed. Then Bryony, you could feel her coming, the lumbering fear of her, hear the clacking of her wheels. *Look*, she gasped.

Don't think about falling off! yelled Lucy. A skid and a clattering bang.

Mum mopped her up with Savlon and dad said *you've been in the wars.* Perhaps wounded people are easier to love.

I grip the wheel tight.

I will bring her soup and water. I won't be able to chat, but she won't mind that. I won't go sitting around, either. I will just take the soup and then leave. She will smile and call me darling. She will get better again, mending in her bed.

I saw her. Paper-thin.

Leaves dawdle across the road in front of me, swinging lazily through the air. Slowly, and then suddenly they slap into the windscreen, catching in the static wiper. Fluttering double quick as they race along with me, tangled up, tearing, falling out. And I am not even going so fast.

Paper-thin she was.

It is hard, staying on the road. My steering is all wrong. You'd think to turn a car this size you'd need some strength behind the wheel, but it goes too far too easily. It is surprising what a little touch it needs. See, I turn too early on the bend by the pig farm, scuff the mud and turn the other way. Brake. Straighten. Carry on, chugging so slowly to start with, and away. I do not look at them as I pass, the little pigs in the yard, but I see them in the mirror above my head once I am safe, and they are all looking at me. Gone, behind the second bend. Pink faces vanished behind the road. I'm driving mum's car. The farmer ought to arrest me.

Out of the overhanging branches, sun washes up over the mossy green bonnet, slashing my face in two. She keeps sunglasses on the dashboard. I grope and put them on, misfiring, poking the right-hand stem softly into the skin beside my eye.

That is better, now I have got the glasses on. The green is not so violent, the world is not so close. And look, her glasses are being worn, her car is being driven, so she cannot leave, not now. Her things are alive and moving and they are part of her. She is in them. We are keeping her alive. My lip trembles with laughter.

A blue saloon glimmers behind my shoulder, passing me. I catch a glimpse of the driver, a man in a marmalade sweater. I never even noticed he was behind me, and now he is gone too, rear windscreen winking in the sun. He overtook me so easily. One more corner before the long straight. Angry, I pull the wheel.

I know I've done it wrong.

Still, it takes a long second to knock me sideways, the grassy bank. I see it coming for an age. And then it is thudding into my metal side like a soft cow. My shoe is jammed on the pedal, going nowhere. Mud flies.

I stop. Pull the key out. It is quiet, so quiet. My feet are stuck to the pedals, knees locked straight. Starting to shake. I open the door and move my legs out into the air. I'm climbing down, and orange leaves are curling out of the pale-blue sky, floating down around me. The morning smells perfectly normal. I see my feet and they are on the ground. I look at them for a while. Then I bend over, to let the sickness out, but my stomach is empty.

We are in the farmland here. Ploughed fields, dark brown, stretch out on the other side of the tarmac. It doesn't look like a road now, that strip of black stuff. Roads are for driving on. I did it, for a bit. I drove on the road like you're supposed to. But now it is just a strip of tarmac again, for riding a bike along, for walking to meet your man, sidling into the verge when the real cars come. Look, my nose is in the grass. Blunted by turf. Glass from my headlights glints in the dry and crusty mud. The car is skewed across the bend, its arse swung across the wrong side of those white lines. The lines run parallel, close together. Mum told me it means you aren't supposed to overtake from either side. You aren't supposed to cross the lines, because that's how people die.

The air is silent. So quiet, as if it is resting after the exertion of carrying our screaming brakes. The car is still, extra still. I stand beside it for a while, not wanting to touch it. I am waiting for the sound of oncoming traffic, I am waiting for something to come and smash it to pieces. But nothing comes.

I cross the road and stand on the opposite verge. I turn my back, looking out across the fields. They are broad, and the hedgerows thin. The soil is steaming in the early sun. Light hangs in blankets just above the ground. No traffic comes.

I glance over my shoulder, thinking the car might have somehow gone. But it is still there. Sitting patiently the wrong way round, glowing like the jade in her ring. I pull a strand of my hair, holding it sideways out from my head. My crooked elbow makes a sign. Scalp tugs after the hair, but does not come away from my head. I stand and feel it, and then I walk.

The key still fits. I sit quietly. Through the windscreen is soggy-headed knapweed. Traffic could come now. Smash me to smithereens. I pull the handbrake up slowly, like a tree root. And now, now it's the beginning again. Firstly, breathe. Then pedals. The key is turning, turning, into reverse. The car crunches as it disengages from the bank, pulling backwards, I can feel the earth wanting to come with it. The bonnet is covered in mud. It bends on one side as if it is trying to wipe its nose. It looks like a car that I would have, not mum. I have not driven well.

The world slides by my crumpled bonnet, but I only catch it from the corner of my eye because I have got to be watching the road. No more mistakes. I see her somewhere up ahead of me, mum, floating across the road where the shadows meet. I do not let her distract me, with her thin white shirt luminescent above the ditch. I know it isn't really mum, because how could I have seen the sand grains smeared on her hem from here? And she was wearing gold flowers when I last saw her, and her bottom half was covered up. Besides, there is no sea for miles. We should be landlocked.

Bonfire smoke in the field to my side, and she is in that, too. I press my knuckles tighter round the steering wheel. I am desperate now, desperate to get to her. I have to pin her down. I have got to put her back. I am the only one who really knows her.

A bubble forms between my lips. I want to hold on to it, but it pops after a couple of seconds. The smell of woodsmoke peters out. I drive faster. I must find her, must find her, cannot let her slip through my fingers. I curse myself for stopping so long. All things grow more possible every second they are not lashed down.

Hot marbles are rolling down my lungs. They are turning corners and burning in dead ends. The pedals give way beneath my feet as I swoop and turn the bends. I cannot see her face, just her hands. Pale and waxy, drawing a white woollen thread across the windscreen. Looping themselves inside it. She is doing cat's cradle. It criss-crosses between my lashes, blurring the road. She is making me a veil. I will not wear it, mum. I won't. It sits there and then it slides slowly down my face. My cheeks sting as the gentler hills roll by.

There are a few cars on the roads outside Perth. I hope that they do not notice me as I go clunking towards my mother, smeared with earth. My engine stalls twice at the lights.

The hospital car park is small and homely. I park across the little marked-out lines and run towards the building. It rises and falls as the tarmac sways beneath my pounding shoes.

The door flaps open beneath my hand. My fingers seem very far away, splayed across its push plate. And then I am snapped across the room of yuccas, standing at the reception desk, saying, 'My mother. I'm here to see my mother.'

The woman's face is soft, scrubbed away into the things around her, part of her desk as she answers, 'We need to know your mother's name.'

'My *mum*.'

'Yes,' says the desk. 'We need to know her name.'

'Mary Gordon,' I say, even though that doesn't sound like my mother, just everyone else's version. I am worried they will send me to the wrong person and I double check with the woman, twice. And now I am following arrows, big and black on white backgrounds. All the doors open for you as you go, and they always go in the right direction. It makes you feel afraid, the way they do that.

'Your father's here,' reception said. Dad will be wondering why I wasn't here already, why I didn't come with her. Lucy will blame me.

Mum is motionless, legs like pillows under the white sheets. As if she has snuck out the window to go to a party and the body in the bed is just a stooge she's left to fool us.

'Where's dad?' I ask.

'Your father isn't here,' says Mr Crawford.

'Yes he is.'

Mr Crawford doesn't answer, just opens out his hands and closes them again. He is standing by the window, blocking the light.

'You should move,' I say. 'Mum likes sunlight on her face.'

'She's dead,' he says.

'Please move.' And he does, he steps sideways and now her

face is washed in morning light. It runs across her skin, tripping lightly over her grooves and hollows. 'That's better, isn't it, mum.' I stroke her hair.

'You should have come sooner,' says Mr Crawford, forgetting his weakness. I carry on stroking her hair, smoothing it under my skin. 'I've been trying to call.' The backs of my fingers trail over and over her soft head. I look up at him. This man she loved. I stroke her face. My fingers rush all over her, over the bridge of her nose and around the lower dip of her eye sockets. Up across her brow and down her cheeks I run. Her eyes do not flicker, but simply look diagonally upwards, as if following a bird or an aeroplane. Oh mum. Why did you have to. I grab her hand tightly, watching her face. Some flicker, perhaps. Some startled look, a sliver of fire. But nothing, just nothing. Where has she gone? And why wasn't I invited? Mum mum mum.

'You should call your father,' says Mr Crawford the idiot. I don't even have dad's number. It's just me and mum. I hold her head in the crook of my arm and sit here, here on the edge of the hospital bed, waiting for her. 'She's dead,' he says again. This stupid stranger in our room.

Anger bubbles the blood in my veins. 'Fuck off,' I say, quietly. And I look at Mr Crawford, not afraid of him any more, not afraid that he will take her away. 'You did this.'

I can see him out of the corner of my eye, raising his hands in mock surrender, saying, 'Fine. Fine.' Picking up his coat. 'I was just trying to help.'

'Fuck you.'

'Very well.'

He is going, thank God. He is gone. The door whispers shut behind him. He didn't even say goodbye to you, mum. Look, I'm here. I stroke her hand and she lets me.

The sun is bright today. Her hair shines under it. Very quiet, she is. Oh mum. I hold her wrist in my fingers and watch her, lying so still. Outside, it is one of those beautiful September days where the sky is so pale with its blueness that it almost lets you see right through it. The sun's disc is clear, the world thin-skinned. Sunlight pours through the glass and on to her white sheets, so that they reflect the light up underneath her chin. It makes her seem to glow. We sit here while the sun moves slowly higher and sideways, through the blue. It is just one day. Look, mum. It is just one day.

I know she wasn't afraid, didn't mean for this to happen, I saw her face. Frightened of death, not of living. She only wanted people to listen, only wanted us to know she was serious. All along.

And Mr Crawford let her die. Him and his lies that killed her. Gone now, to call a taxi, I suppose. To retrieve his car from our driveway, to go home to his wife and sons, to tell Mrs Crawford it's all over and now for once she can believe him.

I sit by her all day long, and still she is not dead. How can she be? My world, cold and swaddled, lying in a bed.

I do not know who called them, but they come. Dad and Lucy, tripping through the door with pale faces. 'Oh God,' says dad. 'Oh God.'

Lucy trembles round the room, pacing and coming close now. She touches mum's face and I want to bite her hand off. 'She's dead,' she says. 'Mum's dead.' Like a commentator on a football match, bland and excited at the same time.

Dad is kneeling on the other side of the bed. Look at his old face, his sad eyes, he is cupping her cheek in his hand. 'Poor Muffy,' he says. 'Poor dear.'

'I refuse to feel guilty,' says Lucy. 'I am going to the cafeteria.'

I don't think dad heard her. He just kneels there at mum's bedside, too late, stroking the side of her face. We can all touch her, now she's dead. We can touch her as much as we like and she can't stop us.

'It was Mr Crawford,' I say, but dad's face doesn't shift an inch. He just keeps stroking her cheek. He seems far away, years ago where I can't go because I never was. And then he looks up sharply, as if he's only just noticed I'm here, that it has been me speaking. 'How difficult for you,' he says. Him who left us behind. My father made of sand. I shrug. And then he says, 'Lucy will look after you. Where is she?'

'In the cafeteria.'

'Why don't you join her? I'll be along in a minute.' He stands up, so I must too. 'Things to sort out with the hospital, I expect,' says dad.

'Yes. I expect.' I nod and leave him, standing there looking like he's waiting for the teacher to leave the room. And I leave the body of my mother, I leave everything, wrapped up cold under the sheets in the dying light. I leave it all and go walking through the corridors. The wind has died, the moon is gone. My heart a glassy pond without her tug.

Chapter Nine

My fingers are shredding something in my jeans pocket. Folded squares of kitchen towel. I put them there yesterday because I thought I might need them, I thought I might cry. But I didn't, they came away with me dry as her flaky ash bones, waiting. Rip, rip. I reduce them to fibrous fluff. Once, these were new. But then once, so was I. Oh please. Just breathe. Oh why did you have to, be you and go before I killed you. I'm crying.

I pull off the covers in my room. I tear off the sheet, and the underblanket, that too. I kick away the pillows. My cheeks are stinging as I fall on the naked mattress and curl tight, tight, too tight to think. Cradling my head in my knees, thin my skin on the stiff cardboard denim, I stroke my long yellow hair, whispering: still, lie still. I know. There. Breathe, swallow the salt, still the gulps, wipe these eyes. I rub them raw upon my knees. My head hurts and my body shivers. I hold myself tighter. Glued eyes. Stop it, still your brain, just nothing, nothing, nothing.

And suddenly all is quiet. Still and grey for a while, I just lie here and let the morning wrap its oblivious arms around me, lull me in its viscous embrace. I will not think of anything other than what I see, I will keep all my thoughts outside. The weave of denim and the weak daylight on the wall. The dust lodged in the mattress stitching, the dead skin, no. Look at something else. Or just breathe, with my eyes closed, forget everything else. Breathe. Only, it makes me more aware of being alive. My being here beats me, and I can't do it properly anyway. Later. Shut up and breathe in time to the music inside my head. Ma-ry, Ma-ry, quite con-tra-ry.

'Are you all right?' Lucy. Poking her nose in.

I scramble up off the bed, upright, arms by my sides. I am smiling and standing to the attention of all rightness. 'Fine!'

How can you show these things? And why, what's the good. I'd rather have it inside me than out there to be pulled about and chewed on. It isn't something I can whip out for inspection because it's all of me. I whip it out and my intestines will come too. Can't tear us apart.

Lucy looks at me a while, and then she leaves me alone again.

I approach my big old wardrobe and tug the door open. It is full of short dresses which I wore in the summer, they hover red and pink above my shoes. Shaking the bin bag open, I slide them cowering off their hangers and drop them in, I do not feel a thing. I stoop and chuck the shoes in on top. Crumpled mundane T-shirts follow them. There is an old jumper here which is dark blue and scattered with holes around the cuffs. It used to belong to Alan. The sleeves are over-long on me, falling down my hands, I used to poke my fingers through the holes and make him laugh.

My bedclothes are all over the floor. I pour the pillows out of their cases, rip the duvet poppers angrily, pull out the duvet. I am sweating. I stuff the duvet in the wardrobe hard as if it is something I can hurt. Fold everything up, stack it against the wall.

I open my desk drawer and pull out the bottle with a bit of vodka in the bottom. I unscrew and finish it, gulping without tasting, because I don't like vodka straight. My little green enamelled bowl is twinkling on the sill. Full of necklaces. One from my mother, a gold rope, paid for. One from Alan, back when we were kids, a cowrie on a string. I don't often wear it because once you've knotted it, it's hard to get undone again. I'm shaking as I tie it round my neck. It's hard to tie the knot behind my head. I can't see what my fingers are doing, and now

I am crying with plain frustration and the soreness in my arms as I finally pull the ends tight. The shell used to hang on my scrawny breastbone but now it sits up in the hollow of my throat. It feels cold and smooth like a marble. I stroke it once over and wipe my eyes on the back of my sleeve. Then I fasten the gold one round my neck, too. It is a lot easier, because it has a clasp.

Mum. She was the only one who understood, because she made me.

Pat pat pat across the smooth black flagstones in the hall, I realise that I still have no shoes on and that my feet are cold like buried stones.

I know there are two kicked-off trainers under the bed, and I pull them out again. Sitting on the bare bed, I am breathing. I haul a leg up, bent, angle its foot into one trainer, which smells of old grass and leathery summer sweat. The telephone is ringing. I listen. It goes on for a while, then there are footsteps across the hall and Lucy's deep, well-practised 'Hello?' And then, 'I'm not sure, I'll just go and have a look.'

But I don't feel like it. But her feet are treading up the stairs, she is coming to my door. Quickly I wriggle my way under the bed, ow. Lying here breathing quietly, like a little mouse. I can't breathe much at all, my lungs are squashed, my head lies on its side. There's not a lot of room under here. She pushes the door and walks into my room. I see the flesh of her golden tan ankles, standing still and then she slimes silkily out. Down the stairs. The footsteps stop, at the pile of washing I suspect. I hear her coming back up, more slowly this time, to check the empty bathroom.

'Ness?' she calls loudly. I hear her in the passage, coming towards my door now. The cramped state of my lungs necessitates quick breathing. Her ankles reappear in my room, also her feet but I try not to look at them. It is very dusty down here but I shan't sneeze.

223

'Ness?' she says quietly.

I can't help looking at those feet. Lumpy, bony-toed, freaky things, with five minuscule squares of shiny pink nail polish, like toads in tiaras. The one nearest me has the added amusement of a jumping vein. Hop, hop, rhythmically hop. And suddenly the curtain falls, the foot is vanished under cream silk and replaced by hands. Lucy's face appears, vastly. She has enormous eyes, the irises are dark brown around black discs, like records, staring out at me from that sudden huge bodyless face. I don't flinch or move at all, I just look back. Our four eyes hang in an invisible rectangle over the floor. Whole balls unblinking and locked. Black holes, tubes to her brain.

She should stop staring at me with them, because I can look harder. I can almost feel the drill of my gaze burning through her cornea. Her eyes are black holes and they don't know what to do. She is stuck to my eyeballs without words, phrase searching. 'Phone for you,' says her voice through her moving mouth. Her eyes don't shift until she's finished saying it, and then the face snatches itself away from me all at once. And the body goes too, gladly.

I stay here, coughing on dust. And then decide to get out and have some breakfast. I heave my body sideways on my forearms, catching my hair in the jaggedy bed. I jerk my head, it tears the hair, out I come, into the room. Roll over on to my back and breathe. I see the ceiling and no one trying to get on top of me, just a lot of air. Suck, blow, breathe. The ceiling, flat cracked white, is disdainfully ignoring me. It's looking sideways, instead of down as ceilings usually do.

I stand up and sit down on the bed. I stretch to reach my other trainer, bend the barefoot leg up and sideways to rest its ankle on the other knee, and I push the trainer on to it. I stand up and go downstairs.

The telephone receiver is lying on the table, like an accidental baby whose mother has gone to sleep, still attached by the curly plastic cord. I put it back. I can hear Lucy and Finlay talking in the kitchen. I tap over to the pile of bedding and I wander off to the laundry room.

I stand on the stone floor, cold in my arms, and also my chest, as I am only wearing a vest. I push the washing into the machine and set it going with a low moan, rhythmically whoosh.

The hairs on my arms prickle upright in a feeble imper-sonation of fur sleeves, pulling the skin up after them into little bumps. My breasts shrink into themselves, spitting out nipple pips.

Water drips down the window. A black shiny leaf is stuck to the glass. I like wet leaves. Down by the river I used to lie in them, lie in the lovely dank mould smell and cover myself, being a squirrel for a while. I smelled the rich rooty earth and heard the little creepy things rustle. After rain the yellowed hazel leaves are soft, they like to stroke your skin. Rowan berries splitting soddenly against you, brown oak leaves covering you, they will hide you, little animal, in the dark afternoon.

I rub my arms to warm up, but the coldness of my hands only chills them further. I ram my hands up into my armpits, squeeze and grimace, burning with it in slivers. My fingers are numb and don't feel cold but they are freezing the rest of me, icy steel fish slices on the ends of my arms. I can't put them anywhere. My brain is numb too, large and leaded, numb a lumb lumb.

She is dead in a pot. Shrunken into a little jar from all her hugeness, like a genie sucked back into its lamp. Everything is over now, my world went with her.

I am starting to feel the coldness of my hands. I ram them in inverted prayer between my thighs and shimmy around a bit to keep warm, except I'm not warm in the first place. Never mind. I am alone. Shimmy in the chair. My hands are warming up, rub a dub dub.

Was it this cold yesterday? I was wearing a coat, I suppose, and a black jumper underneath, so probably it was and I just didn't notice. There was that little chill inside me. But I had a half-bottle of whisky in my coat pocket, ready mixed, so I was prepared for it. Perhaps I drank too much, because my knees got shaky in the standing-up bits, the low slow hymns when everyone else was singing except for me. There were a lot of people. You might be surprised by how many people thought they knew her.

They said nice things about her, little speeches and bits of poems. Vivacious, witty, kind and strong, a tragic loss. I said nothing. I exited before the egg sandwiches, before the service had quite finished, actually. Puked in a privet bush and walked quickly to the bus stop. Nobody came after me. I don't know why I went, anyway. Maybe I needed to see her go, to know it wasn't another of her elaborate tricks. And she did go. She went sliding through the curtains, and look who she's left me with.

A dumb big sister, followed through doorways by the adoring godson. He touches her shoulder with his hand every time she looks out of a window. Watches her boil the kettle, rapt.

A smaller sister, haunting the edges. She stands in the same room, scratching me and I am made of glass. She was there all along. She is here now, somewhere. Her great escape did not last long. Dad took her out the water and put her back. Lucy's idea again. He didn't demur.

Sometimes Bryony stands by the stairs, so thin that she almost slides into the wall. Sometimes I only notice she was there once I have passed her and feel her eyes on my back. At first I thought she was melting into the house, but now I am beginning to think she is melting out of it. I wonder how long she has been there, watching me from the shadows. A minute, a month, one year or two.

Dad sleeps soundly at the Grants' house, the other side of the hills.

*

In the laundry, I can be alone. No one will come here because of the cold.

I sigh and stare out of the window, up at the side of the hill as it rises past us, pale green and cold. You would imagine it was winter already. Low pressure curling off the sea, wind flicking at the trees, taking their leaves early. Three weeks ago, the sun blinded my eyes and I wore T-shirts. I wish it would come back. I hate the cold. And now dad is coming to eat with us and sleep in his old bed again, now is the time, and Lucy and I must be Ready, she says. Life must Go On.

In comes Lucy, right on cue. 'Brr!' She holds out her cosmetics bag. 'Here, Ness,' she says. 'You look tired. Go and put some make-up on.' I take the bag and she smiles and shivers and then leaves, and after a bit I do too.

The bag is full of gold-coloured packages, expensive little creatures, delectable crustaceans labelled Lancôme and Chanel. I open them all up. Full of colour. I close them all back shut again and zip up the bag with them tucked away inside, little eggs, and I look up.

Someone is in the mirror. A woman who grew out of me. Arms poked through my child with hands of their own that do, and don't ask. Don't ask questions. Her eyes harden like salt on the road. Vertigo dives inside them. I don't. I stay outside, eyes firmly on the surface of the glass. Gripping salt. Don't go in. I tuck her hair behind my ears. Oh my skin is quite blotchy. My feet might fall through the floor. I used to be a child, when I was me.

Somebody calls to know if I am in here. I can't speak. I turn on the tap, to signify yes. And I stare back, alarmed, and blink in the same moment as myself do. Won't do. This won't do. Her mouth trembles. I think I am going to laugh. Something swells and catches in my cheeks. It makes my eyes smart. Open the door and walk. I call from behind a door of my own, 'It's all yours'. That voice was hysterical. Bite my finger, hard. If I can just bite through to the bone.

Busy-busy, they are. Tidying up.

'Can you give us a hand, Vanessa?' Her cross face around the door.

Oh not you, no. 'Yes,' I say. Yes don't be cross. I'm coming. The cushions come off the sofa and I throw them in the air. I forget to catch them and they frighten me as they fall. I crouch down with my hands over my head. Finlay says, 'Vanessa, what are you doing?'

I didn't even make a sound, so I don't know how. But here he is. Standing in front of me as I straighten. The dust makes him sneeze. I count the cushions on the floor. 'Sorry,' I say. Very quietly I leave.

Something shivers in the corner of the hall. I know it is Bryony and I don't look up.

My shoes lie piled in the middle of my bedroom floor, where I tipped them back out of the bin bag. I had to undo it all.

I lie on the bed suppressing the flap of bat wings in my lungs. I had a sick bat when I was seven, just for a while. It lived in a shoebox and I used to take it out and stroke it. It was very soft and then it was better and it went. Dad said it probably would be fine on its own. Dad, who stood in the pew with his new girlfriend with burgundy hair. Dad, who gave up on mum a whole year ago and nobody said.

Lucy knew. Lucy kissed the new girlfriend's cheek at the big wooden door. *Hello Frankie, thanks for coming.*

Minutes drip down the walls. I stroke the paper that covers them.

Lucy walks in. 'Vanessa – sorry – Do you think this skirt's okay?'

'Yeah. Yeah, it's fine. Definitely.'

'It's not too short?'

'No.'

Lucy smiles at me and it's almost genuine. 'What are you wearing?'

'Oh.' I heave myself up on to one elbow. 'I think I might just – stay as I am.'

'No, no,' Lucy warmly insists, doing me a favour. 'We should make an effort. It will make us all feel better.' She opens my wardrobe. 'Oh! Where are all your clothes? There's nothing in here.' She rattles the hangers. 'What have you done with it all?'

'It's in the laundry.'

'But then what will you wear? Are you all right?' She peers more closely at my face, and adds, 'Do you want a hand with the make-up?'

'No. Thanks.'

She stands there, on my carpet, for a second or two. 'Oh well,' she says. 'It's only us, I suppose.'

'Yeah.' I pick at my mattress.

She laughs. 'And you never did like getting dressed up.' Then: 'Your bedclothes –

'In the laundry.'

'Too.' She nods. Finishing off my sentence, buckling it down. Making it hers. Wanting to be mum, more than ever. I wonder, though, who she is trying to prove to. Mum is gone, who was the only judge worth pleasing. 'That's really good, to keep your bedroom clean,' says Lucy. '*Mens sana in corpore sano* and all that. Can I borrow a hair-band?'

'Top drawer of my desk.'

She rummages around in there while I lie here on my bed, and there is something surprisingly soothing about the sound of her scrabbling. I wish she would go on looking for a hair-band forever, but already she has one in her fingers and is flipping her head back. Catching her hair in her other hand and I hate her again.

'I'll be downstairs,' she says.

I roll over and bury my head in my folded-up arms. Time passes. Sickness curdles in my limbs.

Someone comes and stands beside me. I hear them breathing, uncertainly. I don't look up, don't move. I always won at Sleeping Lions. But I'm too convincing, because Finlay pokes me and it makes me jump.

'Oh!' cries Finlay. 'Jesus, Vanessa!'

I curl my elbows gawkily, trying to act sleepy as if that was all it was. I rub my right eye and say, 'Wha'?'

'I didn't realise you were asleep.'

'Well, I've woken up now.'

'Come down. We're in the drawing room.' He hooks his finger through the belt loop on his black jeans. I can tell that Lucy sent him. He looks at me, and looks away. I say okay and follow him and my muscles are like cold bacon rind. He coughs on the way down the stairs, for something to do.

I can hear the low boom of dad's voice from here. Have you brought me any sweets, dad? Don't take sweets from strangers. I'm coming, I'm coming down the stairs towards your well-thumbed strangeness. I've read it so many times.

And there he is, talking to Lucy with a glass of wine in his hand. He is in the middle of saying something and he is not going to stop, he is not. I stand on the Chinese rug, a peeled egg on the shop floor.

He turns to me, once he's done. 'Ah, hello, Nessa darling. Very chilly today.'

'I expect you're not used to it,' I say, and sit down. Wondering if I should have touched him somehow. He is looking at me and now he is sitting down too, in the armchair near the window seat.

That's dad's hand, drumming on his knee. Black corduroy trousers. Though I noticed he was also wearing a rust-coloured jumper, which goes to show that it isn't a funeral any more.

In the service, I sat at the back. Couldn't bear their calmness. And now my father is just a few feet away and his skin is always older, browner, and his eyes hide deeper in his face. His sandy hair is paler, almost blond, a thinning angel's mop.

'How's work?' I ask.

'Very busy, Nessa.' Frowns, and brightens. 'But can't complain. It's nice to be back in the same country as my offspring.' He rubs the arm of his chair as if it is my knee. 'Very nice to be back.'

'Back here?'

'Here?' he echoes, picking up his drink from the side table. Ice knocks softly against glass.

'In the house.'

'Really I meant Britain. You know, nice being back in London.' He smiles at me. I wonder what he is thinking? It probably doesn't matter any more.

My words are enunciated carefully: 'Where-abouts in London do you live?' And when I am done I walk over to the table and pour a drink for me, so that I have my back to him as he answers, 'Fulham'.

I glance at Lucy, but she has suddenly become busy with her mobile phone. I take a drink. Whisky and ginger beer. Mum bought the ginger beer just for me. I was always the only one who drank it. Whisky and ginger beer, because I liked it, and then just so mum would keep on buying something for me.

'You'd like it, Nessa,' says dad. 'Lots of little shops and restaurants.'

'Sounds lovely.' How long, I wonder, how long has he been back for? A train ride away, how long. I pick up the little glass bottle and scrutinise its label for clues. Have I been sleeping?

Lucy stands up, smoothing her skirt and saying she is going to check on Bryony.

Finlay scratches the back of his neck, dad sighs, I turn around and watch the fire. Finlay says, 'There's a big lighting emporium in Fulham. My mother goes there.'

'Oh! Lord, yes,' says dad, so quickly it makes me jump. 'I know exactly the one you mean. I walk right past it every day.' He is leaning forward in his chair, sounding delighted. 'Chandeliers. Lamps – bronze fairies in the nude.'

Finlay picks up his glass. 'Pa's got one in his study.'

They laugh. Dad lives in London.

'Holding a torch?' asks dad.

'Yes.'

They both start laughing again, as if the bronze fairy is a woman they have both had.

'Ah, wonderful,' sighs dad, at length. He wipes his eyes, even though they are dry. I tilt my wrist to reflect the light off my watch face, and make it dance across the ceiling.

Finlay coughs and smiles at my great-grandmother. Judith Henderson hangs in her painting quietly and half smiles back, wearing a cloche hat and a springer spaniel at her feet. Her eyes are bright, cheeks lightly flushed, blonde hair set in a curl beside her jaw. Who knows what she was like.

I move my wrist slowly. The dot of light slides across the ceiling, wilting down the wall, on to dad's shoulder. I edge it gently towards his face. It is nestling in the grooved skin of his neck, it is under his chin saying *I Love Butter*, it is on his curving lip. It flicks away as Lucy comes back in.

Bryony lists behind her, wearing black. Black lycra trousers with flared bottoms, clinging limply to the hollows in her hips. Black polo-neck, with hands disappeared up inside its sleeves, swinging its arms. She is sort of smiling, at me. And I am holding an empty glass bottle.

I am going to say something. I am just about to. But then my big sister speaks instead, and it is easier to smile back weakly and turn to face Lucy, to listen to her lilting prattle, than to hammer out a message in pins all by myself. 'Fin, don't you think Bryony looks like a model? Look, she's wearing black. Hot off the Champs Élysées, I'd say.' In Lucy's eyes every public thoroughfare is a catwalk. She is our mother's daughter. Bryony shuffles awkwardly.

I lift my empty ginger beer bottle by a fraction, just enough to shield my shoulder. 'Women wear black in Saudi Arabia,' I murmur.

Lucy laughs. She has been laughing a lot since mum died. 'Bryony hardly looks like an Arabian, does she? Ah, dear. Do you want another drink, dad? No, no it's fine, stay where you are,' and I move away from the drinks table so as not to get in her way. Lucy turns round to look at Bryony as she takes the lid off the ice bucket. It takes a while for her to locate her, because the black clothes have shifted to the window seat. Bryony's face is inclined, watching the flames in the fireplace.

Lucy asks if she wants a drink and she moves her head. 'Models don't drink,' she says.

Lucy smiles and replies, 'Of course!' while trying to open the bottle of tonic water, letting the lid off and screwing it back, three times over to keep the bubbles from overflowing.

When she is done, she goes and sits with the men. They welcome her on to the sofa and the three voices go on and on, arguing and interrupting but mainly laughing, and I stand here for a while and then I go and stretch myself out on the other sofa, which is empty, and pretend to be reading dad's newspaper. Whenever I look up, Bryony is watching the fire.

After a while we all trot through to the dining room and Lucy sits in mum's chair. And I think how much Lucy is enjoying this, being in control and dishing out the spaghetti with its creamy bacon sauce. She is steering the conversation as we eat, stopping at stations, closing doors, speeding off, checking our tickets. I do not bother trying to board it but just sit eating my food, drinking my wine. Lucy isn't drinking, which is unlike her. Maybe it's part of her new incarnation. I watch Finlay's face. It is safe to do this, because he is engrossed in Lucy's moving lips. I can tell when she is lifting the glass of mineral water to her mouth, just by watching Finlay's eyes. And dad, too, watches my sister, with admiration and relief in his face.

Mum, if only you could see them. I take another swig of wine. They have forgotten you already.

And then I look over at Bryony, sat opposite like a cat with her plate of plain spaghetti. Her face, and how it seems to know a million things. Between finger and thumb she is balancing her fork as if it were a tool of divination. She looks up and something behind her eyes, it slides underneath my skin.

My glass is swimming in front of me. Swimming away from me, or coming to get me, I can't tell. I have to grab it to make it stay still. But it just swims out through the top of my fist and lies down with a clunking sigh on the cloth as all its liquid pours out. Oh well. It was nearly empty anyway. Someone is handing me a cloth to wipe it up. And my hand takes it. The exact same hand that used to touch Alan's cheek and open up his shirt. Back in the middle of nowhere, when I was not an apple being dooked at by death. I stroked my little sister's hair, once, when we were young.

'Thanks.'

The voices around me swoop down on each other, pulling bits from the other's beak and flying off with it. I lie down underneath and only slowly blink. If you don't move, you'll never have to know that you can't. Oh mum.

But food, food is rising like a cloth in my gullet, suffocating me. My chair is out from under me now. My arms scrape past. Keep the mouth shut, for God's sake.

*

I'm shuddering, so hard it feels like I'm being paid for it. The wine is acidic coming up my throat. And white pasta strings and more liquid and liquid acid shutting my eyes down, choking me. And then it is all out. I pull the chain. I take water from the tap and rub my teeth with minty paste. Check my cheek for flecks in the mirror. Mum. Leaving me again, and taking my food with you. I don't want to be alone.

I go back and sit with them. They all turn and look. What? What's so funny? Stop staring at me and not laughing. I pick up my wineglass. 'Don't you think you've had enough?' asks Lucy.

I stare at her. 'Do I look drunk?' I demand. She throws me a reproachful look, drops her gaze placidly. Bloody hell.

The evening is light, bright white with falling sunlight as I cross the gravel. I pull my jacket tighter round my wine-warmed body. I smell the cigarette smoke and look over at Finlay, hunched against the corner of the house. The tip glows orange under his face with a Hallowe'en light too early lit, weak by day. He is looking away down the glen, his eyes shrivelled in the wind. His head sits fragile on top of his burly puffa jacket. It looks like it might roll off if you pushed it, but he wouldn't really care. Finlay looks as if he doesn't care about anything, or cares too much. He is sick with it. The orange light flickers.

I keep walking.

The wind catches me as I come over the brow of the hill. It crashes into my ears, sealing them up. All I can hear is the hood of my jacket beating against my ears, thwack-a-wacka-thack. The lochan is dark navy, slurring into the oil-green heather. It has got darker while I was climbing. Night is coming. The air is thick and shadowy round about me, already the moon is risen high. It is a skinny moon, a fingernail trimming just.

Rust still leaks up from the vanished sun, tingeing the horizon in the west. The ridge of mountain tops glows weakly. Only the pockets of snow in high places sparkle. I look back, and already the lochan is murkier. The rocks at its edge are full of shadows. A grouse rises, skimming low across the pale ghostly grasses. A snatch of its cry hits me and then it is gone. I sit down in the heather, just here, and wait until the mountains have all turned black. I watch and wait until nothing is left and I feel the heavy presence of it all around me nonetheless. I press my face sideways into the heather stems, dry and stubby, and they rustle to remind me I am here. There will be no disappearing tonight.

My lungs are warm as I trudge back down the slope. Lights twinkle from the house. I stumble on stones in the darkness, far above. I have earned my loneliness at least.

I am halfway across the kitchen, arms tangled up in shrugging off my coat, when I see Alan. He must have seen me first, though, because he is standing up, unfurling into my eyes as I watch. My footsteps slow beneath me but still I am moving forward, like a curling stone sliding over the ice, carried by its own weight. By the time I come to a stop, it is too late.

'Hi,' he says.

I swallow my saliva. 'Alan.' Tug at my coat sleeves. It's coming off. I shake it and drape it over the back of a kitchen chair, smoothing out the hood. 'What a coincidence.'

'I'm sorry. I should have spoken to you first. I just wanted—' He stops as I look around to see where dad and Lucy and Finlay are. Soft voices carry from the drawing room down the hall. 'I wanted to see how you were.' Alan is putting his hands in the back pockets of his jeans.

'It's a family thing,' I say, staring at the range.

'Fair enough. That's what I thought. I mean, if you don't want me here, then I'll just go.'

'No. Sit down. Maybe I'm just surprised to see you.' I sit myself down, sharply, in one of the wooden chairs.

'Right.' He has to pull his hands back out now, as he sits down at the end of the table nearest me. He leans back, then leans forward, then slumps back again. 'So,' he says, 'I'm really sorry about your mum.' Leans forward. 'Your sister told me quite a lot.'

'I wouldn't listen too much to what Lucy says.'

He gives me a funny look. Then he drops it. 'Anyway, I'm sorry. I should have seen what was going on, and I should have helped you. I feel really bad.'

'There was nothing *going on*, Alan. There's nothing for you to feel bad about.' I look around, at the soft glow of light on the walls, the Turkish tiles stuck safely down in grout behind the range, the pewter tankards hanging from their appointed pegs. The china and glass is gone. Lucy has put tupperware pots in its place. There are only non-breakable items in the kitchen now.

Alan pushes his hand up behind his ear. 'Look, I still care about you. I don't believe what you said before.'

'When?'

'In the restaurant.'

I nod. I draw circles on the table with my finger, following the knots in the dead wood. Knots are where they have cut off the branches. I only found that out recently. I thought they were just patterns before.

'Do you want a drink?'

Looking serious as I approach him with tumblers in my hands, he clears his throat bravely. He's wearing a blazer with crimson and caramel stripes. It lends him the air of an Oxbridge fop, only he's chosen to wear it over a black tour T-shirt with holes in. I place the tumblers on the table, slosh in some vodka. Open a fizzing can of Coke.

'Nice jacket,' I say.

'Thanks.'

His voice sounds so incongruous in this house. We were always somewhere else.

'I hope you don't wear it late at night in the streets of Perth.'

'Fuck off.' He grins at me. I'm filled with the old adolescent urge to kiss him, but it doesn't last long. Fairly soon I merely want to sleep with him again. I attempt to smile at him over the top of my glass as I take a sip, although I didn't even want this drink.

'What's the matter?' he asks me. Because I'd forgotten that I never tried flirting with Alan.

'Nothing.' I put the glass back down on the table and take my hand away from it. 'How's Sarah?'

'She's fine. We split up before I went to London.'

I don't say anything. Neither of us speaks for a while.

'Did you want us to split up?' asks Alan. 'You and me, I mean.'

I shrug. And then I see him staring into his glass, swilling the drink round. So it's safe to say, 'No. Not really.'

'Me neither.'

'Oh well.'

'Everyone said you were after Lindsay Douglas.'

'I don't suppose it really matters now.'

'No.' He looks up at me. 'Do you still see him? Around?'

'No.'

'So you dane have a boyfriend? You didn't say.'

'No.' I rearrange my hands. 'I don't really want one.'

'Oh.'

'How about you?'

'London isnae very conducive to relationships. Either that, or nobody fancies me. I went out with this one lassie, like, but she kind of lost interest after an hour or two. So there you go. Anyway.' He looks around. After a while he says, 'It must be funny being you, Vanessa.'

'Not especially amusing, no.'

'Ha. No, I mean, it must be funny being so totally unimpressed by anything. Except for books written by dead Russians. You're not really like other girls, are you?'

'I think I'll take that as a compliment. Most girls I know are fucking idiots.'

'Aye, but the female intimacy – in some ways it must be nice.'

'You're the expert.'

'Just that the girls at college always seem to have this closeness. Don't know if it's real, is it.' I say nothing. 'Camaraderie,' he persists. 'The girls at school, that big clique of them. You weren't ever part of anything like that, were you.'

I tap the table top with my fingernail.

His cheeks are colouring slightly. 'I'm sorry,' he says.

'Oh, it's okay. Anyway, you're right, I'm not very good at being a girl. Maybe there was a training course I missed.'

He looks at me and says, 'Life isn't a problem to be solved. It's a mystery to be lived.'

'Where did you get that from?'

'Church.'

'Since when were you religious?'

He shrugs. 'I'm not.'

I pull wistful eyes and say, 'Will you come to my room?'

I feel sad just beforehand and I almost don't go through with it. But I want to, I do. Alan kisses my neck, and I run my hands down hard through his hair, on to the backs of his shoulders, my fingers trying to find a hold in the hard muscle. Trying to find a hold in him. The pillowcase is crisp against my cheek. And then my chest is suddenly cold as he pulls away.

'I'm not sure about this,' he says. 'I don't think we should have sex.'

For God's sake. 'Why not?'

'It just wouldn't be right.' He sighs. 'You're like this thing in my head that's perfect, and if we have sex – it'll spoil everything.' He strokes my thigh. 'You're my ideal girl, see. My ideal world.' He smiles a funny little smile like holly, gleaming and prickling and naughty and sad as Christmas.

I sit up. 'Don't you think that's a little unhealthy?'

'No.'

I sit back on my heels. 'Do you want to marry me?'

He grins. 'No way. You're a fruitcake.'

'Then shut up.' Shut up, because we have to do this quickly. I know exactly what Alan is talking about, and that's why we're going to do it. I don't want his perfect ghost in my head any more. So I lean forward and work my mouth down his body, and I'm amazed how much easier I find it these days, now I've learnt how to breathe at the same time. And the world is all Alan, trying to breathe quietly somewhere up above me as I turn my head in this weird place that isn't mine.

I'm curled around him like a baby and his hand is pushing its way between my legs like something just as small. Like there's towels and gin wrapped round us, I'm rising and falling and none. His fingers brush it all away cept him.

Pulling me back, holding my head in his hands. He could uproot me, and I'm scared. But he just strokes my nose, kisses my mouth, tasting of him and relieved. Laying me back on the cloth, he kisses me harder and harder. Sighs as he slides on top of me. Sighs a different sigh as he slides inside me. Oh. Oh. Vowels fall out my mouth. That's it. Right inside me. I think he's actually done it as I start to cry.

'No, no don't stop. No. It's fine. It's good.'

Oh yes. Very good. My eyes are open because I want to see it's him. Alan in his body in mine. And I'm actually in it. I'm here as sweat collects on his forehead, drips and splashes on to my cheek. He is breathing hard and looking at me like I'm the one who's doing it. Drip. He's trying to hold on mto me. It's working, I actually think it is. I'm out of me and into a shared pot as his hips rock into mine. Red hot and surprising. He sees it in my eyes and laughs and pushes faster. Hold tight. Hold on. I'm still here. I'm staying, this time.

I am leaking.

He is folding me up in his arms and his breath is warm on the side of my neck. Beneath my ear it is resting like a tide beneath a rock, carving with feathers. I am tied to him by the hair on my body and the teeth in my mouth. I am falling, and there are pillows at the bottom. I close my fingers round his arm and take it with me. My family are far away.

The darkness is still full when I wake up. These are expensive curtains, well lined, and we drew them closed last night. Alan seems miles away, on the other side of the bed, his back raised against me. A boulder in the sand, lightly snoring. I move close, pressing my body into the length of him, and the sheets seem very loud. I hold my breath, but he is still sleeping. So I just lie here, for ages, with my nose in his skin, and then after a bit I get bored and get up. My scuba watch reads seven and a quarter. I asked for it because I like being ready to go deep-sea diving as I wash the dishes. Anyway, it is early still. I return to Alan's back and close my eyes.

'What you doing?'

'Nothing. Go back to sleep.'

'You going somewhere?'

'No. Go back to sleep.'

He rolls over and pulls me gently towards his chest. We both lie here with our eyes closed, pretending to be asleep. It is too early to get up, so there is not much else to be done.

Alan. This should have made less of him, not more. It has turned out wrong, for reasons I didn't think of. A hollowness in my belly is longing to give myself away. I close my eyes and in my head I say: hormones working over time, any port in a storm, you can never go back. While my heart just aches for losing him.

'Are you awake?' says Alan.

'Yeah. Are you?'

'No.'

I smile into the smell of him. He smells of the taste of wet metal. 'Do you remember making me lick the roof of the shed in the rain?'

A sleepy laugh is rising in his chest. 'Hey, you could have done the bet.'

'I can't even remember what it was. The bet. What was it?'

'I canna remember either.'

'Just the forfeit.' I roll on to my back and breathe out. 'God, that was ages ago. Do you remember how we used to all hang out and play together? We had that base in my dad's study.'

'Course I remember. Your sister was just as bossy, but. And you were just as sexy. Oh man, those pink dungarees. Baby, baby, baby.'

I lie here smiling. As if the past was something sweet and not a place where everyone fought and was scared just as much as now, only not having the power to change a thing. And I quite like this version, so we play some more. And then I say, 'Do you remember when Morna poured lemonade in my sister's hair?'

'Oh aye, cause she wouldn't let her play with the new Sindy.'

'And then when Lucy didn't want her at her birthday party. Do you remember that?' It isn't funny, but I keep bashing away. 'Do you remember my mum and your dad having that big row? And everyone being banned from seeing each other. Lucy said she was glad.'

'Aye, well.'

'I bet Morna did as well, did she? I bet Morna was glad about it.' I can hear the meanness in my voice.

'No, not really.'

'I thought afterwards, Morna and Lucy are too alike, you know. They're both so full of themselves.'

'Leave our sisters out of it.' He is sitting up. I have annoyed him. It was this easy. I lie flaccid in the pillows as he rises, swinging his legs on to the floor and growing up towards the ceiling in the dark.

He moves across the room and then it all stops. I can't see him at all and I can't hear him moving. He is gone into space. He is growing up the walls and over the ceiling and down to meet me, he is coming, he is coming to kill me—

'Alan?'

—my voice is thin and taut. I don't like the sound of it. There isn't any answer.

The curtains glide apart and daylight falls in. It seems diluted, casting Alan in a painting rather than a photograph as he stands to one side of the window, still holding the curtain cord.

'It looks like there ought to be a plaque there instead of a window,' I say. 'The way you're standing.'

'Does it?' He doesn't let go of the cord. He doesn't look very impressed.

'Yes. It looks as if you're pronouncing the world open. Or maybe just the morning.' White light drifts outside the windows, sun shifting through clouds. 'Anyway, you don't look very happy about it.'

'I was just wondering if you were being unpleasant on purpose or by accident, and wondering which would be worse.'

His eyes are scrutinising my face front, but I don't know what it is they're looking for. I don't know what to put there at all, even after all this time. He turns away again. 'Oh, Vanessa,' he sighs, standing there with his back to me, and it sounds like the saddest name in the world. It makes me want to cry, the way he says it. I huddle into the wallpaper, pulling the duvet round me, waiting for him to leave.

After a while he begins to speak, quietly, reciting something.

'I know your rising up and your sitting down,' he murmurs, 'your going out and your coming in.' I don't know what to say. 'The frenzy of your rage against me and your arrogance. Your arrogance.' He turns to face me and his eyes are so still, and solemn, like he wants me to sign something. 'Have come to my ears. I will put a ring in your nose and a hook in your lips,' he says, 'and I will take you back by the road on which you have come.' The weightiness of his words wraps around me, horrifically comforting. So grave and heavy. You could trust words like that, too much, because tears are welling up behind my nose now and I look away. Everything is falling apart, I can feel it go, sliding out through the gaps between my ribs.

Alan is right in front of me, his bare arms gripping my shoulders, he is saying my name, asking my name, over and over, as if I am a question I can answer. 'Vanessa? Are you okay? Say something, Vee. I didn't mean to upset you. You okay?' I nod my head. He puts his arms around me, and my mouth opens against the solidness of his chest. I let it hang there, just relieved that I did not cry. 'I'm sorry sweetheart,' he whispers. He laughs briefly, and it shakes my cheek. 'It just reminded me of you so much,' he says. 'But I didn't mean to upset you.' I am listening to his heart, beating steady. He is explaining now, how he went to the church to draw, and someone was reading it out. He is quiet for a bit, then whispers, 'As if God had met you already, four thousand years ago.' I can hear him smiling as he strokes my head. I let him, wishing the words had been his own.

'There's no such thing as God,' I say. He kisses my shoulder and I let myself stay here, resting, for a while.

And then I am feeling a bit better, so I pull away from him and get to my feet. Pad across the carpet and stand in front of my bookshelf, pretending to be browsing along it. I stroke the spine of *20th Century English Poetry*, but really I am just wanting Alan to look at my naked behind and fancy me, to stop feeling sorry for me.

I'm thinking that it's worked, as I hear him moving behind me. He is coming closer, coming to wrap his arms around me. And then he veers sideways to pull the towel off the peg on the back of my door. He is holding it out to me, saying, 'Don't know about you, but I'm fucking freezing.' He doesn't want to see me naked any more, my breasts are not novel. Alan doesn't want me, he just wants to help me. He smiles, but he doesn't know what at as I take the towel from his hands and wrap it round. I leave the bedroom door open behind me.

In the bathroom I empty Lucy's expensive bottles over my skin. By breakfast I expect I will be beautiful. I rub the stuff in hard. Fuck Alan, fuck him. Suds run slippy round my feet. I bang my wrist hard against the tiled wall, to make it feel like me again. It feels better, so I do it again, and then I get out and dry my hair and go back into the room.

'Are you okay about last night?' he asks, just as I'm pulling up my jeans. 'Aren't you wearing any knickers?'

'Of course I'm fine about last night.' As if the whole thing wasn't my doing anyway. My abruptness makes him look at me as if he thinks he's managed to hurt me, so I smile as genuinely as I can.

'I was worrying you'd regret it,' he explains.

'No. It was fun, wasn't it?' I'm saying it mild and gentle so as he'll believe me.

'Aye.' He looks at me hard and then he seems to shake himself down, saying is it okay if he uses the shower and I say of course. I am feeling high. Until he disappears into the bathroom and I'm alone in the bedroom. I think I might leave him here. Quickly I pull my bra and top on, the sleeveless black silk T-shirt; I pull on clean socks and then my boots. I know it's cold outside but the morning is hot this side of my falling hair. I can't find my hair band. Never mind. I sit on the end of the bed, ready to go. I can hear him in the shower across the passage. I wonder what he was looking at out the window.

I glance at the door and then I go to look, but there's nothing there.

The thick brocade curtains remind me of mum, so I stay at the window a little longer. And then I make the bed, and then I sit on it and wait for Alan.

'You're still here,' he says when he enters the room, and that surprises me. It makes me wonder what else he knows about me. It makes me wonder why he is still here, never mind me. My fingers trace over the bedcover, enjoying the feel of the satin quilt like perfect skin. I nod. My skin is quilted. He tells me he has missed me. As if I am a real person.

Lucy trills her fingers at us from the kitchen table. I think about ignoring her and then I see the way she has already dropped back into conversation with my father, nodding vigorously as she listens and then tapping the table with her coffee spoon as she speaks, while Finlay tries to look involved. I start towards them. I glance over my shoulder, feeling the space at my back, and see Alan still stranded in the middle of the room. I jerk my head and pull out a chair.

'Morning, Vanessa,' says Lucy. I hate her. That is dad's job to say that.

'Hello there,' says Finlay, standing up and kissing my cheek.

'Is Alan joining us?' dad enquires.

'Yeah.'

'*Quelle surprise*,' smiles Lucy, looking all smug and knowing. 'Alan! Did you sleep well?'

'Aye. Thanks.'

'Well, sit down,' says dad. 'Sit down. Jolly good kedgeree.'

'Where's Bryony?'

Dad pretends he hasn't heard me, just takes another sip of coffee.

'She's having breakfast in her room,' says Lucy, as if she's lying.

'Oh. Wish I'd thought of that.'

'Is our company so dreadful?' asks dad. Everything about him seems peculiar, even the way he's talking. Like he's trying far too hard.

'No. How are you this morning, Finlay?'

He smiles. 'Oh, much the same as yesterday.' And you can tell just by looking at him that this is true. That he wants my sister more than anything, that it's an ongoing affliction that could run for years.

Lucy looks shocked. 'Oh God, I haven't introduced you. Alan, this is Finlay. Finlay, Alan. Alan lives in the little house down the road.' She beams at my ex-lover. 'Tell us about art college, Al.'

'Oh, it's not so bad. Maybe a wee bit wanky, but on the whole it's cool.'

'London's brilliant, isn't it. I love shopping in London, compared to Edinburgh, I mean you can just get the most amazing stuff. And all those restaurants, and clubs, there's always so much *going on* isn't there. You really feel like you're where the *action* is.' She shivers with a passable impression of delight. 'And how's Morna?'

Alan casts a wry smile in her direction. 'Oh, Morna's fine.'

'What's she doing these days?' Lucy turns to Finlay and explains how Alan's sister and she used to play together! Like that, with an exclamation mark, as if it is shocking or a joke.

'She's working in Edinburgh,' says Alan. 'She's a PA.'

'Oh, good for her. One of those business parks, is it? The Gyle, that's it. It's got a shopping centre attached. Not a very good one, but it must give the office workers somewhere to go in their lunch hour, does it?'

'I don't know. She's along Castle Terrace.'

'Oh well.'

247

'They send her over to Germany a lot and Morna's mad about Berlin. Like you and London.'

Lucy smiles. She sips her mineral water.

'Anyhow, at least one of us is earning some money,' says Alan. 'I think my folks are quite relieved.'

Dad laughs far too loudly.

Alan is asking Lucy lots of questions about the fashion course she's doing. I butter bits of torn croissant and turn to dad. 'How long are you staying?'

He puts down his cup. 'As long as it takes, Nessie. Mmm. Margie Grant rang earlier. Made me burn the toast. Gillian said she'd love to see you.'

'That was nice of her.'

'I don't suppose nice comes into it. I expect she just likes you.'

I can't help laughing, and dad smiles, glad to have cheered me up. Humbly he picks up his cup again, the big red stranger. I would throw myself in front of him, I would stand between him and the world, if I didn't know he can't see it anyway. It can't touch him. Invisible men can't fire bullets. They just meander through the back of his days dumbly.

Finlay puts his arm around the back of my sister's chair and she doesn't even look up. His fingers brush her shoulder and she just keeps talking. I look at Finlay, but he is busy watching Lucy's mouth open and close. Alan listens, seeming interested in what she has to say, interjecting correctly. He's a natural. The ease with which he does it makes me ridiculous as I pretend to contentedly survey the pans on the shelf above the range. Mum couldn't break them.

'I'm going to brush my teeth.'

'Will you be okay?' asks Lucy, as if I might be about to string myself from the ceiling with dental floss.

'Of course I will.'

The cool air of the hall hits my cheeks and I realise how flushed I am. My stomach is feeling empty in spite of all the croissant.

'What's the rush?' asks Alan, and I'm feeling too sick even to shrug so I just say that I don't feel well.

'You should have said.'

'I just need to lie down on my own for a bit.'

'Do you want me to go?'

'Yes.'

'Okay.' He stops and stands still, his shadow vague on the gleaming flagstones. His hair still damp. 'Well.'

'Did you have a jacket with you?'

'Not really.'

'Are you going back down to London?'

'Thought I'd spend a few days with my folks, you know. Head through and say hi to the boys on my way back down.'

'Right. That.'

'What?'

'Oh, nothing. I'm just – not feeling well. Excuse me.'

'I'll come with you. Up to your room.'

'No.'

He reaches out and rests his palm on the side of my head, cupping my hair, and I think how nothing has really changed. I step forward and kiss the side of his mouth and then I move away.

'Can I see you again?' he asks. 'I know it's not the best time, but if you'd like. Because I still can't be doing without you.' He throws the words out as if they are nothing. I watch him do it.

'Yeah. That would be nice.'

'Great. So, I'll see you this evening, then.' And he lurches forward, holding me tight, pressing my head to his chest. His hands and arms embrace me. And this time it is him who pulls away, partly because I can't move. He is looking at me like I'm

249

still his and I'm just about to go off on a skiing holiday. Like he's saying take care, and come home.

'I'll give you a call,' I say. I mean, I could, if I wanted to.

He just nods and turns round and starts walking.

Chapter Ten

I try not to make a noise as I climb the stairs, so as not to disturb sleeping dogs and the morning. And then I hear him in their old bedroom, up ahead. At least, I hope it's dad. I hope it's dad and not Lucy, with her dusters and notepads. Someone is in there, shuffling sporadically on the carpet.

I sneak the door open slowly. Edge my throbbing face into the room, wishing my eyes were nearer the edge of my head so I wouldn't have to stick out this far before I can see. Oh, it's dad all right. I notice again how much older he looks. It's a long time since I unwrapped an electronic keyboard at Christmas. Mum said he probably got it cheap in duty free, but I didn't see that it made a difference if he did.

'Dad?'

He looks up, not in the least bit surprised to see me. But then, why would he be? He knows I live here, doesn't he? 'Hello, sweetheart. What are you doing?'

'I was just looking for you.'

He looks perplexed. And then he rubs it out. I can almost hear the voice inside his head saying, *oh well, not to worry.*

'Shouldn't dwell, but – it's rather sad, all this, isn't it,' he says, looking at me and then turning to look out of their old window.

I fidget with my fingers in my palm.

He doesn't say anything. Just stands there, staring out over the garden. After a while, he says, 'We really were in love with each other, you know. When we married.'

I have not seen him like this before. He seems detached from his usual buckets of stones, the rocks of blissful conservatism that hold his tarpaulin down. I feel afraid for him as he carries on, thinking maybe I shouldn't have come in here. 'These things just seem to happen,' says dad. 'Our generation married young, and people change.'

I pick up the silver nail scissors from the dressing table. They have not been packed or wrapped. I open and close the blades. The screw is a little stiff.

He turns towards me, asks, 'What do you think? Nobody really asks you.'

It lames me for a second, till I find a question. 'Did mum change?'

He doesn't even bother answering me. Just puts his back to me, and then I notice his shoulders are trembling.

'Dad?'

Shaking, shaking, helpless tree. Car that will not start. Then goes too fast. Father who never shakes, shakes like she did. Shakes like I have. He lets out a deep cry. Out of control.

I slide against the wall and close my eyes and wait for him to stop.

'She changed,' he croaks, 'she changed and I let her.' I can hear the air and water sobbing in his throat. 'I lost her,' he intones, over and over.

I open my eyes and watch the quiet convulsions in his neck.

His body solidifies. I see him beginning to turn towards me and I close my eyes again, to save us both the embarrassment. I feel him looking at me, and then not.

He is sitting on their old bed, and his face is wrecked. He is staring at mum's everyday life, set out innocently on her bedside table. Her books, her tissues, her spectacles (spare pair), the incongruous tapestry she was working on. Mum, sitting quietly with an embroidery needle, drawing the thread carefully through her fabric. I know it wasn't her fault. She never meant to hurt us.

The scissors are on the floor, where I dropped them, and I stoop to pick them up. The blades open and close.

She was not bad.

'You shouldn't have left,' I say.

Dad sighs. His voice is shaky. 'It's hard to understand at your age. When love is still rather an idealistic thing.' I laugh out loud and he looks at me, sharply. 'For Christ's sake,' he says, and I shut up and he carries on. 'We thought it would help our marriage, to be apart a little. If anything, your mother was keener on the idea than I was.' How little he chose to know her. I almost smile. 'Things weren't perfect between us, Vanessa. I suppose we thought that, if we saw less of each other, we might be able to prevent things from coming to a head and breaking down altogether. Keep things amicable. For you lot.' He sounds almost tired of his own excuse.

His watery blue eyes fix upon my face. I suppose it's as good a place as any for them to rest. 'But it's important you know that I really did love her,' he says. 'It's important that you know that.' It is meant to cheer me, but instead I am sickened. Understandable, to abandon something you never cared about. But how depressing to give up on something you truly loved. How useless. I rub my thumb hard against my wrist. Dad looks at his hands.

A sudden shower slings upon the window, making us look up. Rain blows in drifts beyond the glass. It is battering the skylights in the attic. The glen fades out of sight behind its mist. There is nothing but rain, it takes up all the world, and I am glad of its pure hammering inside my head. Water flows down the window-panes, melting us in.

'Anyway,' says dad, after a silence, 'I don't think there's much fruit to be had from discussing this with you.' So prim. The horse is out of the fire, but the ash is sticking in his hair. He shakes his head and flicks his tail. The rain is spluttering to a stop.

He picks up her embroidery, unfinished in its frame. Sun washes over him, twice as bright as before. He is standing up and holding the embroidery out to me. 'Do you want this?'

I look straight at him. 'No,' I say, and I say it for mum.

Dad inspects it more closely, with a curious lack of interest. 'Perhaps Bryony would like it.'

Lucy and Finlay have been busy in the kitchen. They are engaged in an unseasonal campaign of spring cleaning, mirthful purifiers in rubber gloves. I can glimpse them in the garage now. Lucy's laugh rings out around the sunshine. I open the cupboard door. The canisters are gone, the lining paper wiped down.

Two mugs are turned upside down on the draining board. The canisters bob soaking in the sink. Oh mother, your cupboards are bare and your heart is cold. Your hearth. They have been drinking cups of tea over your dead body.

I go stand in the hall like a child.

Mum. I'm so sorry and so very relieved that you're gone. In the end, look at me, I am relieved. Relieved of the laws of gravity. I am lurching into space, queasily without you. I float through the house in my spacesuit.

The drawing room is empty. It is full of upholstery and mahogany, cushions and carpet, and portraits, the young faces of the dead. But it has the curious stillness of an uninhabited place, ticking over by itself as if it's got a mind of its own. The air sighs, and then it just seems to drift away. I am scared, for no reason. Indecisive sunlight smudges the carpet and shines on the dark wooden arms of the chairs, petering out and returning. Over and over. My tummy rumbles.

'I thought it was best like this,' Lucy explains, standing in the doorway.

'Sure. Where's Bryony?' I feel anxious, like she might have been spirited away again.

'I'm going up for her separately. She's still getting ready.'

'What for?'

'Life, I think,' says Lucy earnestly. 'Tell me, how did you leave things with Alan?'

'I don't really think that's your business, Lucy.'

She smiles back at me. 'So you're seeing him again.'

I shrug. 'Maybe.'

'I'd be glad if you were, you know. I'm not such a snob as I used to be. I arranged for him to come, didn't I?' Lucy turns on her expensive heel and heads off in search of the littlest one. The room swoops in towards me, and when it rushes back out it seems to suck at my skin. Breathe, Vanessa, breathe.

I look around me, smelling flowers. A vase of yellow roses, cornflowers and sea thistles, on the little table stranded by the door. We're long past the flowering season. Finlay must have bought them for Lucy, imported from a warmer place. Or grown under plastic. How do they do these things?

Dad pushes the door open. Nods at me, puts his whisky down on the table. Pulls a book from the cabinet, with deliberation, and settles down. Making himself at home.

He has rinsed his eyes and thinks it is splendid when Finlay comes in with the coffee pot. Finlay leaves us to it. We sit and wait. Out of nowhere, dad slaps his knee and says, 'Do you take sugar? I forget.' His book sits open on the sofa next to him. I can see his fingers itching for the page. I can read this small restraint. He drums his knee to mark its poor return from me.

Lucy is opening the door and, like puppets, we look up. Her face is solemn. She is holding Bryony's hand.

'Hi,' I say, trying to smile warmly. Bryony snorts and chews her lip. It's almost the only bit of fat left on her.

I become aware of Lucy watching me. I suspect she is enjoying herself immensely. She is bending over the coffee table now, saying, 'Oh good, Finlay remembered your hot water. Here you go, Bryony.' Showing off.

'So,' says dad, 'we've all come here to close the door on the past and make some progress. To make some practical decisions on the future as a family.'

Lucy stirs milk into his coffee.

'We stopped being a family when you flew off to Saudi,' I point out.

'That's enough,' says dad, in a gentle voice I didn't know he owned, a secret shadow underneath the table.

'And don't think you can sit here vilifying mum just because she's dead, you can't blame it all on her.' We all could have been fine.

'Oh *shut up*,' snaps Bryony, and she's looking at me.

'What?'

'Right,' interrupts Lucy.

'No, shut up. I want to talk to Bryony.'

'It's a bit late.' Bryony is staring at the wall. 'You could have started caring a bit sooner. You knew fine what was going on. At first I thought you didn't, but you did. You knew fine.'

'About what?'

'You just ignored it.'

'It's okay,' murmurs Lucy. 'It's okay, Bry. Daddy and me took you away, didn't we.'

Bryony sips from her cup of hot water in silence. She whispers something inaudible into the china. Shaking her head, and I am sure she is laughing at me and I really don't like it.

Nobody says anything. We all just sit here, dad constantly glancing at Lucy to see what he should do. But Lucy is sitting calm as a doped sea, head slightly bowed, a funny smile dancing over her face, like she's just waiting and she knew this would happen. She's just waiting.

Bryony starts to look uneasy, and shifts in the chair. She unglues her eyes from the cup, flitting a glance to Judith Henderson and back. Then another, this time to the floor. And in no time they are going everywhere, those little spiky looks, javelins darting into every point in the room except our eyes. 'Sorry,' she says. 'I'm sorry.' She bites her lip again.

'It's fine,' says Lucy, touching her thigh. 'We all understand. Even Vanessa—'

'Don't say you're sorry,' I tell her, trying to override my big sister. 'Bryony. You haven't done anything wrong. Don't say you're sorry.'

Lucy gets up and bends forward, obscuring Bryony from view as she puts her arms around her in the way I never could. 'There. It's okay.'

'We're all here for you,' says dad, and I stare at him. Lucy withdraws and now I can see Bryony gazing at dad too, before turning her eyes on me as if to say *well well*.

Bryony doesn't speak again, just sits in the chair trying not to exist, a ghostly little carapace floating on our lips.

Lucy and dad explain the options with the house to us. Bryony fails to muster any kind of enthusiasm for what's going on, but listlessly nods and squeezes a flap of cardigan. Dad is telling us he will be continuing to live in Frankie's house in Fulham; that the most sensible thing would be for him to sell the house up here and buy us each a flat, except Lucy, who can have the flat in Edinburgh; that we can keep the cottage on Mull; that he won't be able to take much furniture with him to London as Frankie obviously has all her own furniture there; and does anyone have a problem with the sale of the house going ahead? Bryony?

Bryony just sits there, looking at him as if he's still speaking.

'Bryony? Are you going to be okay about this?'

She nods as if she doesn't understand the question. All the time looking to see if a nod is the correct response.

'Are you sure?'

She just stares at him now.

'I think Bryony will be fine,' says Lucy. 'Vanessa?' How come Lucy is asking me? Presumptuous cow.

'Sure. Whatever.' But I'm thinking – *oh house*. The only bit of me that was ever certain still lives here, and I can't bear the thought of it going.

'Now, Bryony, this concerns you,' says dad, slowly and carefully for her to understand. 'Have you thought any more about the clinic we talked about?'

Bryony nods, shifting her weight sideways.

'Do you feel it would be constructive?' Dad's voice has shrunk to a whisper. It's like he's trying to make it small enough to match her, small enough to fit inside her shrunken frame. She nods again. Coughs out.

'I know, I know,' says dad. My understanding father. 'I'm glad you want to try this, sweetheart. And Essex isn't too far from London, so I'll be able to come and visit as often as you like, so you can rely on plenty of moral support. Frankie would love to have you to stay, eventually. I know you and she get on. She's very fond of you.'

'Is she?' Pathetic, almost laughing.

'Frankie's so lovely,' says Lucy. 'We had so much fun going for lunch together.' Bryony goes back to squeezing the cardigan.

'How's the writing going, Bry?'

Bryony glares at me. 'Fine.'

'You still writing a book?'

'No. I just write poems now.'

'Why?'

'*Why?*'

'Yeah.'

'I don't know. They're just nicer, you know.'

'How?'

'They're smaller. There isn't so much crap blocking the view.' She laughs in miniature. 'Poems are thinner.'

'I'd love to see them,' says Lucy.

'You wouldn't like them.'

'And Vanessa,' dad interrupts, trying to keep things on track, 'what are your plans for the future?'

I remember Stuart asking me the same question in July, and it seems like years ago. 'I don't have any.'

'It might be an idea to start thinking. About careers. Your qualifications, or lack thereof, needn't necessarily be a drawback.' I love the way dad talks. His conversation always sounds like the final draft. 'You just need to decide what you want to do and then go about getting your foot in the door, so to speak. You aren't stupid, and if you can get experience then no one will be too bothered about exam results, I shouldn't suppose. As long as you don't want to be a doctor or a lawyer, but you aren't the type for those sorts of professions anyway.'

'I honestly don't know what I want to do, dad.'

'Well, make up your mind. You can't drift around for the rest of your life. How about journalism?'

Why? Is that the usual profession of choice for difficult daughters? 'I'm not really into writing,' I explain. 'And anyway, it's very competitive.'

'So are you, as far as I can remember.'

'Things have changed.' Have they? 'I like photography.' I haven't picked up a camera since Christmas '92.

'Splendid.'

'But I think I'd like to go travelling for a bit. I haven't really done much. Maybe it'll clear my head.' Yeah, right.

'Yes, you could photograph your travels.' Dad looks so relieved. I can almost hear him trying out the phrases in his head: *And my second daughter is a photojournalist, she's travelling at the moment. And my second daughter is in the Hindu Kush, she's a photographer.* He's seeing coffee table books with my name on, he's saying, 'I think that's a very sound idea, Nessa. Where would you like to go?'

'Spain.'

'*Spain?*'

'Oh. Well. I suppose I could go down to Morocco. And then – across Africa?'

'Ah! I see,' he approves. 'Yes, that sounds like a good plan. You'd be able to photograph all the Berbers.'

'Yeah.' I don't even have a camera. I don't even particularly want to go travelling. It's just that there's nothing left to do, and maybe I can put things off for another year or two. 'But I don't think I'll actually do people, dad.'

'What?'

'I'd rather photograph the plants.'

'*Why?*' asks Lucy scornfully. 'I think people are *so* interesting. I could sit and people watch all day long.' This is the biggest load of rubbish ever. Lucy would get bored rigid watching other people after all of five minutes.

'Good for you,' I say. But there is no way you would ever catch me going up to people and trying to take their picture. Imagine what might happen. For a start they would all look at you. And then they might start saying things. They might want money, or they might want to ask you about being a photographer, or they might get angry, or they might invite you to drink coffee with them. And you just wouldn't have any way of knowing. I think I will photograph plants. Plants and mountains, the Atlas Mountains, and deserts like dad's.

'What sort of camera do you have?' asks dad.

'Nikon,' I lie. I had a pocket Canon but I lost it two years ago. 'Anyway, I'm mainly going just to travel. Not to photograph.'

'Gillian Grant had a great time in Nepal. She's got some wonderful photographs, terribly pretty children. You could ask her about it when you see her,' says Dad. And thankfully Lucy produces a plate of sandwiches and my future is off the hook.

Bryony eats half an egg mayonnaise triangle.

There is masses of food left over. Bryony holds out a plate. 'Lucy, you've only had three halves. Do you want another one?'

'No,' says Lucy nervously. 'I'm fine.' Adds, 'I'm just full, that's all.'

Bryony looks unimpressed. So I say I'll have another one, and take the plate away. She still can't help glancing at Lucy, sizing up her thighs.

'I like a light lunch,' pronounces dad, licking mayonnaise from his pale coarse lip. 'You know, I think I might have some Stilton. Crackers. Where do the crackers live these days?'

I go to find them.

We all have to make small talk until dad has finished his food. Then Lucy says that we've got to discuss the assets, which turns out to be the paintings and chests of drawers. She has drawn up a list of the house contents which dad doesn't want and which he would like to be divided between us. Bryony and I are handed copies. Lucy instructs us to write our names at the top, and then write a number against each item, starting with 1 for the item which we would most like to have.

So we sit here for half an hour, playing bingo with bits of memory. Bryony keeps looking up to see if she's the only one still trying to work out what she wants.

I chew the pen and write things down, and all the time the feeling of leaving Alan behind is swelling up inside me.

Lucy finishes first; but then, she knew what was coming. She organised it all; she has thought it through. Lucy, anchoring herself as Bryony and I drift away. Drawing lines round herself and closing the hatch. She puts down her pen. She is done.

I walk around the house alone. I sit on the bed in the room that is my bedroom. I sit with my back against the wall and hunch my knees up in front of me, like I used to. This was my home.

She is not here.

I leaf through my childhood diaries, lay out stale and fuzzy photographs, kneeling on the floor, hunting for something that

I do not find. Some explanation. Exculpation, more like. I smile at my own grim fooling. Finally crank my legs out from under me, ankles pained numb from bending the wrong way for so long.

'It wasn't my fault,' says Bryony, lost between the walls of her bedroom. They are smothered with pieces of paper, her drawings spreading, blooming into space.

I didn't even know she'd heard me come in. She sits with her back to me, the setting sun making her insubstantial hair seem like a solid sheet of glass. Colour lost in the brightness, it simply reflects.

'Can I sit down?'

'Why? You usually run away.'

I don't answer.

Bryony turns round, examining my eyes for a second or two. 'I suppose you're trying to be clever,' she says. She gazes at the armchair as I sit down behind her on the nearest edge of the bed. Bryony's bedspread is a different colour from the one in my room. It's the colour of butterflies: sky blue. I look up and now I can see the side of Bryony's face, the hollowness of her cheek and the slackness of her ear lobe, hair falling behind it. She looks very tense. 'Why did you come to my room?' she asks.

'To talk to you. To say hi.'

'Well don't.'

'Okay.'

We both sit here for a while, and I watch Bryony's back moving slightly every now and again. She moves as if her body is terribly heavy, as if she is a heavily plated armadillo and not a few dear sticks lashed together with sinew. The sun is sinking. You can't see shadows any more, just sweet marshmallow colours dragged over the glen outside. You get a good view from here, right down over the garden and across the river to the hills beyond. In my room you can only see the side of the hill and Alan's house obliquely in the distance.

In the room, everything is grey.

Bryony glances around nervously. 'I always loved her,' she announces. 'I always really, really loved mum. Did you?'

'Yes.'

Her voice drops. 'I wish she was still alive.'

'Do you?'

She nods. 'I don't know why she loved Lucy so much, though. Lucy was always her favourite, wasn't she?'

'Do you think?'

'Oh, come on Vanessa.' The way she speaks surprises me. 'You know she was. And Lucy said to me that she never loved mum at all, not even when we were little and dad was home. She said you just had to learn how to play her. I wish mum was alive so I could tell her. Except she probably wouldn't believe me.'

'You wouldn't tell her.'

'No. Probably not.'

'She'd go mental.'

'Lucy says she had mental health problems.'

'Lucy thinks unhappiness is a disease. It isn't, it's just the flip side of happiness. You have to spin, don't you? To keep moving. It's only human.'

Bryony picks philosophically at the dirt behind her fingernails. 'You could just lie still, I suppose. There's nothing wrong with lying still, right side up.'

I watch the last light snagging on water as the river runs under the trees on the other side of the road. Curled leaves hang like paper earrings from the crumbling lichened branches, falling as I watch. 'There's no such thing as perfect,' I say. 'Not in the real world. You think you can find the perfect position and just hold it, for the rest of your life? It won't happen, Bryony. Things change, they just can't help themselves.'

'You haven't changed. You're just the same as always.' Her voice takes on that sing-song tone. 'Locked in a box, running away.' She laughs, and her laugh is surprisingly liquid given the tautness of her face. 'I envy you your capacity for self-delusion,' she says, and catches my surprise. 'You're not the only one with fancy words for things, Vanessa.' Swallows. 'Dad and Lucy think it's your fault, you know. Not mine.'

I say nothing.

'Calling the ambulance too late on purpose.' She sits there, picking at the quilt listlessly. As if her accusations are boring to her. Horror shoots through the muscles of my calves, in a reflex. And then it subsides, and it surprises me, how little I really care what dad and Lucy think of me. There is only one piece of familial care left inside me, somewhere behind my knee, and it is all wrapped up in Bryony. I grit my jaw.

'It's okay,' she says. 'I know that wasn't how it happened, Ness. You wouldn't have done that. I know you loved her too. Like I do.' She looks me in the eye and there's a challenge in her face. She wants an admittance, or denial. She wants me to choose. 'I know exactly how you loved her,' says Bryony, with a trembling voice. 'I know exactly.'

I get up and cross the room to close Bryony's curtains. Outside, the stars are stretching into focus through the gloaming. My sister sits quietly on the bed behind me. I stand at the window, nothing special after all. But then I knew, didn't I, wasn't there always a sneaking hum of it in the air? Wasn't I always the great dissembler?

I close my eyes as I close the curtains on that land, longing for Alan's body again, for its certitude.

When I look up she is still there, watching me. Sad anger flickers in my heart and dies. For a moment I wanted to snap her bony arm in two, but what would I have done with the pieces?

'Mum used to have such long hair,' says Bryony, pulling it from nowhere to wave across my face. Mum's hair: the sleek rope swing of it crashing down her spine. But if you read your books you know long hair never comes to any good. Look at Samson and Rapunzel.

'She let us plait it on the beach, remember.'

I nod. I remember her big sunglasses too, on the dashboard that day, and the black beach towel in the cupboard, and the straw bag on the hook in the cloakroom. I remember it all being hers on the sand, with juice and Penguin biscuits. Me and Bryony plaiting her hair and dad, with a harder body and softer face, saying she looked like Bo Derek. Mum laughing and wondering drily whether it was more Bo Derek or dressage pony. Me hoping that these were good things. Lucy saying *Don't you dare do mine.*

'I cried when she had it cut,' says Bryony. 'But you never cried at anything.'

'She said she was too old.'

'That's not the point.'

I sit down in the armchair, wondering what is. Looking around the room. I have never spent much time in here before, Bryony used to always come to mine. There are photographs in here, too. Not in a dusty pile under the chest of drawers, but pinned into a shining and orderly panel on the wall behind her desk. We are all there: mum, Lucy, Bryony, dad. Me, lots of pictures of me too and it surprises me to be included. There must be forty or fifty pictures. We are all smiling. There are only one or two of us in each snap, but Bryony has stuck us together into one family. It makes me feel guilty, how much she has needed us.

'She cut my hair off too,' says Bryony. I think about it, think about maybe I knew, think about how could I not have done, think about how I managed not to know, somehow. Feel the timbers creaking, the gluey bones of me coming unstuck far too easily, as if they're tearing along ready-made perforations, like they saw this coming. 'So maybe you were sensible. Maybe you were just being clever, not to cry, never to get cross. That's what I used to tell myself. That it was just cleverness.' She does this weird smile. 'You kept your hair.'

Not cleverness, no. Just the only way I knew how to be. I rub my sleeve through my hair, make myself look at Bryony properly, looking back at me, the softness stretched out around her eyes. 'I'm sorry,' I say. The words rasp stickily in my throat.

Bryony shakes her head. 'You don't have to say sorry. I only wanted you to stop thinking you were better than me.'

'I never thought I was better than you.' Oh, but I did. What a liar.

'I believe you. It's okay.'

How can she be so easy? It makes me so much worse. I laugh.

Neither of us speaks, not for a while. We just sit here and listen to the house, the creaks of ourselves in its walls. Bryony bends fingers inwards and outwards from the clasp of her hands in her lap.

'Can I come with you?' she asks me slowly, cheeks dull in the lamplight. 'I think I'd like to run away with you.' Sighs softly. 'Lucy's driving me mental.'

'I thought Lucy was your role model.'

'Well, you were always somewhere else.'

'What about the clinic?'

She sighs again. *Yeah, spose.*

Oh Bryony.

The sheets are cold tonight, and I wake seven times and wish I wasn't on my own.

The night is bland and starless. Third time I wake, I think of ringing Alan. Lean on my elbow for half an hour, can't decide. Blearily lift my finger and delete his number from my phone.

266

Slam back into the pillow. Wake again an hour later. At quarter to five, I eke his number out in beeps which are luminous through the dark. I knew it off by heart.

'I was wondering when you'd call,' he says.

It's a beautiful morning, misty but split open with sunshine. Dad seems contented; his turning of the newspaper is perky, the way he tilts his face up to the window and lightly flicks the page with his thumb.

It's all so easy, I think, as I cock my head. I roll my eyeballs upwards in my skull and see a lid of sunlight flickering over the kitchen ceiling.

I lift the spoonful of cereal to my mouth, dripping milk.

Bryony turns the radio on.

I know what's coming as I step on to the terrace, but still, it's shocking somehow. The whole glen is lying there, waiting, when I feel it should have changed.

I walk into the garden but the bench stays empty. The flowers have receded into the earth, leaving just a few greeny brown sticks here and there behind them. I feel the grass squelch beneath my soles as I wander across the lawn. The shed is bolted, and through the window its interior is nothing but darkness. You cannot make out the shapes. The shapes of pots, and wire, hanging in loops from nails, and old cloths and jam jars, and the loppers hanging on the wall. They never did come and nip me in my sleep. Me and her, her too, all along.

You can't see any of it, you can just see dark.

So. I wonder, who will look after the garden?

Of course. The new people. The people who come, they will take care of it. They will come and live a life on top of mine and cut her flowers in July. They will stick their noses in and smell honey; they will sleep in our beds.

But, at least they will look after the garden.

*

The step and the bell.

Mrs McAlpine's face is pale and smooth. Apparently it's nice to see me. She will get Alan. Then she changes her mind and calls over her shoulder while keeping me chatting in the hall, as if I might turn and run away.

He is there again, just the same as yesterday morning. He is smiling, saying to come through to the lounge, and again I hear it is nice to see me. So soon, he says. Tossing me a grin in the old careless way. Like at the very beginning. Like nothing has changed, not really. His mother has the radio on in the kitchen. He slings an arm around my shoulder. 'How are you doing?'

'Fine.'

'Really? You're all right?'

'Yeah. Yeah, I'm fine.' I turn to admire the view out of their floor-to-ceiling window. The trees are dark against the wan grasses, pinching their leaves in grey fingers. The river is high and the sheep have gone. They must have taken them round the other side of the hill.

'It doesn't feel like September, does it,' I say. 'Even with the sun.'

'No. I ken what you mean.'

I'm bored of the view already. I don't like the way it just sits there. I turn back to the room, seeing Alan standing in the warmth with his hands in his pockets. Master of everything, even a hearthrug, without really trying. I could shelter behind that for ever. Maybe, if I stayed and watched him long enough, I could learn it myself.

'What are you thinking?'

'Nothing,' I say. 'Just, it's funny how you always seem so at ease.'

'Me? At ease? With what?'

'Everything. I don't know. Yourself.'

He shakes his head. 'It's you who's the queen of composure.'

'Well, everyone composes themselves, don't they.' And then I'm embarrassed and sit down on the chocolate-coloured sofa.

'Ya-ha. Like Schubert, you mean?'

'Whatever.'

'You're in a bit of a bad way.'

I shrug. I was going to say no, but maybe he's right.

'You can stay here as long as you like. I'll stay too.'

'No. I can't. I'm going away.'

Alan drops down on to his haunches, right in front of me, so he can get a hold of my eyes. He is resting his hands on my knees. I look at his fingernails, harder than mine, solid like plates, cut square, and look back at his eyes. It really is him. After all this time, he is the same person. 'Away? Away where?'

I don't want to tell him about Africa. 'Spain,' I say.

'On holiday?'

'Kind of. But for quite a long time, well. I don't really know how long.'

'So you're going travelling?'

'Yes.'

After a while, he nods, as if I've answered some difficult question that's really been bothering him, and he says, 'Maybe that'll be a good thing to do.'

He comes and sits on the sofa beside me. We both look at the coal-effect fire.

'Not really,' I say. 'It was just to make it look like I was planning on doing something.' He laughs, always where I least expect it. Then he asks, 'And now? Now, why are you going?'

He pins the tail on me so exactly.

I shrug. 'It's like maths. I'm subtracting.'

'Subtracting what?'

'Me. From the wrong side of the equation. Numbers don't just walk across the equals sign, they have to disappear in between.' I pick at the small rip in my jeans at the knee. 'Besides, I can't stand being reminded of her. Even this whole country is too small. I want to go somewhere where they speak a different language.' I try to laugh. 'And I always wanted to run away properly.'

'I'm sorry. You didn't need to explain.'

'Oh, I'm fine.'

He asks me about dad then, and Bryony, and I tell him about dad's new girlfriend who isn't actually new, and about how Bryony isn't very well, that's how I put it, and how maybe she'll come out to Spain and meet me, maybe not, it depends how she goes. Alan doesn't ask me what's wrong with her.

I tell him about how we're selling the house. 'You'll have new neighbours,' I say. I can see them already, the new people. They will be excited by our house, because they will have come from somewhere smaller or less beautiful. They will be taken by the scenery and have barbecues in the garden during summer, to make the most of it. They will always be making the most of it all, of everything we have left behind us. Perhaps there will be a girl, less complicated than me.

'I kind of liked the old neighbours,' says Alan.

I pick at my jeans some more. 'Do you love me,' I quietly ask.

'Jeez, Vanessa,' he says. 'You must know the answer to that.' Smiles. 'Why do you want to know, anyway? You're going away.'

'I'm coming back, aren't I. Thought you might offer me a spare bed down in London.'

'I don't have a spare bed,' he says.

'Ah well.'

I reach out my hand and touch the side of his face. My elbow is awkward. I can feel his skin under the tingling of my finger. He bends his head towards mine. Our faces are only inches apart, and I go even further in. My lips are on the roughness of his cheek. He moves around to kiss me. It races through my brain with a trail of yellow smoke. How much I love him. How this will always be here.

*

We sit in silence for some time, hands clasped around each other's necks. One of us should say something, and we both know what it is.

'Goodbye, then,' I say.

Alan smiles, and I am glad. 'Goodbye, Vanessa,' he answers. 'Don't be gone too long.'

He is standing on the doorstep of his house, watching me walk all the way back. I can feel it, but I do not turn round until I am almost home. He seems small from here, a dark figure on a shadowy step amid the daylight. He stands with his hands in his pockets, legs apart. I raise my hand and wave. He lifts his arm in reply and watery sunlight splashes off his hand.

He is still standing there when I get to my house. I go inside and look out from the kitchen window and see him over the hedge and down the glen, one arm resting on the doorpost now. I don't know if he can see me or not. He taps the doorpost. Seems satisfied with its solidity, and turns to go in. The door flicks closed behind him.

I don't have much to pack. Lucy wanted to take me shopping this morning. I turned her down, on the basis that Perth's September swimsuits were unlikely to be of great merit: the dregs from the summer sales, with monster cups. Lucy had to agree. 'I can buy what I need when I get out there,' I told her. But my bag is awfully small. Look at it: tiny blue rucksack, holding underwear and T-shirts, a spare pair of jeans and a jumper, a couple of dresses (one pink, one green) rolled into its side pockets. Trainers on my feet. Fluttering in my stomach.

I am leaving. On the back of a throwaway sop to my father, I really am. The cheeky terror of it shakes my fingers.

I pick up my bag. Still room for a book and a bottle of water inside. And suddenly I wish I had more, I wish I had a

first-aid box and a Swiss army knife and a camping stove and
a shiny tin mug to hang from my strap. I wish I had a good
picture of Alan.

One of these days.

Bryony says she will come with us. Maybe she wants to say
goodbye to me, or maybe she just doesn't want to be left in the
house by herself, I don't know. She smiles at me as she slides
into the back seat. The leather upholstery is cold.

I feel happy, though. It's nice, just the two of us sitting in
dad's car in the garage. I could almost stay in here all evening,
smelling dust and polish and listening to Bryony's quiet
breathing. I turn round and she smiles again. I had thought
she was weak, but perhaps it was always only niceness. I smile
back. Turn around again and pull down the vanity mirror.
Look at my eyes, and flip it back up. Partly human. Not
entirely lost.

I pull the seatbelt across my body, click it in. That's better,
that's better now. There is always some comfort in restraint.

Dad jogs out to the car, apologising, he couldn't find his keys,
got them now. He is chatty, almost high, as he reverses the car
and swings us down the track. 'Got everything you need?' he
asks, and I nod. The house bumps past us. Big and red, dark
red, like a scab or a rose. But it is starting to shrink already. I feel
like there is a wasp in my throat as I watch it fade.

There is a light left on upstairs, in mum and dad's old
bedroom. Dad was always useless at switching off the lights
behind him.

I lean my cheek against the icy glass and watch the white
bungalow slip away to my left. Everything I need. Dad starts
talking again, about some book he has nearly finished reading:
something to do with a long-ago gardener at a Scottish palace,
and a poisoning plot. Ah, mum. The poisoned gardener. Or was

the gardener the poisoner? I ought to listen more closely. That was always one of the things.

I turn my neck one last time, before we round the bend out of the glen. Looking out of the window at the place I used to live. The light left on by accident is glowing now, in the sloppy dusk.

I watch the night thickening in the fields. Dad drives fast.

Amulree, Buchanty, Methven. They sound rougher when you leave. Back to front, coughed up. Lights and darkness. Homes and fence wire. Dad's voice rumbles on and he injects measured coughs into his silences as the headlights swing round sharp corners. The fields are black, and absolutely limitless in their possibilities. I stare hard but I can't make anything out other than that they are not the sky. That this is earth is all you can know for sure, looking at their darkness.

'It's dark,' I say.

'Autumn. Winter's coming. Can't stand winter,' says dad. 'Lot to be said for the Middle East in that respect. London too is an improvement.' And it's Frankie, and it's London, and it's not a bad life, not bad at all, as we carry on through the black countryside. Blank. Like a white sheet of paper that has been scribbled on so much that it has become plain black – it's that sort of black and that sort of blank. There could be anything in it.

We will go south, all of us. Dad and Lucy and my skeleton sister, a skeleton key, and who knows what might happen if we can only get her to work?

There's a big fat allowance for me, a travelling kitty to be kept purring monthly. And I keep thinking how weird it is, the way that all of a sudden everyone seems to approve of my running away. As if I'm going on some holy quest, and not just trying to avoid dad and Lucy. The flapping skins of just plain people who never knew me, all along. And ghosts of mum. Mum mum mum even the word is magic numb, you were. But she's gone. Scribbled until the ink ran out and threw the pen at the wall.

I suppose I should buy a camera.